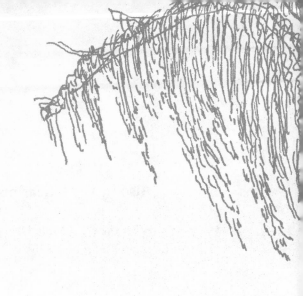

G. D. GEARINO

Also by G. D. Gearino

What the Deaf-Mute Heard
Counting Coup

BLUE HOLE

A Novel

Simon & Schuster

SIMON & SCHUSTER
Rockefeller Center
1230 Avenue of the Americas
New York, NY 10020

This book is a work of fiction. Names, characters, places,
and incidents either are products of the author's imagination
or are used fictitiously. Any resemblance to
actual events or locales or persons, living or dead,
is entirely coincidental.

SIMON & SCHUSTER and colophon
are registered trademarks of Simon & Schuster Inc.

Designed by Deirdre C. Amthor

Manufactured in the United States of America

10 9 8 7 6 5 4 3 2 1

Library of Congress Cataloging-in-Publication Data
Gearino, G. D. (G. Dan), date.
    Blue hole / G. D. Gearino.
        p.   cm.
    I. Title.
PS3557.E214B58   1999
813'.54—dc21   99-32922
                                    CIP

ISBN 0-684-83727-7

Acknowledgments

There is only one name on most title pages, but that's almost always misleading. There are lots of people who make contributions, large and small, to any book and this one is no exception.

Jane Dystel, my literary agent, and her associate, Miriam Goderich, proved once again that I was a lucky man the day I found them. Roslyn Siegel, my editor at Simon & Schuster, took a manuscript (which came to her by default when my original editor left) and became its champion, for which I am inexpressibly grateful. Elizabeth Hayes, also at Simon & Schuster, has sought to spread the gospel at key moments. Preach it, sister. And Charles ReCorr, a friend and ex-soldier, provided valuable lessons in how to behave when people are shooting at you.

Finally, my colleagues in journalism have been supportive and tolerant, probably more so than I deserve. My gift to them, then, is that for the first time in my literary career, I make no pointed observations about the sorrier edges of our craft.

For Karolyn, who will see Paris

Chapter One

Frances Selkirk finally shed her secret that summer, but three people died before she did. She regretted only two of the deaths, however. The third made her happy.

She was a widow and mother who disproved the widely held notion that a small town surrenders its confidences readily, that among its citizens there is little that isn't known or soon won't be. It's true that a small town gives its inconsequential secrets a wide circulation: in beauty shops, barber shops, bait shops, or anywhere that encourages lingering, the minor indiscretions of a town's inhabitants are reported quickly, commented upon firmly, compared to other past indiscretions for evidence of a pattern, and finally archived in the memory of the few people for whom gossip is a higher calling rather than a softly malicious way to fill a few idle moments.

A real secret, however, can stay buried for years. Until it was set free by an anonymous, luckless boy, Frances Selkirk determinedly and successfully kept a secret from the other residents of Barrington, Georgia. It was an old and weighty secret, too weighty, in fact, to be borne by a woman who was barely thirty years old when her tragedy struck. The secret bowed and isolated her for a long time, made her seem aged and unapproachable. It was so palpable a force in her life that its presence was almost like a third member of the family when she and her son sat together. Without the weight of that secret, she could have remarried and perhaps lived a happy and fruitful life, for she was an attractive woman and had, as she eventually proved, an uncommon strength and fortitude. Or she could have moved away from the secret, simply bundled her clothes and son into her car and driven to another town to start fresh. But she didn't, because for years the secret drew the verve from her as effectively as a poultice draws poison. Besides, she couldn't bear being away from his grave. So she stayed in Barrington, a town set in the low hills north of Atlanta where she had come as a young bride. Her son, Charley, grew up there and was on the lip of becoming a man before she finally shed her secret and reembraced life.

Little is known of the boy who set everything into motion. His was a short life and the things that marked it are lost to history. No one even learned his name. But what can be said of him is that in death he achieved what was unlikely to have ever occurred in life: he became the object of attention from many people, among them state officials, police investigators, prosecuting attorneys, newspaper editors, and television reporters.

Much is known about Charley Selkirk, however. He was seventeen years old that summer and coming up to eighteen quickly. The other boy was about that age, too, but beyond that the two of them had little in common. Where Charley was bright and thoughtful, the other boy was vaporous and naïve, a barely-there presence in the lives of the few people who remembered him. Where Charley felt a visceral need to stay close to his mother, despite her inattention and neglect, the other boy had left his home for reasons no one ever remembered him explaining. Where Charley would grow into a fine man, the other boy wouldn't grow at all, because, of course, he's dead.

In short, little can be said about the other boy, but much can be said about Charley. So, this is Charley's story.

●

In truth, Charley was bored and unhappy and angry at just about everyone that summer. He was at that precise age when he'd begun to develop adult sensibilities but hadn't quite learned the benefits of treachery and malice, which are the usual tools adults use to make their way in the world. He had been kicked out of school just a couple of months before graduation, had no job or even the promise of one, and was beginning to understand how perfectly bizarre his childhood had been. His girlfriend had rejected him, his fellow white people thought he was a fool, black people didn't trust him, and a whole staff of football coaches was ready to kill him. His food didn't taste good, his truck wouldn't run right, and he hadn't caught a fish in ages. Oh, and he was still a virgin, too.

He blamed Baby Girl Sanderson, his girlfriend, for most of that, especially the last.

The way Charley saw it, Baby Girl's problem was that she couldn't decide whether she wanted to be a homecoming queen or a sexually liberated social activist. So, her solution was to be an activist pretty much all the time except when he wanted her most to be one, meaning, of course, when they were parked alone somewhere, whereupon she suddenly would remember the unspoken responsibility shared by every Barrington High School homecoming queen to remain unsullied and pure. As a result, he spent most of his last year in school listening to Baby Girl preach the virtues of equality between the races and—this being 1969—the notion that love is all you need; meanwhile, Charley got the raw end of the first and none of the fruit of the second.

It didn't help that virtually every black male student that year suddenly decided he didn't want to play football anymore. The black schools had been closed at the end of the previous year and their students accepted into the white schools, which wasn't nearly as progressive as it sounds because there was only a couple of hundred black students anyway and when the Barrington zipper plant closed and took its property-tax money back up north with it, the school board decided it could both save money and put the federal Justice Department off the scent by simply integrating. The first salt-and-pepper year for the schools in Barrington, then, began in September 1968, and the town saw an immediate payoff when the football team burned through its conference schedule and made it to the state championship game, which it lost only because a referee didn't call pass interference even though Charley was practically mugged in the end zone by a linebacker on the last play of the game.

But racial harmony is easy when you're winning games and you're involved in a sport that requires so many players that no one feels left out. Basketball, however, was quite another matter. The school only dressed twelve players a season, and the basketball coach, reluctant to cut any white boys who'd made the team the previous year, decided that he'd only take a sufficient number of black boys to fill the positions left open by graduation, juvenile-court convictions, or dumbness so chronic that it prevented an athlete from meeting even the minimal academic requirements for participation in sports. There were two of the first and one each of the other two that year, meaning that there was a grand total of four spots open on the team. The problem—as was clear to Charley or anyone paying even a little bit of attention and unencumbered by modern values that discouraged any suggestion that one race might be better at something than another—was that the worst ballplayer among the black kids was far better than the best white kid that the coach could put on the floor. The white players could see it, the black players could see it, anyone except the most willfully blind fool in the world could see it. And the coach was that fool.

The black students had the perfect Sixties reaction: they boycotted. The four of them who had been issued basketball uniforms returned them to the coach, who promptly gave them to some of the no-jumping white boys who'd washed out during tryouts. So the team was all white and the crowds at the games were all white, and, by the end of the season, the won-loss record was pretty much all white too, which, of course, means all losses. No matter: Barrington High School had always had mediocre basketball teams, so that carried the comfort of the familiar. Besides, it gave the old men who hang around in crossroads stores and gas stations something to complain about.

Still, everyone had liked having a winning football team. As a result, the boycott became a serious matter when it was extended into spring football drills.

To Charley's dismay, Baby Girl was right in the middle of it. She'd never learned a thing about football, despite having served as a cheerleader for several years—mostly because it gave her the social sanction to twitch her barely covered, almost-liberated delicious little butt in public, he suspected—but from the way she carried on about the boycott, she must have thought it was the most dramatic moment in civil rights history since Selma. She was constantly declaiming about the rightness of the whole thing, exhorting her classmates to acknowledge its moral purity, and generally carrying on in the most annoying fashion. Charley ignored her as best he could because the boycott seemed to be working just fine without his involvement, and he was just a couple of months away from graduating anyway—meaning that it all had the flavor of someone else's business. But Baby Girl was his girlfriend, or so it usually seemed as they clinched in his truck at night and he whispered things in her ear, hoping to hit the right combination of pledge and endearment that would lead him to the promised land. So he should have known it was impossible to not get dragged into the whole mess.

Nevertheless, he might have avoided it if two other things hadn't happened. The first was a request from the school's football coach that Charley participate in spring drills, even though his playing days were over. "You don't have to run the sprints or anything, just fill in wherever I need you when we go through the formations," the coach explained to Charley. "What with the boycott and all, I want to make sure I've got some hard hitters out there." They were words he'd later regret.

The second was the appearance of Leander Jackson Jr. at spring practice.

Leander was a preacher's son, a soft and large-bodied creature whose natural habitat was the library and the chorus room. He'd never played football before, as much as anyone could remember, and nothing in his sweet nature would lead anyone to believe that there was the killer instinct of a defensive lineman buried in there somewhere. He hung around with girls a lot, made good grades, was fussy about his clothes, and was a member of several of those after-school clubs in which students sit around and talk clumsily to each other in foreign languages or argue about which Broadway musical to stage. In short, if someone had asked a hundred Barrington residents to guess who would be least likely to be standing in the middle of the football field on the first day of spring practice, equipment still creaky-new and bewilderment apparent to all, every one of them would have scratched their heads and said, "You mean, aside from Leander Jackson Junior?"

So Leander was no football player. What he was, however, was black.

Leander's problem—and eventually, Charley's problem—was that his father saw the boycott as a divisive and unnecessary move. Lean-

der Sr. was a courtly old gentleman and typical of many black minis-
ters of the time, as far as Charley could tell. He had an almost saintly
belief in the inner goodness of people, even white people, and a fundamental faith in the notion that one turned the other cheek in the face
of provocation. The boycott had been widely debated in Barrington's
black community—not that white folks knew or even cared much—
and Leander Sr. had preached against it. When it moved ahead anyway, he had but one gesture of healing and reconciliation left to him:
he had his son join the football team to show that even in tense times,
the races could find a way to live together.

Somebody, however, forgot to tell the white boys that Leander Jr.
was a racial olive branch. They mistook him for a punching bag.

"You've got to look after him," Baby Girl told Charley a couple of
days after practice had begun. "They'll kill him."

"They're not going to kill him," Charley said, knowing where this
was going but hoping to head it off anyway. "Anyone who's new gets a
bad time. It's like an initiation."

She didn't buy it. "No, it's not. It wasn't like that in the fall when the
other colored boys were playing. The white boys didn't dare treat any
of them like they're treating Leander."

Charley knew she was right. They'd had a few pushing matches at
the early practices, but it was clear right away that the black players
were big, tough, quick, and proud. He'd noticed how quickly a certain
sense of racial equality had settled over the team after the white boys
had to line up a few times against someone who'd given them a forearm
to the face mask on the previous play, then stood over them and said,
"Man, I'm sure sorry about the way my arm got integrated with your
head like that."

Charley thought Leander could have done himself some good if
he'd simply lowered his head and planted his helmet into somebody's
gut a couple of times. He considered suggesting this to Leander early
on, but knew it was pointless: he might as well have asked Leander to
change the color of his eyes. Leander was a mild, affable guy with no
anger in him. Charley would have practiced a few tackling drills on
the father who'd insisted that he be there as some symbol, but Leander wasn't even mad at him. He claimed to understand his father's

point, although it was lost on everyone else, black and white alike.

The first couple of practices were a sort of dry run of torment. Leander had his regular clothes thrown in the shower, meaning that when the first day's drills were finished, he had nothing to change into; he was told to lace his shoulder pads loosely for comfort, so that the first time he hit a blocking dummy he looked like a big goof when they slipped off sideways; and somebody poured baby powder into his helmet at one point, which prompted great merriment when he took it off during a water break and his hair had become snowy white.

"Hey, Leander, how you gonna break the boycott if you ain't black anymore?" crowed Donny Chambers, the team quarterback and torment organizer. Everyone else cackled enormously; this passed for high humor among Charley's teammates.

But it was clear things would not remain this benign. Leander had already taken a late hit or two after a play concluded, and it was only a matter of time before somebody nailed him with their helmet and broke a rib. So, as Charley soon discovered, Baby Girl was right.

"How am I supposed to look after him?" he asked. "If he's smart, he'll just quit. He's never going to play, anyway."

"His daddy ain't going to let him quit," she replied, ignoring his question.

"There's something else I'm not clear about," Charley said. "You've been behind this boycott all along, but here's Leander trying to undermine it and you want me to save him from his own foolishness. I'm having a little trouble keeping track of which side of this issue you're on."

"Leander's making a statement. I may not agree with him, but he's brave to take a stand."

"He's not taking a stand. His daddy is. He's just suffering the consequences."

"That's why you need to look after him," Baby Girl said, giving Charley a smug smile. He was not going to win this.

"You like it when people make a statement?" he asked. She nodded. "Here's a statement, then," Charley continued. "I'd like for you to get naked."

That didn't work for him, either.

●

Actually, Charley had never liked Donny Chambers. Donny was a bully, a whiner, and he paid just a little too much attention to Baby Girl. So when Charley finally popped him, it didn't have much to do with Leander at all.

It happened just a few days later, pretty much as Charley suspected it would. The offense was practicing a short pass play. The ball was bobbled, and Leander—stuck in the middle of the field where he could do the least harm—somehow found it in his hands. He stood for a moment until a coach yelled at him to run, then began lumbering along, carrying the ball awkwardly and clearly unsure as to where he was supposed to go.

He headed first for the near sideline, but when he saw a tackler angling toward him, he turned and circled around behind his team toward the far sideline. When he got there, he saw his way blocked again, so he repeated the process, circling back once more. Each time he did it, his arc got wider and he lost more ground. The third time Leander ran between the sidelines, he was easily forty yards back from his original starting point, and almost everyone had quit chasing him because they were laughing so hard. If he'd had the stamina for one more circle of the field, he might have scored—had he started running in the right direction. But Leander was winded by that point and he ended up stumbling over his own feet, dropping the ball and adding to the merriment.

Only Donny didn't see anything funny in all this. It was his pass that had been intercepted, and perhaps he thought that Leander was showboating—although any fool could see that this preacher's son was terrified of getting tackled and practically running backwards to avoid it. So Donny had drawn a bead on Leander before he fell, and, coming at him full speed, didn't slow up a bit after he went down. Leander was defenseless on his back with the ball rolling away when Donny speared him, lowering his helmet and launching himself into Leander's soft abdomen as hard as he could. It was the cruelest thing Charley had ever seen on a football field.

Leander probably would have howled in agony if he'd had any

breath in him. But he didn't, so he just held his sides with both arms as he tried to breathe, looking for all the world like some great pudgy fish that sits at the bottom of the boat while the fisherman mulls whether to throw it back. After a minute or two, he was finally able to talk.

"Feels like a knife sticking in me," he gasped.

"I don't doubt it," the coach said. "Are you breathing better now?"

Leander nodded. "Don't want to, though. It hurts."

"I don't doubt it," the coach said again. "You probably broke a rib. That hurts, but it's not going to kill you. We don't want you to get a collapsed lung, though. You still breathing?"

"Lordy, it hurts," Leander said. That apparently was his answer—if you're talking, you're breathing. "I thought you said to not tackle people on the ground."

No one could say that Leander hadn't been paying attention at practice. He knew he'd gotten a late hit. The coach gave Donny a sidelong glance as he patted Leander on the leg. "Yeah, there was no call for that. Donny's going to be running some laps after practice," he said. "Listen, in a few minutes we're going to walk you out to the parking lot. We'll get you to the clinic and see about those ribs."

The rest of the players were herded to the far end of the field, where they resumed their drills. As they did, Charley heard Donny mutter, "Well, I guess we're an all-white team again." His buddies snickered.

The coach's diagnosis was right, as it turned out. One of Leander's ribs was broken and another cracked. He would miss a couple of days of school, and, when he returned, would move through the halls with all the lithe grace of a mummy, his torso wrapped tight and the pain still apparent. Leander's three-day-long football career was over.

Donny's football career ended the same day.

Charley didn't have to wait long. The car carrying Leander to the clinic had barely gotten out of the parking lot when the huddle broke with a clap of hands and the team settled over the ball. As Donny squatted behind the center, Charley could tell exactly which play was about to be run.

There's little mystery or beauty to football. It essentially comes down to the notion that it's best to smash people as hard as you can before they smash you. Charley had spent the previous two seasons catching passes from Donny, so when Donny brought the team up to the ball, Charley could tell from where everyone lined up which play had been called. Donny was going to pass the ball to the far side of the field, and, as he did, he'd be looking away from Charley—virginal boyfriend, temporary fill-in, helper of coaches, the boy who wanted only to graduate peacefully and get on with whatever career awaited an unmotivated and mildly befuddled seventeen-year-old.

Yet as the play started, Charley found himself suddenly and unreasonably angry. It wasn't as if Leander was his pal, but he was a harmless fellow who belonged in a choir robe, not on his back in the dust writhing in agony as Donny stood triumphantly over him. And Charley knew that Baby Girl was going to hold him somehow accountable for it, which only fueled his anger. Later, he understood that he should have just left the field. At that moment, though, Charley decided to give Donny a taste of football justice.

Donny had just let the pass go and was watching its arc when he must have sensed Charley coming fast. He wasn't facing away from Charley, exactly; his head was turned away, mostly, but his body was in profile. So when Donny heard Charley's step, he had just enough time to square his shoulders to him and swivel his head before Charley hit him at full tilt.

Charley put the top of his helmet into Donny's chest right under his chin, and Donny's head snapped back so hard that it seemed it would fly off his neck; his helmet did pop off, rolling ten yards before coming to rest at the feet of one of the astonished assistant coaches. Charley didn't slow down as he hit him, heeding the countless instructions he'd gotten over the years to drive through the tackle—to wrap the ball carrier firmly in your arms and keep your legs moving, so that you overcome his force with one more violent of your own—and Charley's momentum carried both of them several steps until Donny's feet gave up trying to keep pace with his now-naked head, which was moving backward a lot faster than any other part of him.

Donny landed on his shoulders and Charley landed on him. He gave a small "oof" into Charley's ear as they hit; it was the only sound he would make for five minutes or so. The two of them skittered across the ground a little ways, Donny on his back and Charley on top, hugging him with his head snugged against Donny's chest. When they finally stopped moving, Charley raised his eyes to look into Donny's face, but Donny had stopped seeing anything the instant he was hit. Charley had knocked him literally into another dimension.

An enormous hubbub broke out. Every coach on the field was blowing his whistle hard enough to tremble the walls of Jericho. As Charley climbed to his feet, the others players surrounded them, jostling one another as they strained to get a better look at Donny but being yanked back by their collars as the coaches waded into the circle. Charley had laid a cheap lick on Donny, but he knew it was no worse than what Donny had done to Leander. The reaction, though, couldn't have been more different.

"Jesus, Charley! What are you doing?" the head coach yelled into his face. Someone was patting Donny's cheeks, which made the quarterback's head roll loosely to the side. "Jesus," the coach yelled again. "I think you killed him."

"Nah, he's breathing. He's just knocked silly," one of the other coaches said, but that didn't seem to help matters much.

"Get off the field!" the coach said, still yelling and still just inches from Charley's face. "Get out of my sight."

Charley left his pads and helmet in a pile in front of the equipment-room door and dressed without showering. There was no one else in the locker room, and the unfamiliar solitude of a place normally crowded with his teammates gave Charley a sudden feeling that he'd crossed over some invisible divide. As he walked toward his truck, he could see that practice was over, but no one was leaving the field. Across the way, Donny was being helped to a car. For the second time that afternoon, someone was headed for the doctor's office.

Charley wondered if Leander's ribs hurt too much for him to laugh when they brought Donny in.

●

By the end of the next day, his locker-room premonition had been confirmed. Charley found himself in complete social exile.

Baby Girl set the tone for the day early. She usually rode to school with Charley, who'd pulled his truck to the curb in front of her house just as he'd done countless times before. He never knew who was going to emerge, hippie chick or cheerleader, but she rarely made him wait more than a few minutes before banging out of the side door near the kitchen, jamming books and papers into her bag as she hurried to the curb. He'd always found her slapdash energy enormously appealing. Her motors hummed all the time, and even if they sent her careering around in inconsistent directions, she had a verve that few others her age possessed.

What she also had, though, was a father who was best friends with Arn Chambers, progenitor of the still-woozy starting quarterback for the Barrington Bengals.

"You are in trouble," Baby Girl announced when she climbed into Charley's truck. She had been uncharacteristically slow in coming down the drive and carried no evidence that she was ready to depart for school.

Charley knew instinctively what she referred to. "It was a tough hit, but he'll get over it," he said.

"Arn"—this was another way Baby Girl had embraced the cultural revolution; she'd begun calling adults by their first names—"says he's thinking about going to the police. He says that wasn't football as much as it was an assault."

"Well, why don't you tell Arn that, in fact, it was the second assault of the day." Charley sounded edgier than he meant to, but then again, he'd expected something different than the cool reception he was getting from Baby Girl.

"That's the other thing. What happened? I thought you were going to look after Leander."

"Look, it's football," he said. "You can't protect somebody. There ain't much to it except people smashing into each other."

She finally seemed to understand. "So if someone sets out to hurt somebody, there's not much to be done about that."

"That's right." Charley mistakenly thought they were still talking about Leander.

"So Donny was going to get clobbered one way or the other," she said.

"Wait a minute. We've apparently forgotten what happened to Leander."

"You just don't understand," Baby Girl said. "You responded to violence with violence. Why didn't you just talk to Donny?" Her face carried that why-can't-we-all-just-love-each-other? look that Charley had seen so often recently and was suddenly sick of.

"Yeah, why didn't I think of that? He's a thoughtful, sensitive guy. He would have seen right away that he was violating the spirit of racial harmony." Charley's head was bobbing sarcastically. "I'm sure that deep down inside, he has nothing but love for his black brothers and sisters."

Baby Girl's face reddened as she reached for the door handle. "God, I hate you sometimes. I don't think I ever want to talk to you again."

Charley got the same feeling that he'd had the previous day in the locker room. Somehow he knew that this was going to be a bad day and that he'd need every ally he could get. "Hang on a minute," he said. "I'm sorry."

It was too late. She pushed against the door to open it—the latch was chronically sticky—and ran back into the house. Charley waited at the curb a few minutes—not only to see if she'd change her mind, but also because driving off right away didn't have the proper taste to it; other guys were always getting mad at their girlfriends and screeching off into the night, leaving twin rubber marks on the road as their version of the last word. Charley had always thought that that was stupid: bad for your tires, hard on your transmission, and like hanging a sign on your back that said, "Yes, I'm girlishly emotional."

As the minutes stretched on, however, and it became clear Baby Girl wasn't relenting, Charley eased away from the curb and drove to school. He had barely gotten in the door when he learned that his premonition had been sound: he was ordered to the school office, where he was ushered in to see assistant principal Harrison Stover, Barrington High School's happily merciless disciplinarian.

"Have you bothered to check on your teammate's condition, Mr. Selkirk?" Stover asked. He was known for his aggressive formality; the more mannered he became with a student, the more likely it was the punishment would be harsh. Being called "Mister" was a famously bad sign.

"No, sir," Charley said.

"He has a concussion, Mr. Selkirk. He spent the night at the clinic and probably will miss several days of school. And, of course, he can forget about football for a while." Before continuing, he hesitated for a moment to let Charley dwell on the horror of his crimes. "Do you have anything to say for yourself?"

Charley briefly considered explaining that in some indirect way, none of this would have happened if Baby Girl hadn't been so fiercely protective of her virtue. But Stover was a straight-line thinker. Charley knew he wasn't going to make him understand the connection, which was a little muddled even to Charley. Besides, Charley was young and didn't understand that a man's willingness to do whatever it takes for sex is universal. He thought it uniquely his own weakness.

"No, sir," Charley said simply.

"Do you agree this was an unprovoked and unwarranted attack?"

"No, sir," Charley said for the third time.

"Oh?" Stover said, making it sound like an order for him to explain.

"It was no worse than what Donny did to Leander," he said. "Sir," he added.

Stover seemed genuinely confused. "Leander who? What are you talking about?"

"Leander Jackson Jr. You know, that black kid in the eleventh grade? He went to the clinic last night, too, after Donny tackled him."

Stover shook his head. "I haven't heard anything about that. It's beside the point, anyway. We're talking about your behavior, not someone else's. How do you plead?" This was another of his mannerisms: Stover always finished every disciplinary proceeding with a judgelike demand that a student declare himself guilty or innocent. Because there was no court of appeal, and because there was a widely held perception that acknowledgment of your sins helped temper the punishment, most students ended their pose of innocence at this point. Charley thought it seemed wise for him to do so, too.

"Well, there's no denying I laid a tough lick on him," he said, trying to sound regretful but not groveling.

But Charley had walked into a sucker punch. "Yes, you did," Stover said gleefully. "And that's why I'm suspending you for the remainder of the year. You won't graduate, of course, but if you'll come see me at the start of the summer session, we'll let you take the equivalency test."

It wasn't even nine o'clock in the morning, and Charley had already been rejected by his girlfriend and kicked out of school. Then, just to make the day a complete loss, he had two visitors as he cleaned out his book locker. The first was Jimmy Joe Hand, a beefy teammate who was Donny's best friend.

"Goddamn, Charley," he said. "When did you become such a nigger-lover?"

The second, minutes later, was Orlando Watson, a strapping black kid who would have been the team's best linebacker, were it not for the boycott. "Hey, ofay. It's best you keep out of this. When there's butt-whupping to be done"—he tapped himself on the chest—"I'm going to do it."

Charley was accustomed to aloneness. Some years before, after his family had shrunk to two, Charley and his mother somehow had arrived at the unstated agreement that talking was the same as hurting—in conversation there is pain and misunderstanding. So, Charley had learned to keep his universe small—Baby Girl and a small number of buddies—because the larger it got, the greater the potential for disappointment and heartache. Finding himself that morning almost completely isolated from everyone might have been unhappy, but it carried a familiar taste.

It was so familiar, in fact, that he didn't even realize that what seemed like a bleak day was actually a fresh start.

●

Much of what he also later came to know wasn't apparent for a long time. For instance, it wasn't until the following football season that it became clear that Donny Chambers's career as a quarterback was over. He missed the rest of spring drills, and when he appeared in the first game later that fall, everyone could see that he was tentative and fearful. He hurried his passes, threw over his receivers' heads, and scrambled backward in a panic whenever an opposing player seemed to be getting close. The memory of his collision with Charley was etched too deeply in his memory for him to ever be an effective player again. Life on a football field is no more forgiving than life around a watering hole during a drought: you know you're going to have to butt heads in order to survive. Donny forgot that, and by midseason, he was on the bench, with someone else in his place on the field. In one of those sweet bits of justice life occasionally offers to the patient, his replacement was a black kid. The boycott, and the issue that sparked it, had been worked out in the intervening months. The football scholarship that had seemed sure to be offered never materialized, and Donny shortly after graduating launched into what would become a lifelong and dead-end career at the local chicken-processing plant.

Leander's football career also was over, although more happily so. He returned to the choir, went on to attend one of the black colleges in Atlanta, and eventually became a gospel singer of some fame. He turned the story of his football days into part of his act, making himself even more hapless than he actually was and making Donny seem tough but sporting, with the lesson, of course, being that God works in odd ways and that a broken rib or two, in the scheme of things, sometimes can be a divine nudge. Leander never nursed a grudge about the incident; some people are born decent and never get over it. Charley bought a number of Leander's albums over the years, but found it hard to listen to them often. They made Charley unaccountably sad.

Baby Girl, ever wavering between hippie chick and cheerleader, finally discarded both those choices in favor of a third. To Charley's mind, it would have helped enormously if she'd made her pick a little sooner.

Charley jettisoned something of his own that summer. When he looked back with the perspective of an adult, it was clear a bright line was drawn in those few months. He couldn't pin it to a day, exactly, but he began that season with the sensibilities of a child—a large child, no doubt, and one with an unusual gravity, but a child nonetheless— and finished with those of an adult. And if he can't tell precisely which day it happened, he can tell the day it began: When he encountered Tallasee Tynan on the street and she ended up offering him a job.

Chapter Two

He was, Tallasee noticed, still a boy. Charley was grown up, of course, in a physical sense, tall and trim, but with the same big hands and feet that Michelangelo so cleverly put on his statue of David—big enough to tell you that while he may not get taller, there was still bulk yet to come. Charley was strong, too, though he was uncertain about it; she saw that he was always careful and gentle, as if afraid of inadvertently hurting something.

With her photographer's eye for the hidden, Tallasee also saw that there was something else: Charley was right on the edge of figuring out a lot of things. She could see that soon, perhaps even before the summer was done, he would be a man. He carried himself purposefully, with none of the airy insolence that propels most young men through that stage of their lives, and had a mannered, watchful calm. Yet, for all her instinct, Tallasee could not have known—when Charley stopped on the sidewalk as she sought to wrestle a case of developer chemicals out of her car—the role that she would play as he learned the lessons a boy needs to learn before he can think of himself as a man.

"Ma'am, let me give you a hand," he said. That made Tallasee grin. She was still in her twenties at the time, had spent the last couple of years hanging around with hippies, and led what was, in Barrington at least, an unusual existence. In short, she was not a "ma'am"—she hadn't earned it and didn't much want it. But from Charley, it was so sincerely and instinctively polite that she liked it.

It also made her grin because it was the perfect setup for an old joke. "I don't need applause," she said. "I need help lifting this box."

She could see it confused him for a moment. Then he smiled back.

"Then why don't I lift the box while you clap," he said. She stepped aside as he horsed the crate off the backseat and carried it into her studio, setting it on the table that she pointed out for him.

She called it a studio mostly for appearances. Truth be told, she didn't want a place to pose people for formal portraits. She needed only a darkroom; the assignments that she shot for magazines were sent directly to their offices for developing and editing, and the things that she shot for herself were sold through a gallery in Atlanta. But her mother, who had never quite grasped the nuances of the photo industry, fretted that unless Tallasee had a studio, she would never be a real photographer like the guy at Sears who took baby pictures and shot weddings on weekends. So Tallasee kept a studio to comfort her mother as much as she did for any other reason. Besides, she had outgrown the darkroom that she'd set up in her bathroom at home, with the developer trays sitting in the tub and the enlarger braced on the sink. She'd eventually grown tired of shuffling things around every time she wanted to brush her teeth or shower. So Tallasee had searched for a place she could turn into a permanent darkroom, finally settling on an empty storefront downtown.

The place was perfect for her. It was a single big, airy room, but with enough space for her to close off an area for a darkroom. She scattered a desk and some chairs around, and also draped a backdrop against one wall and set up lights for the perhaps ten portraits she did a year, a number kept deliberately low by her high fee and her un-Searslike demand that they be scheduled months in advance. Though Tallasee talked about portraits as if they were a horrible burden, she secretly appreciated them. A portrait, when done properly, requires much concentration while it's being shot and meticulous attention to detail in the darkroom as the print is prepared. In other words, it's good practice. But, like practice of any kind, it's routine and boring, so she was happy to steer people as often as possible to Sears for their portraits.

After setting the box of chemicals down, Charley looked around. She could see that he was curious. She spent most of her days at the studio when she wasn't out shooting pictures, so she had tried to make it a nice place. She kept a sheer curtain across the front window, where the mannequins used to be, which gave her a little privacy and softened the light, and she had hung pictures all around the walls. The chairs were clumped together to make a sort of sitting area, with magazines and books piled on a table and a couple of lamps nearby. Tallasee didn't mind if people came in and read while she was working; her friends understood that while they were welcome to hang around, she felt no obligation to entertain them. They didn't take it personally when she disappeared into her darkroom and didn't come out for an hour or two.

As Charley studied the prints on the wall, she could tell that he was pretending to not notice the nude. It was nothing all that revealing, really, just a photograph of one of Tallasee's friends with only her back and buttocks showing. Tallasee, testing a new lens one day, had asked the friend to model. She hadn't expected to shoot anything worth keeping, but one frame caught the friend just as she had turned, and the light made her every ridge and curve stand out beautifully, a slim woman made lush and exquisite. So Tallasee had printed and mounted that frame. No one but the friend and photographer knew who it was, and the friend loved to watch people studying it.

She would have been disappointed with Charley, though. He worked hard at not seeing the nude, right up until the moment he turned back to Tallasee and said, "Interesting place here."

"Stay as long as you like," she said. She meant it, but Charley—apparently accustomed to the overweening politeness of Southern society, in which good manners sometimes aggressively disguise intent—took it as his cue to leave.

"Thanks, but I've got to get going," he said.

"Appreciate your help," Tallasee said, then remembered that although she was pretty sure who he was, she hadn't nailed it down. "You're Charley Selkirk, right?" she asked. He nodded.

"I'm Tallasee Tynan," she said, shaking his hand.

"Yes, ma'am, I knew that," he said.

"Aren't you supposed to be in school?" she asked. Even as she said it, she realized that it sounded abrupt and scolding. "What I mean is, are you out of school already? The years are starting to get by me."

She could see a flush climbing toward his face. "I got kicked out of school."

She suddenly recalled a conversation from a day or two earlier. "I think I heard about this. You got in a fight, right?"

"Sort of," he said.

"You get into fights?" she asked. It didn't fit. He seemed like a calm sort.

"Hardly ever. This was . . . an odd circumstance." He didn't seem inclined to explain.

"Isn't your girlfriend the one with the unfortunate name?" Hearing herself, Tallasee knew that she wasn't rating well for tact or conversational continuity that day.

"Baby Girl," he confirmed. "You seem to know a lot."

"It's a small town."

"It's not her real name. Her name's Dorothy. But her daddy called her that when she was little and it stuck."

"That would be considered child abuse in other places," she commented.

He grinned. "Actually, I don't think she's my girlfriend anymore."

Tallasee would have asked why, but at that moment the phone rang.

●

Charley could see she didn't know at first who was on the phone. She sat at her desk with her face squinched up in a confused sort of way for a few moments, until she figured out who was calling. She didn't say much, actually, aside from the occasional "uh-huh" and "oh, dear." Whoever was calling had something to tell and was telling it at top speed.

He felt uncomfortable about being there. He was pretty sure they were finished when the call came—after all, she'd only needed help with one box, which had long since been put away—but she'd been asking him questions, and now it seemed impolite to just leave. Thus, he wandered around and looked at the pictures on the wall again, though that also made him uncomfortable because one of them, a nude woman, was embarrassing and he didn't think it was right to look at it.

But seeing as she'd hung it right in the middle of the wall, it was hard to keep from seeing it. Still, the longer he stood around, the more he felt he should leave. So when she looked up at one point, Charley waved and headed for the door.

"Ma'am, can you hang on just a second?" Tallasee asked into the phone. It was the most that she'd said since the conversation began. She then held the receiver against her chest and called across the studio to Charley.

"Do you have to go? I might need some help with something else, it turns out."

"Sure, I can stay," he said.

"That's your truck out there, right?" she asked, motioning through the window to the street. He nodded.

"You're my man, then," she said, putting the phone back to her ear.

"Why don't I just come see you?" Tallasee asked the caller. She listened for a moment, then said: "This afternoon, probably. Let me check." She looked at Charley for assent.

He nodded again, although he had no idea what he was agreeing to.

●

Tallasee's problem was that her car was just not going to make that trip again. She'd done it once, a few years back, and had bottomed out several times on the steep, rutted track that led to the old woman's home. That time, she'd had no idea how far away the house was located, so she'd kept going on the hope that it was just around the next turn in the road. By the time Tallasee had arrived, she could smell gasoline from the leak in the tank that had resulted from a particularly hard skip across a rock between the ruts. She'd done better going back down the mountain, driving off to the side on the high ground whenever she could, but those thieves at the dealership still claimed the tank couldn't be fixed and had to be replaced. A discussion with a mechanic was one of the few things that could make her feel girlish and inadequate.

So, she felt lucky that Charley—or more precisely, Charley's truck—was handy when the old woman called and asked for help. The truck already had seen some hard driving, from the look of it, and Charley himself didn't give Tallasee the impression that he had anything pressing to do. They were away within thirty minutes, after she'd tracked down some of the photos of hippies she'd taken in the recent past.

She explained as he drove. "We're going to see this old gal I took pictures of one time. She lives way up in the hills beyond Rabun Gap. It's going to take a while to get there. You sure this is not a problem for you?"

Charley shook his head. "It's not a problem."

"Well, I did sort of hijack you."

"I don't mind. Really."

"God only knows where she called from. She lives about ten miles and a hundred years away from the highway. There's no telephone at her home, and if I remember right, there's no power either. She lives there alone in a house that looks like it's going to melt into the ground one day."

"What does she want?"

"Probably what everybody else wants," Tallasee said. "A fulfilling sex life and someone else to do the dishes after dinner."

Charley blushed, but his reply surprised her. "I meant, what does she want from you. But maybe you just answered."

Tallasee laughed. "Whoa. Score one for the kid."

They had come to the first switchback curve on the highway that led through the gap, so she waited until Charley had slowed the truck and geared it down before resuming the explanation.

"Her grandson has run away. From the sound of it, he's her only grandchild and she dotes on him. Apparently, he used to spend his summers up there with her. She says he's a good kid who may have fallen in with the wrong bunch in high school. When he first ran off, she was sure he'd show up at her place. But he hasn't, so now she's worried."

Charley nodded, but said, "Well, I still don't understand why she called you."

"She thinks he may have joined up with the hippies. You know there's a commune up here, right?" He nodded again. "I've taken a lot of pictures there, had some of them published. *Life* magazine ran a bunch of them—"

"Yeah, I know," Charley said. "I've still got that issue."

"You do?" Tallasee was pleased. "I'm working on a book on hippies now."

Most people in Barrington had ignored the fact that Tallasee's pictures had been published in the leading magazine of the day. Someone else's success is a lot easier to tolerate if you don't have to face it every day. But because she hadn't moved away, her neighbors did the next best thing: they pretended it hadn't happened.

"Baby Girl was in her hippie period at the time," Charley explained. "When she gets involved with something, she tends to see it in the purest terms. So, I'm always trying to show her that things have both a good side and a bad side. I thought your pictures were really good. When you looked close, everyone in them looked sort of unhappy."

Tallasee bobbed her head in agreement. "Interesting you noticed that. They talked all the time about how happy they were, how they'd achieved spiritual peace. But anyone who talks a lot about being happy is usually trying to talk himself into it. So, yeah, they were a miserable bunch. Cold in the winter and hungry most of the time. If your girlfriend's not a hippie anymore, what is she?"

"She's finding spiritual peace in the leading of cheers," Charley said. "I think I get it now. The old lady wants to see if her grandson ended up in one of your pictures."

"Clever boy," Tallasee said. "If you were any smarter, you'd be a woman."

●

Tallasee almost let him drive past the turn. She was fiddling with the radio, trying to find a station whose signal wasn't discouraged by the steep hills all around them, when she looked up. "Oh, hell, hang on. This is it."

Charley stopped the truck. There was no shoulder to speak of, but as they were on one of the rare flat, straight stretches on the highway, he didn't worry about getting clobbered from behind. "This is what?" he asked.

"The turn. Back there where that can is stuck on a stick."

He backed up the truck about twenty yards to a spot where a beer can was hung on a branch jammed into the ground. A narrow dirt road, almost hidden by the growth on either side, opened up from the highway and disappeared into the woods.

"This is her driveway, if that's what you'd call it. Just pull in there," Tallasee directed.

Charley turned onto the road, bushes slapping both sides of the truck until they got deeper into the trees and the underbrush thinned out. For a few miles the road skirted the side of a long ridge, following the path of a creek that was occasionally visible from Tallasee's side of the truck. Then the road made a big sweeping curve to the left and they began a series of turns that had them climbing to the peak of the ridge. It was slow going, but the road was better than Charley thought it would be.

It was so good, in fact, that Tallasee apologized for it. "I remember the road being much worse than this," she said.

"Someone's been in here with a blade. You can see dirt pushed over to the side in a few spots."

"So who made a liar out of me?"

"Probably the Forest Service," Charley said. "A lot of this is national forest around here and I'll bet they use this as a fire road. So they come up here every few years and scrape it smooth."

"You seem to know a lot," she said, repeating his words of just a few hours before.

"It's a small town," he replied, appropriating her answer. Tallasee began to be aware that little escaped this young man's attention or memory.

"Pull over here," she ordered.

They were at the last turn before the top of the ridge. The trees had been cleared from the downhill side of the road, giving them a long view of the surrounding hills, and as they got out of the truck Charley understood why she wanted to stop: it was an exhilarating sight. The ground at their feet fell away sharply into a deep swale perhaps a mile wide, with a collection of successively higher ridges across the way telling them of other valleys even more remote and wild. Spring was fully upon the forest, but the leaves had not yet become the impenetrable mass they would soon grow into; instead, they were a dusting of that special shade of green that only nature can produce, and only then in the nascent stages of growth. A breeze rustled the branches and a pair of hawks rode the updrafts, shifting their wings but never flapping as they circled leisurely over a spot that held their meal, or at least their interest. In the distance a stream winked where it ran over a bare spot of rock. Everything seemed still, yet there was movement everywhere, barely perceptible shifts in motion that individually didn't count for much but collectively made this ridge and its companions seem like a single large being. Charley and Tallasee stood for several long minutes, leaning against the truck's fender and unconsciously imitating their surroundings: seeming to be still, but shifting their gaze continuously as they took it in.

Tallasee spoke first. "Beautiful, isn't it? It's hard to imagine anything bad could happen here," she said.

"Has something bad happened here?"

"I don't know," she answered. "It sure feels like it, though. There's something weird about this whole thing. This lady we're seeing, Mrs. Bullock, first said her grandson had run away. But then she said he'd never run away, that they were too close, so something must have happened to him. I kept getting this odd feeling the whole time I was talking to her." Tallasee paused a moment, then added, "To be honest, she gives me the willies. I would have hated to come up here alone. I'm glad you're with me."

"What if she spots her grandson in one of your photographs?" Charley asked. "What do we do then?"

"We?"

"Well, you just said you were glad I'm here." Charley was confused—one moment they were pals, and the next moment he felt like she'd seen him drop his chewing gum into the collection plate at church. With his argument with Baby Girl still vivid in his mind, he wondered whether he was going to spend the rest of his life sparring with women.

"I did, indeed," she said. "I don't know what *we're*"—she drew out the word—"going to do. In fact, *we*"—damn her if she didn't do it again—"aren't going to get there at all if *we*"—once more—"don't get moving."

"We're sorry we asked," Charley said.

She was grinning as she climbed back into the truck. "You push right back, don't you?"

"I'm beginning to think that hanging around with you is like being on the football field," he answered. "You're either taking a lick or giving one."

"Actually, let's talk about hanging around. I want to make sure I understand. You're out of school"—it wasn't a question, exactly, but she paused as if waiting for him to confirm it, so he nodded—"and you're looking for work, right?"

He nodded again.

"Well, I've got some work. I've got thousands of photo negatives stuck in boxes all over the place. I bought a cabinet for them recently, but I need them sorted and organized. It's not hard to do, but it's tedious. Everything has to be cross-referenced by date and subject matter. I'll pay you by the hour, assuming you're not moving in slow motion. You interested?"

"I might be," he replied. "How are the retirement benefits?"

"I need help with some other things, too," she said, ignoring his question. "There's painting to be done and, truth be told, the carpet in the front ought to be pulled up. I think there's a hardwood floor under there you could refinish. Tell you what—I'll put you on the clock as of an hour ago." She leaned back in the seat ostentatiously. "I feel like such a tycoon. I've got my own driver."

The matter seemed to be settled, even though Charley hadn't actually said yes.

●

The road became much steeper in the last mile before her house. There was actually another turn, which Tallasee didn't recall until they were right on it, so for the second time that afternoon Charley had to stop the truck and back up a bit. She felt better about her memory after they turned; the last stretch of road was rutted and washed out, causing the truck to lurch about as they climbed the steep grade. Charley kept the truck in first gear, though, and it felt surefooted as he drove. After a few minutes, the road reached a flat spot high on the ridge, where the trees had been thinned years ago. The house squatted down in the middle of the clearing.

It looked even more decrepit than Tallasee remembered. Built at least fifty years prior, the house's plank walls apparently had never tasted paint, and the weather had left them a feathery gray. The metal roof, also never painted, had acquired its own special color, this one the deep shade of rust that develops only when decades of rain finally triumph over galvanization. A wide front porch blocked what little light filtered through the trees, keeping the interior of the house in a permanent twilight, and the boards had a spongy feel under their feet. As they knocked on the door, they could see gaps in the siding where the wood had warped, a few of them so big that the newspaper that had been crammed down in the space between the interior and exterior walls for insulation was visible. There was no answer to their knock.

"She probably heard us coming up the road and ducked out of sight," Tallasee said. "If you wanted company, you'd live in town, I guess. This happened to me the first time I visited, too."

They walked back to the truck. Tallasee leaned in through the driver's-side window and honked the horn. It blared through the woods and startled a small creature, which they could hear scurrying through the leaves nearby. The noise was unnaturally loud in that forest clearing, and even Charley jumped despite watching her and knowing it was coming. He found himself wishing that Tallasee hadn't mentioned the creepy feeling she had about coming here. Maybe he now wouldn't be so unnerved by the oppressive stillness of the place.

"Mrs. Bullock?" she called. "It's me, Tallasee Tynan. We're here just like I said we'd be."

They leaned against the truck and waited. After a few minutes, they heard the creak of door hinges from the back of the house; a moment later, the old woman appeared at the front door. Tallasee and Charley stepped up to the porch again and the woman pushed open the screen to let them in, nodding her greeting as they entered. She didn't seem inclined to explain where she'd been. In fact, she hadn't said a word yet, although she'd been quite the chatterbox on the phone just a couple of hours before.

"Well, we're here," Tallasee repeated, feeling stupid for stating the obvious. The old woman still said nothing, but cocked an eye toward Charley. Not for the first time, Tallasee marveled at the profoundly suspicious nature of people who lived apart from others.

"This is Charley Selkirk. He's . . . my helper," Tallasee said.

The old woman finally spoke. "The unhappiness just drips off that boy, don't it?"

•

They'd met a few years before, when Tallasee decided to stop changing clothes every forty-five minutes and instead learn something about the other side of the camera. For no better reason than the fact that they fascinated her, Tallasee had begun taking pictures of the old women who lived in the deep mountain hollows. The twentieth century had largely passed them by, leaving them to live as their own mothers and grandmothers had, but it was an existence that would probably not survive beyond them, and Tallasee thought it was important to make a record of it. They were the last link to another time. The luckier among them had a power line to the house to run the pump and provide lights, but it was just as typical to find one still hauling water and using kerosene lamps at night, stalking a chicken every once in a while for dinner, and making her toilet in an outhouse.

Yet Tallasee never met one of these women who felt deprived or oppressed. There's a deep streak of isolationism and independence among the mountain folk: by nature they're contrary and self-sufficient, suspicious of any authority that doesn't originate within their families or settlements. In one county of north Georgia, lore has it that this sentiment was so firmly held that the families there even wanted nothing to do with the Confederacy; they seceded from the secessionists and threw their lot with the Yankees, who, of course, were nowhere to be found—which was probably the point.

Tallasee would take a tape recorder with her and set it on the table as she took photos. At first, she had only wanted a way to record the proper spelling of their names, their birthdates, things like that, and it seemed easier to just tape their answers rather than take notes at the very moment she was trying to set up a picture. After a while, however, Tallasee realized that she had something special under way. She would keep the women talking as she worked, try to make them less conscious of the camera, and the stories the old gals told were amazing. In these matter-of-fact voices, with their thick Southern accents and Scottish or Irish rhythms lingering just underneath, they would recall things that made it clear that their world was a much, much different place from the one that other people live in.

That first became apparent on the afternoon that Tallasee photographed Mrs. Annie Lily Murchison at her home near Bolt's Gap. She noticed that Mrs. Murchison's right hand was bandaged and that she held her arm close to her body, looking awkward and stiff as she used her other arm to reach for things. Tallasee asked her if she'd hurt herself.

"Oh, honey, I did a silly thing," Mrs. Murchison replied. "I found a copperhead in the garden and killed it. He'd been around for a few years, getting bigger and fatter all the time. I used to always just shoo him away 'cause he never ate anything I wanted to eat, but he scared away them that did. Rabbits and such. So I'd poke him with my hoe and off he'd go somewhere 'til I was done. It was peaceable between us.

"Then one day, I suddenly took scared of him. I don't know why, exactly, but he frightened me something fierce, all curled up there looking sassy and mean. So I took my hoe to him, whacked him a few times 'til he was dead. That's when I did my silly thing. I looped a piece of twine 'round his tail and hung him from a branch of a tree next to the garden. I meant for it to be warning to his kind, I guess.

"Now, a snake understands he must die by human hands—it's always been that way. We fell from grace together, and the snake accepts that man will kill him in memory of that. But what we must never do is make a ceremony of it. You don't glory in it. They must have thought that's what I was doing when I hung him in that tree.

"So they set out to even up with me. The next day, as I reached down to pick the okra growing close to the ground, his brother bit me on the hand. He was as brown as the dirt itself, and I never saw him until he put his mouth on the fat part of my hand, right here between the thumb and the finger. It burned as he put the poison in.

"Now, a copperhead usually won't kill you, even if he wants to. His poison's not that deadly. But he'll make you so sick that you want to die. It was three days before I could move much, and as soon as I could I went out there and cut down that snake from the tree. Once I did that, I felt better. I still can't use my hand much, though. It's been five weeks now."

Tallasee was enchanted by this tale, with its biblical references and implicit assumption that beasts will conspire against men. The book was born as Mrs. Murchison told it. Even as Tallasee photographed her, she knew how the picture would look on the page and where the type would go. She knew that it would be a large book, printed on top-quality paper and filled with glorious photographs of these wonderful old women accompanied by the tales from their own tongues. Tallasee knew exactly what she wanted to do, although she later had to fight with the publisher about almost everything related to the book.

His apology came with the third printing. He eventually sold a hundred thousand copies, which made him a genius to the rest of the publishing world. He got very good, too, at analyzing for reporters what social trends that he, in his genius, alone had seen and capitalized on: the growing strength of the women's movement, the nostalgia for a simpler time that comes during periods of social upheaval, and the willingness of the rest of the country to forgive the South its sins, especially now that places like Watts and Newark and Detroit had come to have as sinister a ring as Mississippi. Tallasee was tempted to remind him that the book's success probably was rooted in something much more simple—great photographs and wonderful stories that combined folklore, mysticism, wisdom, and a fundamental grasp of human nature that lives only in the very old—but why argue? Despite his genius, there was only one name on the cover. Besides, his checks cleared. She was happy to let him talk.

Tallasee had almost left Pearlie Bullock out of the book altogether, however. She'd visited nearly sixty old gals over the course of two years, learning about one from another, and photographed all but the dozen or so who politely listened to her request before shaking their heads no. From among those who agreed, Tallasee had selected twenty-five to be featured in the book, sending the others a framed copy of one of the better pictures she'd made of them as compensation for their time.

Twice she had removed Pearlie Bullock from her stack and replaced her with someone else. And twice Tallasee had second thoughts and returned Pearlie Bullock to the lineup.

Tallasee feared that Mrs. Bullock's would be a jarring and inconsistent chapter. The other women, in both their pictures and their stories, were lively and happy, wearing their years and circumstances comfortably. In contrast, there had been a darkness about Mrs. Bullock. Tallasee had seen it through her camera, had sensed something faintly sinister that accompanied them as she tracked Mrs. Bullock across her house and grounds for two days. And it was captured on film and in her words

Still, Tallasee kept coming back to Mrs. Bullock's pictures as she worked on the book. Eventually, she realized that if she was drawn to the old woman, others would be as well. Mrs. Bullock would provide the leavening that the book needed, the subtle reminder that a hard life in a remote place can leave its mark in different ways. Her story— a bleak tale of children lost to sickness, a husband lost to accident, and optimism lost to nature, which invariably delivered storms and freezes at the worst moments—may not have been uplifting and inspirational, but it at least carried a lesson of survival: you can always endure more than you think you can.

Among the things you endure is the odd conversation.

"How have you been?" Tallasee asked.

"Fine," Mrs. Bullock said without conviction. They were still standing just inside the door. A long moment passed and Tallasee suddenly wondered whether the old woman even remembered calling her. She'd aged considerably in the two years since Tallasee had last seen her, a period during which forgetfulness could have taken up permanent residence.

"I imagine you're pretty worried about your grandson," Tallasee prompted.

That did the trick. "Yes, I am. Thank you for coming. My road's washed out pretty bad, so I hope it wasn't too hard getting up here."

"It wasn't bad. Charley drove."

Mrs. Bullock gave him another wary look, then said, "Well, y'all come sit down."

She led them to the back of the house, to a room that was half kitchen and half back porch. She motioned toward the table, and they sat.

"I brought as many photographs as I could find, but I don't print nearly all my negatives," Tallasee said. "Just contact sheets." As soon as she heard herself talking, she felt foolish; the old woman didn't know what the devil a negative or contact sheet was. Her confusion was immediately apparent.

"I ain't signing no contract," Mrs. Bullock said. Tallasee suddenly remembered the difficulty she'd had trying to explain the permission form she needed the old woman to sign before Tallasee could use her photograph in the book.

"No, ma'am, of course not. Let me just show you the pictures I brought."

There were fewer than a dozen for Mrs. Bullock to review. Tallasee had brought only those photographs that showed groups of people, or those with panoramic shots of the communes that she'd visited. Most of the other shots had been of individual hippies, all of them adults aside from the occasional infant love child, and all of them clearly not runaway teenage boys.

No matter, because Mrs. Bullock got no farther than the first photograph. It had been taken at the commune closest to Barrington, and it showed nearly all its residents gathered to display their garden's bounty: a couple of bushels of potatoes, some melons, a gourd squash, a few handfuls of tomatoes, and a wicker basket full of pole beans. The hippies had been inordinately happy with their harvest, and in the photograph their faces clearly showed their pride in what surely was the first step toward a new society. But the produce had been buggy and wormy, and Tallasee recalled that their desire for the fruits of farming had never quite overcome their disinterest in doing things like weeding the garden every day and staking up plants properly. So, what they held in the photograph was the sum of what they had at all. It wasn't representative of their harvest—it *was* their harvest.

The old woman looked at the picture for a moment, then set it flat on the table and tapped her finger on one of the faces in the group. "That's him," she said.

Tallasee took the photograph back and studied it. The boy was standing near the edge of the group and was partly obscured by the person in front of him. He was skinny and bland, with straw-colored hair that still carried an echo of an amateur haircut on a back porch somewhere. He seemed older than Tallasee expected him to be. During Mrs. Bullock's explanation on the phone, Tallasee's mental image of the boy was that of a young teenager; this was somebody older than that. Somebody Charley's age.

Tallasee recalled him vaguely, remembered that he'd been waved over to join the gathering as she was setting up the shot. He hadn't said anything, and when he'd been given a melon to cradle for the photograph—in a truly egalitarian society, everyone has a trophy for the camera—he'd held it listlessly against his hip. His was the only bit of produce not visible in the picture, and he was the only person not smiling. Tallasee had visited that commune many times, but hadn't noticed him before the day the picture was shot, and hadn't noticed, during recent trips, whether he was still around.

"When did he run away?" she asked.

"Couple of months ago, best I can tell. Nobody bothered to tell me," the old woman said. "He's a good boy and he's got no business hanging around with those people. He cares about me and he always comes to see me."

Tallasee missed it, but Charley caught the time problem right away. "When did you shoot the photograph?" he asked Tallasee.

Tallasee had gotten in the habit of stamping a date on the back of every print, a useful exercise taught to her by a newspaper photographer who once helped clear a man of a murder charge by producing a dated photograph that showed the man at a ball game, just where he said he'd been, when the murder occurred. She turned the picture over.

"Nearly four months ago."

"This doesn't fit then," Charley said. "He runs away two months ago, but he's already living at the commune four months ago."

Mrs. Bullock either ignored or felt no need to address this inconsistency. No one said anything for a few moments, each of them turning it over privately. Charley had taken the photograph from Tallasee, and he studied it during the lull. He ended the silence with another question.

"What's this he's wearing?"

There was printing visible on the part of the boy's T-shirt that wasn't obscured, along with what seemed to be a large emblem or crest. But the letters were too small to be distinct.

"I don't know," Tallasee said. "But I've got a loupe in my bag."

Both of them looked at her blankly. "It's an eyepiece, like what a jeweler uses," Tallasee explained. "They're good for looking at contact sheets."

Charley stood up. "How 'bout if your assistant gets it for you?" he said. Tallasee couldn't discern whether he was being sarcastic.

He came back a minute later and handed her the bag. She found the loupe in the bottom and placed it over the boy's image, then leaned down to look. The letters were immediately clear.

"It seems your grandson was a Notre Dame fan," Tallasee said.

Mrs. Bullock brightened. "Yes, that's right. He was always wearing that shirt. I don't know where he got it, but you know how children get attached to some of their clothes."

They all smiled giddily at one another, as if an imposing obstacle had been surmounted. Mrs. Bullock eventually brought them back around to reality.

"So," she asked, "can you find him?"

Chapter Three

He was supposed to stay in the house like Charley told him to, but since when have little brothers ever done what they're supposed to do? And Charley was supposed to look after him like he was told to do, but since when have big brothers ever resisted the lure of a baseball game being played down the street?

There also was a pair of more specific questions, although it wasn't until the summer of his adventure with Tallasee that Charley learned the answers. Where had his mother gone that afternoon? And whom did she see?

There'd never been a mystery as to where Charley's father was at the moment it happened, because a troublesome drinking habit has a way of being all too public a thing. Lee Roy Selkirk had left work at lunch that day and not returned, but in the aftermath of events, his presence at a roadside tavern in a neighboring county was easily confirmed. There was nothing, however, to establish Frances Selkirk's whereabouts beyond her own word. When the people whose job it was to make an official record of tragedy asked her where she'd been that afternoon, she claimed that she'd gone for a drive in the country. That's all. When the authorities exchanged doubtful glances among themselves and invited her to elaborate, she wouldn't. She'd simply gone for a drive, she said. There was nothing more to explain.

Official interest eventually faded, because Frances Selkirk's driving habits weren't central to the issue. But Charley's curiosity never waned.

He was nine years old; Shay was five. It was an earlier summer, one grown old and flat, having traded its early promise of adventure and freedom from school for the numbing reality of empty, endless days.

One morning, Charley was sitting on the back porch reading a comic book when he smelled his mother behind him, fresh and fragrant. She was attaching an earring when he turned around, her head cocked fetchingly as both hands worked near her neck. She was dressed nicely and was clearly ready to go out, as had become her habit that summer.

"I'm going for lunch at Corey's," Frances Selkirk said.

"Can we come?" Charley asked.

"Now, why would you want to spend two hours with a bunch of women in a department-store lunchroom?" She grinned and gave him what she meant to be a sly wink, but she wasn't very good at it. She had to squinch her whole face in order to get one eyelid to drop.

"You never take us anywhere," Charley said. It was a reflexive response; he didn't actually want to go, but in the chess game between parent and child, no move ever goes unchallenged.

"Well, if my children behaved better, maybe I could take them places," she said. Checkmate—Charley and Shay had fussed at the grocery store the previous day, quibbling over who got to sit in the shopping cart and prompting Frances to finally declare that they both could walk. They'd then spent the next half hour trying to trip each other as she strolled the aisles, a contest that Charley won by inadvertently nudging Shay into a stacked display of canned green beans, which came clattering down noisily and brought the store manager running. Frances's fury had only the next morning seemed to wane.

"It was an accident," Charley said, offering his explanation yet again in the hope that it might register.

She ignored him. "Fix your brother a sandwich in a little while. The bread and peanut butter are on the counter. I don't want any trouble while I'm out, you hear?"

He nodded. "How long will you be gone?"

"A while. I'll be back in a few hours."

"That's a long time for lunch," Charley complained.

"Honey, when you're a grown-up there's more to lunch than eating," she said, then blushed inexplicably. "Look after Shay. And you know the rules: don't turn the stove on and don't let anyone in the house, right?"

He nodded again.

"Give me a kiss," she said, then walked into the living room, where

Shay was watching the black-and-white television. Charley heard his mother give the younger boy a shorter, simpler explanation of where she was going, then a moment later heard the car backing out of the driveway, scraping the tailpipe like always. If his father had been home, he would have hollered at her. Like always.

Charley joined Shay in the living room. Two of Atlanta's three television stations had signals strong enough to reach Barrington, and the station in Spartanburg, South Carolina, also somehow managed to put enough beef into its broadcast to get it over the hills that bunched around the town. The boys spent an hour idly flipping between channels until it was clear that all three had completed the segue from morning cartoons to midday soap operas. Finally, Charley turned the set off.

"What do you want to do?" he asked.

"Science spearmints," Shay said.

Shay had become a scientist that summer. He had some vague notion of what constituted science, and had spent countless hours devising elaborate and usually hilarious ways of tinkering with the natural order of things. He had a fine collection of insects in the shed behind the house, stored in empty instant-coffee jars whose lids were punched to provide air, and he was forever concocting breeding combinations that would improve upon the appallingly slow process of evolution: bees and butterflies together in one jar, for instance, in hopes of creating a creature that didn't move quite so fast as it tried to sting you.

He also was enthralled by gadgets. A couple of months before, he'd gotten fixated on divers' face masks and had nagged his mother until she'd bought him a child-sized version at the five-and-dime. The thunderstorm that had been brewing all that day broke as the family arrived home from the store, and it was a couple of minutes before Frances had shaken out the umbrellas and noticed that Shay was still standing outside, diver's mask on and facing into the driving sheets of rain.

She had stepped out to the front porch and shouted for him to come inside. As he climbed the steps, his clothes soaked and dripping, she kneeled down to look at him through the face mask and asked, "What on earth were you doing out there?"

"Mom," he explained patiently, "I was trying to keep my face from getting wet."

It was a story she was to tell often in later years, for it captured Shay's essence in a single tale: uncommonly bright and unknowingly funny, the sort of child that parents hope for and teachers delight in. He'd never been fussy or troublesome, even as a toddler, and even though he was only five years old, few doubted that his happiness and generosity were permanently in place. Charley would complain about him occasionally, because that's what big brothers do, but his heart was never in it. If Shay had claimed the greater share of their parents' favor, even that was acceptable because he never solicited it and never stored it for later use. And Charley couldn't have resented Shay even if he'd worked at it, because Shay liked him too much.

"I'm glad Charley's my brother," Shay said one night as their mother was tucking them into bed. The boys shared a room, with their beds pushed against opposite walls, and even in the dim light Charley could see his mother smile.

"Why?" she asked.

" 'Cause we do fun stuff together, and 'cause if he wasn't born I'd still be waiting."

"Waiting for what?"

"Waiting to be born," he said. "I wouldn't get my turn." Shay thought that all souls got assigned to earth on a strictly sequential basis, sort of the way someone takes a number and awaits service at the butcher shop.

"Honey, when you're born, you're born," Frances told him. "It doesn't matter who came first."

"Yes it does," Shay replied with irrefutable logic. "I couldn't be a big brother. I don't know all the stuff he knows."

But Charley didn't know quite enough, as it turned out.

"What sort of experiments?" he asked.

"I want to make frogs," Shay answered. He meant he wanted to catch tadpoles and keep them in a bucket as they grew legs.

The boys rummaged in the shed until they found the net their father took with him on the occasional fishing trip—during which he never seemed to catch anything but always returned home smelling of beer—then picked up a bucket from the corner of the back porch where it sat beneath the leaky part of the ceiling that Lee Roy never quite got around to fixing. They crossed the yard and went into the woods bordering the back of the lot; the ground sloped down to a spongy, flat area just a hundred yards from their back door, a two-acre wetland that no one had ever attempted to clear and drain for more homes. A small stream trickled through the middle of the marsh, its water barely energetic enough to move itself to the pond that filled a low spot a quarter mile away. The frogs had been loud earlier that year, croaking their love calls all through the night, and the fruit of their efforts now swam thick in the stream. The boys previously had spotted a half dozen eddies in the stream where the eggs had been laid, and had monitored them for weeks as the tadpoles got fatter. Their plan was to now capture a few dozen and watch as they made the amazing metamorphosis from fish to frog. Charley wondered how long it would take Shay to decide that a many-legged frog would jump better than the standard model, and start trying to mate one with a caterpillar.

This day's expedition, however, was a failure. The swarms of tadpoles had disappeared, presumably having migrated to the pond, and the few strays they saw eluded their net. Shay's disappointment in this interruption of scientific endeavor was unmistakable.

"Where'd they go, Charley?" he asked.

"I don't know. The pond, probably." Charley knew what Shay was going to ask next, so he headed him off. "Mom says we can't go there. We'd better just go home."

They trudged back to the house, and as they came up to the back door, Charley saw a half dozen boys from the neighborhood moving down the street in a loose clot, with baseball bats and gloves in their grip. One of them spotted Charley and waved. "Hey, Charley, we're starting a game," he called. "Come on and play."

Charley hesitated. He knew that a game of baseball would keep him busy for the afternoon, salvaging a day that was shaping up as yet another of those late-summer stretches that made him long for school, if only for something to do. But he was supposed to be looking after his little brother, and even though Shay was a great scientist, he was no athlete. Neither team would want him, but Charley would insist on taking him on his team so Shay wouldn't feel bad. Then they'd lose.

Ultimately, the threat of boredom overrode his sense of responsibility. "I'll be there in a minute," Charley shouted.

"Can I play?" Shay asked.

"Nah, you stay home. Tell you what—I'll fix you lunch, then you can watch TV or something."

Shay pouted until Charley made his favorite sandwich, bologna with peanut butter, and poured him an extra ration of Kool-Aid. Charley then excavated the bedroom until he found his baseball glove, and, as he headed outside again, stuck his head into the kitchen. Shay was contentedly chewing, elbows on the table and sandwich held in front of his mouth ready for the next bite. It was another of the things he did that was unintentionally hilarious: he held food close to his face, as if he was afraid that it otherwise would squirm away.

"I'll just be down the street," Charley said, then relented a bit. "C'mon down after a while, if you want."

"Okay," Shay replied from behind his sandwich.

The game was just starting when Charley arrived. He joined the team on the field, and for the next hour played with the energy and abandon that only the young can seem to muster. However, midway though one of the innings, Charley felt the need to check on Shay. It wasn't a concern that crept up on him gradually; it was instead a sudden knot in his stomach, some subliminal instruction to hurry home right then.

Charley was panting as he came through the kitchen door. Shay wasn't there, but he'd obviously finished his lunch and cleaned up, which in reality meant that he'd merely moved his mess from the table to the sink.

"Shay, where are you?" Charley called. There was no answer.

He checked the living room, but the television was off. He looked in their bedroom, then opened the closet door—Shay had gone to sleep in there once a couple of years before, nestled on the floor among a bunch of stuffed animals, which set off a minor panic when Lee Roy— who, instead of keeping an eye on them while his wife was at the store, had allowed a beer and a ball game on the radio to distract him—finally realized that the boy was missing. It turned out fine that time, as Shay was found sleeping peacefully, but it marked the first moment Charley had noticed the tension between his mother and father.

"I was just forming a posse to look for him when he turned up," Lee Roy had said when Frances drove up to the sight of several neighborhood men milling around the front yard. He said it jokingly, but there was no amusement in Frances's flat stare.

"How about if I stitch a Miller High Life label into all his clothes," she'd replied. "You'll keep track of him then, won't you?" Charley recalled the other men turning away with embarrassed looks on their faces.

Shay wasn't asleep on the closet floor this time, though. And when it was clear that he wasn't anywhere in the house or yard, Charley went next door to see Mr. Boggs.

Mr. Boggs was a retired schoolteacher who puttered happily and competently around his house, and who surprised Charley and Shay every couple of months with something that he'd built for them: bookshelves and rabbit pens and such. He also regularly offered to help Lee Roy with maintenance on the Selkirks' house, pointing to a sagging gutter or ripped window screen and cheerfully saying, "Let me know when you're ready to fix that," but Lee Roy neither asked for help nor fixed it himself. The boys adored Mr. Boggs, and Charley often wished that his father would take up the offer so that the three of them could work together. Mr. Boggs was adept with tools and patient with the youngsters, and Charley—much as Shay sought to do with his breeding schemes—hoped that if they all labored together, in close company, the characteristics of one man would rub off on the other, that Lee Roy magically would metamorphose into the father that Charley fantasized having. Instead, Lee Roy would only complain privately about Mr. Boggs and call him a busybody.

Charley found him in his shed, with parts from a lawn-mower engine spread out on a board in front of him. "I can't find Shay," Charley said.

"Well, everybody's got to be somewhere. Let's look around," Mr. Boggs said.

They retraced Charley's original steps, then fanned out to neighboring yards, calling Shay's name as they went. At one point, Mr. Boggs stopped as if a thought suddenly had occurred to him.

"Where's your momma?" he asked.

"She's having lunch at Corey's."

"We'd better call her," Mr. Boggs said.

They walked back to Mr. Boggs's house and he went inside. Through the window Charley saw him look up the number in the phone book, then jot down another number when the Corey's operator presumably told him how to call the lunchroom directly. The second call was brief.

"They said she hasn't been there," he declared when he came back outside. "Your dad's at work, right?" Charley nodded.

The process repeated itself. Mr. Boggs called the plant and was given another number to dial, which rang near the door of the loading dock where Lee Roy operated a forklift. But when Mr. Boggs came back outside that time, he just shook his head. His normal cheerfulness had left him.

And then, suddenly, Charley knew.

He ran as fast as he could. He ran heedlessly through branches and brambles, ignoring them as they whipped his face and clawed at his clothes. He lost a shoe in an especially mucky spot near the stream, but still he ran. His chest felt as if there was a steel band being tightened around it, but it was fear, not exertion, that suffocated him. Still, he ran—he wanted to run so hard that he would die before seeing what he was sure to see.

Mr. Boggs was guided by Charley's screams. It was a long way for an old man to run, and it likely seemed even longer coming back as he carried Shay in his arms. Yet he, too, ran each way, moving as fast on the return as his old-man legs could propel him.

All their running made no difference, however. Shay had been in the water too long, spent too many minutes face down in the shallows of the pond where he'd gone to capture the tadpoles. They were there, too, just as Charley had predicted, swimming lazily near Shay's head and occasionally nosing into his clothes in search of food. They'd scattered when Charley first plunged in and grabbed the back of Shay's shirt, but as he sat on the bank crying after Mr. Boggs ran away with Shay—as he sat there wishing he could be just as undeniably dead as his little brother—Charley saw that the tadpoles had returned, wondering where their new friend went.

●

Mr. Boggs never seemed to be as happy after that. He still did the same things, but there was a joylessness in his puttering. He moved away sometime later, even though he'd lived in that house for most of his adult life. The Selkirk family got a card from him the next Christmas, but they never heard from him again after that.

Lee Roy moved away, too. He and Frances had terrible fights after Shay died, long periods of screaming that went on until it seemed like they had drained themselves. Then things would be calm for a while until, with their rage recharged, they would start again. They carried on like that for months, until one morning when Charley got out of bed and saw that his father was gone.

Lee Roy had come home right on time the day Shay drowned, just as if he'd been at work all along. A policeman had been sent to wait for him, or with Charley—it wasn't clear which—and when Lee Roy arrived, he was jaunty and happy, as he always was after drinking. Only his breath, sweet with whiskey and mints, gave him away, and then probably to Charley alone. The policeman didn't seem to notice as he told Lee Roy what had happened, didn't seem to notice that Lee Roy's incomprehension lasted until they were almost to the patrol car for their ride to the hospital. Lee Roy kept asking the policeman questions about what had happened, but the officer couldn't, or wouldn't, answer. So Lee Roy would twist around in his seat and look at Charley, sitting in the middle of the backseat like a suspect being brought in for questioning, and demand to know what had happened and where Frances had been. Charley would try to answer, but he kept remembering the sight of the back of Shay's shirt billowed up out of the water, a strange bubble of red on the pond's surface, and that image would cause him to cry again. Then Lee Roy would shoot another question at the policeman, starting the exercise all over again.

The scene at the hospital was horrible. The policeman left Lee Roy and Charley at the front desk, where an officious nurse flipped aggressively through several patient lists before informing them that she had no record of Shay's arrival. "Try the emergency room," she suggested, waving her hand in the vague direction of another part of the hospital. They arrived there just a few minutes ahead of Frances, who was hysterical even as she came through the door. The family was ushered into

a small room so that their unhappiness wouldn't infect the other people who sat in the waiting room while surgery was performed on family
members; the hospital staff clearly worried that other people's secret
fears of bad news could be easily stoked.

In that room began the argument that Frances and Lee Roy were to
have so many times over the coming months.

"What happened? Where were you?" Lee Roy asked. He'd started
to hug his wife, but she'd shrugged off his arms. No one can be a com-
forter when they sound like an inquisitor.

"Where was I? You spend half your life boozing and you dare to ask
me where I've been?" She was screaming, and her fury caused Lee
Roy to back up a step. "Get away from me. Both of you get away."

Charley already had begun to move toward her, seeking both comfort and to comfort her, when Frances pushed him away rudely. She
dropped herself into a metal chair set against the wall, leaving Charley
alone and sobbing in the middle of the room. Lee Roy, with tears on
his own face, patted Charley on the shoulder, but he had no natural
talent for intimacy. After a few moments he also sat down and put his
face into his hands. When the emergency room physician entered the
room a minute later to confirm what they already knew, that was how
he found them: mother and father sitting against opposite walls, alone
with their grief and guilt, with Charley standing suspended between
them quivering.

In later years, Frances sought Charley's forgiveness for that moment. But a nine-year-old boy's failure to stay with his little brother
was the only lifeline she had at that moment, the only thing that saved
her from being eviscerated by her own guilt. As long as the blame
could be shared, or be wholly assigned to Charley, she could survive.
So it hadn't mattered much at the time that Charley was left alone to
his own sorrow, a child with guilt humming like a tuning fork in his
gut. Charley just stood by himself and cried. It's pretty much all he did
for a long time.

The thing is, that humming never went away. It somehow made
Charley extraordinarily sensitive to the world around him. Anything—
the smallest shift in mood, an eye that looks away too quickly, the wandering of a hand that suddenly seems lost—caused the humming to
start. Noises startled him all out of proportion to their actual loudness;

any movement caught his eye, regardless of how far into his periphery it may have occurred. It was as if Charley's awareness was on a dial that couldn't be turned down.

Years later, that awareness helped him see something that no one else saw and helped him set off a chain of events that ultimately, and painfully, made things right between him and his mother. But it also was disconcerting for him to meet Pearlie Bullock and realize that she had a touch of that awareness herself. The unhappiness indeed just dripped off Charley.

●

The Selkirks were the talk of Barrington for a while. There was much speculation as to where Frances had been; even though Shay's drowning clearly was accidental, the police had questioned both Frances and Lee Roy before determining that their absences didn't rise to the level of criminal neglect, so the fact that she hadn't been at Corey's after all became widely known. It was universally agreed that she'd been with another man, but the mystery never was solved and the people who care about such things soon found other lives to discuss. Frances gave them no other reason to talk after that, anyway: Shay's death seemed to have permanently squashed whatever restless impulse had led her away from home. But while it was years before Charley sensed that she might have had a lover—a realization that came only when his own longings caused him to understand that all adults, even mothers, are subject to desire—he always wondered where Frances had gone that day.

He never missed his father as much as he thought he should. For a few years after Shay's death, Charley heard from Lee Roy on a timetable known only to the older man, through a haphazard series of letters sent from different places as he took different jobs: oil-rig roughneck, trucking-company tire changer, warehouse night watchman. Occasionally, Lee Roy would enclose a five-dollar bill, along with a recommendation that Charley spend it frivolously, as if he suspected that it wasn't something Charley would do on his own. Sometimes Charley would write back, but Lee Roy often would have moved already and the letters would be returned. Charley got a birthday card from him on his thirteenth birthday, then never heard from him again. A year or so later, Lee Roy's sister in South Carolina wrote Frances to tell her that he was dead: it seems Lee Roy had lost a debate in a bar when his opponent used a pool cue to the temple during the rebuttal period. The letter carried a cool, just-thought-you-should-know tone, making it clear that whatever remote family connection there had been was now truly severed.

So, it was just the three of them: Charley, Frances, and the memory of Shay.

●

Just as Pearlie Bullock had measured Charley, he'd deftly plumbed her essence, too, and came to a conclusion. The difference was that he was too polite to state his analysis: she was demented.

He considered telling Tallasee, but decided against it. As they drove back down the mountain, it was apparent that Tallasee already had grown cool to this venture, anyway. It was one thing to help an old woman determine where her runaway grandson might be; it was quite another to be recruited to search for him. Tallasee had a book deadline looming and countless hours to spend in her darkroom. Even if she had a new employee to help out around the studio—an eager lad, and uncommonly bright for a high school dropout—this was not a chore that she had time for. Mrs. Bullock's madness would have been just one more reason to simply pass the matter off to the sheriff and let him poke around the commune.

But still, Tallasee's skill had held true. Even in a photograph of a family of hippies, she had captured something in the runaway boy's eyes. Charley was sure that he knew what it was: the look of unhappy anticipation that children get when events supersede them, when they realize that life has suddenly accelerated beyond their understanding. Charley recognized the look, and he wanted to find the boy to tell him that whatever had happened, it probably wasn't his fault.

Chapter Four

T hings just got away from me. That's about the only way I can explain it. I would try to fix one problem, but then another problem would pop up. And it got a little worse each time. Weird, isn't it? I started out with a small bit of trouble, but when I tried to deal with it, more trouble resulted, and when I tried to deal with that, even more trouble came. Pretty soon, I had lots of problems. More than I could handle.

So, that's how I got here. You boys are pretty smart, I'll give you that. But it helps when people do foolish things, doesn't it? It's not like you had to be some kind of Sherlock Holmes to figure this out. I walked right into it. I'm not going to insult your intelligence by denying things. I was there, it was clear what I went there to do, and you boys were waiting for me to do it. I'll bet it doesn't get much easier than that for you.

And I'll tell you something else: I'm not going to insist that I have a lawyer here while we talk. I'm just going to tell you what happened. I know I don't have to. But I have to say, I don't recall that you boys have read me my rights. Hey, I watch television. I know how this works.

That's a joke, by the way. Goddamn. What's it take to get a grin out of you two?

You look a little young to be doing this. I feel like I ought to ask for some ID. Now, your partner there, I can relate to him. He looks like he's done some honest work in his life. You're sure your boss knows about this? Oh, hell. That's a stupid question. I was sitting right there when he called. Or at least you said it was him. I don't know—you're a little tricky. Maybe I should ask to speak to him myself.

Tell you what—why don't we go through this one time and let me explain what happened. I'm not a bad guy. It's like I said—things just got away from me. I meant no harm to anyone, and I'm confident I can make you boys understand that. Hell, maybe you'll even let me leave when we're done here. Can we make that deal?

No? Well, I had to ask. It's like they say, you can't win if you don't enter.

Chapter Five

Barrington didn't have much of a spring that year. When Charley and Tallasee drove up the mountain to see Mrs. Bullock, the leaves were only then beginning to uncurl on the trees. When they came down a few hours later, the leaves had popped out completely. Or at least that's what it seemed like to them.

The temperature also showed no taste for gradual change. One day, as if there was a switch somewhere that had been tripped by a capricious god of climate, it suddenly turned hot, a still and muggy heat that put a permanent glass of iced tea into the hands of natives and made visitors wonder if they'd developed a lung condition that prevented them from getting a good breath. It happens that way in the South. For a long time, summer was the region's best weapon as it fought the leavening influence of Northern commerce. A Yankee company might establish an outpost in a larger city like Atlanta or Birmingham, or send a manager or two to oversee a factory located in a community civilized enough to support a country club, but it wouldn't consider a wholesale relocation to such a torrid place, even if the residents were legendary for their willingness to work for nothing and inclination to believe that unionism was blood kin to communism. So, until air-conditioning became common, heat was the device that kept the invaders from feeling too comfortable in their captured lands.

But if air-conditioning is what made the South tolerable to outsiders, it also eroded whatever tolerance for heat that some of its natives once had. Tallasee didn't remember, as a child, ever being uncomfortable in the summer. She'd lived in a house her mother always called "modestly large," which meant, Tallasee later concluded, that it was bigger than the ones around it, but not pretentiously so. It had a wide, deep porch on the front, which faced east, so by the time the sun got high enough in the sky to begin making trouble, that side of the house already was shaded. Behind the house, two large pecan trees stood shoulder to shoulder, so there also was shade when the day ended. The only time that the house was at the sun's mercy was when the sun was directly overhead, but open windows and doors helped air circulate on all but the most still days, when an attic fan mounted in the ceiling of the central hallway took over nature's job. When thunderstorms blew in and necessitated the regular scramble through the house to close windows, turning the interior muggy within moments, the family simply decamped for the front porch, where they thrilled to the thunder and competed to see who could kill the most flies, which seemed to seek a dry place with the same instinct that drives humans to run for cover when it rains.

Later, however, Tallasee always seemed to feel hot. Nearly every building in the South eventually became air-conditioned, of course, and most cars too, but she realized one day that those improvements perversely made the heat more oppressive. There was a constant twenty- to twenty-five-degree difference between the indoors and the outdoors—not to mention an even wilder swing in the humidity level—and the body quickly lost its ability to adjust between the two. Stepping outside wasn't just mildly uncomfortable, like it used to be; it became a trauma, leading the once-hardy natives to do their praying, eating, and fornicating exclusively indoors.

But the sudden heat that spring didn't seem to bother Charley, even though his new job required much hauling, and movement in and out of buildings. He'd decided that it didn't make sense to organize Tallasee's negative files first if he was just going to have to haul them out to refinish the floor. Instead, he would pile all the cartons and boxes into the back of his truck and take them to Tallasee's house for storage while he pulled up the carpet in the front room of the studio. He would work on the files later, he said.

She was busy in her darkroom the morning he loaded the truck, so Tallasee gave him the key to her house. When he returned, he said, "Somebody must have broken into your place."

"They did?" she said, walking right into the punch line.

"I don't think they took anything, but they made a terrible mess. Left dirty dishes on the counter, messed the bed up, threw stuff all over the floor. It's vandalism, is what it is."

Tallasee felt herself blushing. "Yeah, it's a little messy. But now that I've got some help, maybe the help can tidy up over there."

"Sorry," Charley said cheerfully. "I don't do widows."

His slip hung in the air for a long moment until he retrieved it. "I mean windows," he said. By then, however, they both were blushing.

●

It seemed to run in Tallasee's family. Her father had died before she was born, leaving her mother alone with two children and most of her life ahead of her. But where Tallasee's parents had a typical courtship, a marriage of sufficient length to produce two children, and enough years to build a foundation—both economic and emotional—to support the widow after her husband died, it was much different for Tallasee.

She was a wife for fifty-eight days. He was a musician on tour when she met him, the front man for a British band whose handlers were convinced that the Beatles and Rolling Stones already had done the heavy lifting, and so any collection of presentable boys from any English city would attract attention if they had any shred of talent. It was a smart bet, as it turned out: there was indeed a bare shred of talent in this band, enough to produce an album with a single good song among ten execrable ones, and on the strength of that song the band was sent on a lightning-strike tour of the United States. They arrived with the usual hype and their shows sold out, but one magazine editor who sensed that there wasn't much behind that single good song—and who further sensed that there was a nifty article on the rise and fall of a phenomenon ready to be plucked—decided to assign a writer and photographer to the tour. A properly surly and dyspeptic writer was easy enough to find, but when he looked through his pool of available freelance photographers, all he found were middle-aged men who thought that Frankie Avalon was cutting-edge contemporary culture and couldn't distinguish between hippies and beatniks. That wouldn't do, of course, because the editor—disguising his true intention—had worked out an agreement with the band's manager to have his photographer join the tour, so he needed someone whom they'd feel comfortable with. That led him to Tallasee, whose work was good enough to catch his eye when she'd sent it to him unsolicited.

Because any good editor is an expert manipulator, he didn't explain the working theory of the article to her. The editor understood the likelihood of Tallasee forming, over the course of the tour, some protective kinship with the band and therefore hesitating to take the very pictures he wanted. In fact, he selected her in part precisely because he believed that just such a kinship would flower, that over the course of time her access would become unfettered and the band's moments unguarded, and in that combination would the curtain be pulled away and the machinery of hype exposed. And that's exactly what happened.

Nigel, the band's front man, had an adequate voice, thanks to some early years in an Anglican cathedral choir, and an un-English set of perfect teeth that made for a deadly smile. He grinned at Tallasee the morning she was introduced to the band, grinned a little wider when he heard that she'd be tagging along for three shows over the next week, then grinned even wider when she shed the coat that she, alone among everyone else, was wearing—this was, after all, March in New York, and her thin Southern blood still felt winter even as the natives and their British visitors felt spring. He was unabashed in his appreciation of Tallasee, and even though a few years of modeling had left her inured to the stares of men, his look was so nakedly and happily anticipatory that she felt a minor version of the same electrical charge that clearly was finding its way to his loins.

"So you'll be taking some snaps, then," Nigel said, and his accent, enchanting to Tallasee, helped increase the charge's intensity a few notches.

She nodded. "Just pretend I'm not here," she said. "Go about your business as always."

He turned to the other band members. "You heard her, mates. No looking at her delicious little bum while she works, eh?"

They smirked lasciviously as his gaze came back to Tallasee. "It's a bad idea to tell them to go about their business, 'cause their business seems to be bagging birds," he said. She knew just enough British slang to understand what he meant.

"What about you?" she asked. "Is that your business, too?"

He shrugged. "I suppose."

"Be glad you're in a band, then," Tallasee said. "Otherwise, I can't imagine you'd be in business very long."

His grin was sheepish as his bandmates hooted. "Cheeky one, eh?" he said. They nodded their agreement.

"So you'll be with us how long?" Nigel asked.

"A week or so," she said. "That should be long enough."

Tallasee didn't know how prophetic she was. A week was indeed long enough.

●

He was solicitous and kind, it turned out. That initial surge she'd felt had quickly cooled as he'd stepped into his role of rock star/satyr, but had rekindled when, later that first day, he'd dropped into a chair next to her to talk. The other band members were elsewhere, along with the assorted handlers and helpers, and he was bored—a condition that Tallasee already had concluded was common during any touring musician's offstage hours. He asked about her cameras, paid attention when she answered, asked more detailed questions, and eventually fixed a wonderful smile on his face when he grasped the capture of light. He then asked how she'd become a photographer, so she explained that, like him, she'd started asking questions one day while in the thrall of boredom, idle queries that came after she'd been fitted, trussed, and left to wait as light was measured and adjusted. The answers had been grudging and curt at first, because models are an annoyance to any fashion photographer to begin with; they are the one unstable element in a world that otherwise is shaped by his whim. So, his reaction to having one of these precious creatures loose at his elbow posing a seemingly endless series of questions was to be as rude and abrupt as he figured he could be without sending Tallasee away in tears, which, while satisfying, would mean yet another delay in the shooting schedule.

But she was tougher than he thought. She had persisted, ignoring his rudeness, and he'd softened, eventually coming to be flattered by her implicit admission—rare among those upon whom all attention normally is focused—that what happened on his side of the camera was more important than what happened on her side. He taught as he worked, and when Tallasee had learned what she could and acquired what she needed, she told her agency one day that her portfolio could be stored away and her assignments given to someone else. "And here I am today, photographing famous musicians for a national magazine, thank you very much," she concluded.

She meant to be wry: it was a plum assignment for a high-profile publication—the promise of much space inside and the possibility of a cover if things turned out right (which to the editor meant if the band bombed as he expected)—and she tried to give it a little-ol'-me tone. It sounded wrong to Nigel, however. He must have heard a sarcastic echo of his own private doubts. Tallasee was indeed there, and she was indeed on assignment for a magazine. So, to someone already inclined to believe that his success had been bestowed and not earned, there was only one part of that sentence capable of drawing blood. Nigel was a performer, perhaps even a singer, but he'd never called himself a *musician,* although he had wanted so desperately to be one that he had lent himself to this slickly packaged enterprise in hopes it could, somehow, make him into that. To hear Tallasee make careless use of the word could only mean she, like everyone else, took it as a joke.

Nothing else she said in the coming months seemed to make up for it.

●

Still, they engaged in an extended minuet. They were elaborately courteous, professional, and arm's length in the presence of others and commitedly revelatory when alone, each presenting the other with a steady trickle of secrets and desires. Once their protective coverings were peeled back and it was certain that the tender parts wouldn't be damaged, they talked about anything that came to mind, lingering on the points of agreement and skating past the others. His self-doubt was enormously appealing to Tallasee, suggesting currents deep below the face that he'd been coached to show; in her he loved that uniquely American sense of being sure that whatever she did was exactly the right thing to do. That, and the fact she filled out her jeans quite nicely.

At the end of the week, Tallasee returned to New York and prepared the photographs. On her own, she then rejoined the tour as a quasi-credentialed hanger-on, loosely assigned the job of press liaison but unofficially acknowledged as chief consort. Three weeks after that, Tallasee and Nigel were married by a justice of the peace in California.

The day after that, with the impeccably vicious timing that life sometimes invokes, the magazine was delivered.

●

Tallasee had been willfully blind, of course. The writer who worked with her on the story, a fellow whose naturally unhappy disposition made any secret prepping by the editor superfluous, had made little effort to hide his sneer. He'd decided early on that the band's manager was manipulative and soulless, that the band itself was a creation of marketing and hype, and that Nigel—barely talented and visibly aware of it—was the very personification of all that was wrong with rock 'n' roll at the moment. But even if it was clear that he thought that, Tallasee hadn't expected him to write it.

He did, in brutally effective terms. It was the magazine's cover piece, as it turned out, and it contained the full measure of malice and attitude that the editor secretly had hoped for. There were a couple of shows left on the tour, in San Francisco and Los Angeles, and when the reviewers from newspapers in those cities had their say—naturally, they'd read the magazine piece first—they made sure that there was no chance of their being identified as the last remaining gullible fools. So they'd piled on, adding their own mocking analyses to the growing body of disdain, and radio stations began easing the band's one decent effort out of their song rotations.

When the end came, it came quickly. The day after the last concert,

the hired help was paid off, the band members were given airline
vouchers and told to find their own way home, and the manager himself decamped for some remote Caribbean resort, leaving his secretary
to give cool, noncommittal answers to Nigel's transatlantic phone
queries.

Only Nigel was wounded. The manager had made his costs and a
good bit more, and it was just business to him, anyway; every base-
ment or garage turned over to any group of young dreamers held the
possibility of his next investment. The other band members had been
journeymen musicians who'd treated the tour as a lark, so they'd never
harbored any ambition greater than simply returning home after they'd
drunk their fill of American women. Only Nigel had wagered anything
of himself on the tour, so it was he who sustained the only real loss.

Worse yet, Tallasee actually benefited from her husband's public
humiliation. The band's real-life moments had been captured on film
artfully and precisely: the difference between the faces they presented
to the world while onstage for a couple of hours and those they wore in
private moments was vivid and lasting. Her ability had betrayed her.
In another writer's hands, that difference could have been explained in
gentle tones, attributed to weariness, the jarring effects of hopscotch
travel, and a perfectly understandable desire to wear the face that
ticketholders came to see. But the photographs instead became supporting evidence for the writer's bill of indictment. He had asked the
band members many times about their music, had given them countless opportunities to demonstrate that there was a foundation of art and
craft supporting them, and they'd muffed each chance. They had
played the role of good-time lads too well, had not appreciated the
subtle social shift that now encouraged rock bands and their fans to
take themselves seriously. America was beginning to want its musicians to be committed and have a conscience. Tallasee's pictures,
which seemed to capture a profound cynicism in the band members'
haggard faces and offstage smirks, only helped the writer prove that
there was something rotten at the center: commitment and conscience
were conspicuously missing.

This never had been done before. Until then, the British Invasion of
pop-music groups had been portrayed as a series of visits by happy

chums engaged in lighthearted antics, with even the edgier, darker bands being credited with having good souls behind the bad-boy facades. But when the magazine published its piece, the editor's instincts were confirmed: the world was ready for what another publication later called "the maturing of reporting on rock 'n' roll." And almost everyone decided that the photographs were worthy of special mention.

"But look at the snaps you took," Nigel said repeatedly when Tallasee sought to explain. He neither understood how the machinery of hype could have turned so viciously against him, nor intuitively grasped that however much America loves to see a fraud unmasked, it loves redemption even more. The fact that he was now in the land of fresh starts and second chances never quite overcame his irretrievably British sense of caste and fate.

"It'll pass," Tallasee always responded, but he couldn't make himself believe it.

They lived in a borrowed apartment in one of the unhappier edges of Los Angeles. He spent his days calling record-company executives and journalists, trying to simultaneously arrange the future and rewrite the past. He had no luck with either. The executives, when he actually got them on the phone, gave elaborate explanations about how they already had too many artists in development, that they preferred to see people perform in clubs a few times before doing a deal, and that maybe he should burrow into a studio somewhere and cut a new demo tape. But each of them assured Nigel that it was really, really great to talk to him, and if their atrociously busy schedules ever eased up, they'd call him for lunch or something. Not understanding the code, Nigel would offer the phone number at the temporary apartment, sounding touchingly naïve as he did so.

The journalists—who, unlike record people, didn't have a salary tied directly to the ebb and flow of music trends and therefore didn't feel the need to even pretend to be friendly in case Nigel's fortunes indeed somehow righted themselves—were rudely abrupt. "Look, I'm in the news business," one of them said. "Your story has come and gone."

He spent his nights drinking. He would start at the apartment, yanking open the refrigerator door when the day's frustrations hit a certain point known but to him, and extracting the first of several beers. He would then complain about America's brewing industry, making unfavorable comparisons between whatever brand had found its way into his hand and the stouts and ales that he was accustomed to drinking in England. Then would come a few minutes of unfocused bitterness on any number of topics—the city's bad air, the unapologetic phoniness of its citizens, the inability to get anywhere without a car and the nightmare of driving if you had one—before he finally circled around to the main event: Tallasee's treachery.

"How could you not have known what that bloody writer was going to say?" he would ask. "And would it have killed you to use a little care when you lifted your camera? It's almost like you waited for my worst moments."

Tallasee stopped trying to explain it to him after a while, and he stopped inviting her to accompany him when he set out for the evening. He'd learned that between fame, even minor fame that was eroding by the day, and his accent, there was always somebody ready to spring for the next round. And that combination must have been good for more than drinks. Twice, Tallasee found the smell of another woman on him.

It was as if someone had pushed the fast-forward button on their married life. They were in Los Angeles for six weeks, and in that time they proceeded from ardor to boredom to disenchantment, then to carousing and infidelity. The whole cycle of marriage had been compacted into a bare month and a half.

The end was destined to be unhappy. God only knows where he was headed—a party or a woman?—or why anyone would loan a drunken Englishman a left-hand-drive car for a nighttime foray into the hills. Whatever the answers, his plunge off the canyon highway put to rest the debate over whether Nigel would recover from the grievous wound that Tallasee had helped inflict.

Ironically, he found redemption in death. The obituaries were heavy with fulsome praise from some of the very record-company executives and music critics whom Nigel had fruitlessly courted just weeks before. On the cusp of a promising career, they said. A light dimmed too soon. No mention was made of the world's previous judgment of him, save this: "He is survived by his wife, photographer Tallasee Tynan, whom he met when she was assigned to document the group's recent American tour."

The photograph of Nigel that ran with the obituaries was provided by the same magazine that had brought him to his ruin. It was one of Tallasee's "snaps." He looked happy and handsome in the picture, relaxed and innocent. She had caught him in a good moment, after all.

●

Charley seemed to be driven by a need to look for that boy. Tallasee was driven by a need to avoid it. She had learned to keep a camera between herself and her subjects. She had come to believe you can take pictures of people or you can help them, but it's not wise to seek to do both.

She could control the outcome of a photograph: determine the light, the exposure, the mood, and the setting. She could capture a dozen different expressions on someone's face and select one that suited the moment. She could look through a viewfinder and decide if the world, as it appeared in that instant, was worth making permanent. Even when she did nothing—when she decided that what she saw wasn't worth capturing, wasn't worth the minor energy needed to trip the shutter release or the expenditure of so much as a single frame of film—Tallasee still was in charge.

She realized that there was an almost theological flavor to photography. When people and light and events arrayed themselves into a specific pose at a precise moment, and no one photographed it, did that moment exist in any meaningful sense? If you could stop all time and movement to examine any small sliver of the world, you'd see that there are an almost infinite number of ways of focusing on it, each with a precisely nuanced difference. So the act of taking a photograph is to select a single image at the expense of a countless number of other images that could have been had at that instant, multiplied itself by the endless number of moments available in the continuum of time. It is a singular act of power.

The answer, then, was "no." Tallasee knew that if she didn't capture it, it didn't exist. She could, in a sense, rule the world with a camera.

But the moment that she set the camera down, she lost control. Everything then took on a life of its own. The world became as perversely contrary as the one she saw through the lens was orderly and submissive to her will. Her marriage was proof of that: she had failed to keep a camera between herself and Nigel.

She knew that she'd made a mistake by agreeing to visit old Mrs. Bullock, and that would only be compounded by launching a hunt for a runaway grandson. Mrs. Bullock was of the world Tallasee shaped and ordered with her camera, but the boy was loose in that other world, where treachery and reality existed independent of her viewfinder. After Nigel, she had no footing there.

Tallasee felt that no good would come of a search. And, of course, she was right.

Chapter Six

The more Tallasee resisted, the more determined Charley became to undertake a search for the missing grandson. At the most superficial level, it simply was something to do: currently, few other things in Charley's life seemed to have a point or a direction. He had never reckoned how much of his life was occupied by school and Baby Girl. With the peculiar conceit of the young, he'd always assumed the world to be a place that both automatically invested every life with meaning and made every life the center of its own universe. To find himself now working in a temporary job with nothing more promising on the horizon—and relegated to the ignoble position of former boyfriend of one of the town's more-desirable young women—was to give lie to both of those assumptions. So, being recruited to look for a missing boy, even if his was a tag-along recruitment, had an appealing whiff of adventure and meaningfulness. Besides, Charley kept recalling the look on the boy's face in the photograph. And each time he did, the tuning fork in his gut hummed a bit louder.

At first, Tallasee was just vague, pretending they'd get to it in a day or so and murmuring noncommittally whenever Charley suggested a specific moment. Then she became doubtful, wondering out loud how likely it was that they'd actually accomplish anything, and after that businesslike, making pointed reminders of her book deadline and declaring the urgency of Charley's chores. Finally, she just said no.

"Let's forget it," she said. "It's a bad idea to get involved in other people's family problems. What are we going to do if we find him? Kidnap him?"

"We'll just make sure he's okay," Charley answered. He wasn't sure how to explain his desires, so this response was the best he could do. It sounded lame even to him.

"Of course he's okay," Tallasee said impatiently. "It's not like it's a concentration camp up there. It's a bunch of hippies living in the woods. The worst thing that can happen to him is he'll get the clap." She regarded Charley for a moment. "And if I know anything about teenage boys, that's a problem any of them would be happy to have."

"Not true," he corrected. "We'd prefer to avoid it. But we don't mind the process of getting it."

"Thanks for clearing that up for me," she said, then changed the subject: "Are all the negative files moved yet? How are we doing on that?" Charley knew that asking how "we" were doing was her way of sidestepping the admission that she was anyone's supervisor, so he met this fake equality with cheerful insubordination.

"I don't know how we're doing, but I'm doing just fine," he said. "I've got a question, by the way. Do I get any days off around here?"

"You're tired already? You've only worked for three days."

"Exhausted. I'm already wondering if I made the right career choice."

"Oh, dear. And I just dismissed the executive search firm," she said.

"The weekend's coming up," Charley prompted.

"Fine. Take the weekend off. Do you have plans?" Her tone was mocking.

"Yeah, I thought I'd drive up to that commune."

Charley expected her to be annoyed, but she surprised him. Tallasee just looked at him for a few long moments.

"I don't understand why this is so important to you," she finally said. "We'll go tomorrow, all right?" Charley nodded.

"But you'll be off the clock," she added. "You can crusade on your own time."

●

The trip carried echoes of the previous one: Charley drove while Tallasee explained about the commune, giving haphazard directions as she did and ignoring him when, after the second sudden turn, he suggested that she draw a map for him so that the slim Selkirk bloodline didn't come to a quick end in a rollover accident.

"The thing about these communes I've discovered is that they're all doomed," she observed. "A lot of them have been overwhelmed by disorder and the rest of them eventually will be. It's as sure as sunset."

"Why?" Charley asked.

"Well, for one thing, no one wants to work much. I've never seen anyone put in what the rest of the world calls an honest day's work— it's bourgeois," she replied, sarcastically drawing out the pronunciation and making Charley think that she'd heard someone invoke the word earnestly at some point. "Besides, order and structure is antithetical in most communes."

"I have no idea what you just said," he said.

"I'm sorry. I forgot I'm in the company of a high school dropout."

"I'm a high school *kick* out," Charley said. "It's an important distinction."

"What I mean is, the people who form communes have decided the world is too rigid and structured. Too many rules. Too many bosses. Too many people ready to thwart desire and impulse. Too many people who think you should just do as you're told. So they've created these little worlds where there are no rules except one: No rules, man."

"So nothing gets done."

"Exactly. Anyone who shows an inclination for organizing things or suggests that certain people do certain tasks will get called a fascist. And there's no accounting for human nature in Utopia. The people who are industrious enough to actually tend to the gardens or bake bread every day eventually resent the ones who are sitting on their butts. But it's tough to shame the lazy ones into working, because you've founded the whole enterprise on the notion that shame and guilt are bad trips, man." Again, Tallasee seemed to be mocking someone else's phrase.

"It sounds like they could use a few days with Turner Smallwood," Charley said.

"Oh, God. I haven't thought of him in years." She laughed at the memory.

"So he was around in your day?" Charley asked.

"My day? Listen, sonny, I'm only ten years older than you."

Turner Smallwood was the physical-education teacher at Barrington High School. He was legendary for his customary speech to the new class of students each fall, in which he informed them that they eventually would run an eight-minute mile. They will not merely *try* to run a mile in eight minutes, he'd say, nor will they discover some medical reason why they *can't* run a mile in eight minutes. They *will* run a mile without stopping. Period. And that mile *will* be covered in eight or fewer minutes. Period. Girls got an extra two minutes. Period.

Turner Smallwood—and he was always called by his full name, never "Coach" Smallwood, as most of the other male teachers preferred even when their coaching was limited to some minor duty with a fringe sport like volleyball, and not "Mr." Smallwood, despite the fact that any Southern-bred child usually would rather risk telling Jesus jokes in Sunday school than be heard addressing an adult by his first name—Turner Smallwood would foil all anticipated excuses by citing some vague medical study that purported to show that a person could run until he puked or even passed out cold, but suffer no lasting harm and in fact be capable of running more as soon as he revived or his stomach stopped heaving. In other words, nothing short of full-blown polio was going to keep Barrington High School's freshmen from making four turns around the quarter-mile oval that surrounded the football field. The only question was how many weekly timed attempts would pass before they finally managed their mile without stopping at the high-jump pit, itself conveniently located close to the track and helpfully sandy, for relief of what Turner Smallwood delicately referred to as "stomach distress."

"So how long did it take you to hit your time?" Charley asked. That was Turner Smallwood's signature phrase. He would stand at the finish line, stopwatch in hand, and call out the seconds as the first runners stumbled across, red-faced and panting. When the eight-minute mark or ten-minute mark arrived, he would click the stopwatch back to zero and announce to those who had failed once again, "Sorry, ladies"—as anyone who fell short of his requirement was thusly labeled, regardless of their actual sex—"you didn't hit your time."

"I had pansy time until the last week of school," Tallasee answered, proving that she indeed had attended Turner Smallwood's physical-fitness boot camp. "Pansy time" was another of his phrases. "I made it on the last try."

"Well, a mile is a long way." Charley meant for it to sound comforting, but it came out condescending.

"A mile's a breeze," she scoffed. "I was helping a fat girl."

"What do you mean?"

"There was this girl in my class I felt sorry for. She was overweight, and walking a mile was tough for her, much less running it. She was never going to hit her time unless somebody helped her, and all Turner Smallwood did was make snotty remarks. So I ran with her. We'd get a little faster each week, but it still took me the whole year to get her around that track four times without stopping." She grinned unexpectedly. "Actually, we cheated the last time. Turner Smallwood was talking to somebody while he timed, not paying attention to us, so we cut off a whole corner on the last lap. She wouldn't have made it otherwise."

Charley had a sudden image of Tallasee as a student. He could see her navigating the halls of the high school or sitting in the gym during an assembly, fetching and friendly. She would have been the girl who is uncommonly pretty, but popular in that remote way accorded to people who have no demonstrated need for popularity—the sort of regard acquired only when one has somehow made clear that the approval of peers is inconsequential. Her friends would have ranged across the whole spectrum of high school society, but she would have had a distinct taste for underdogs, cause-bearers, poets, and troublemakers. It was the same quality in Baby Girl that Charley always had found profoundly attractive. Yet Charley suspected that unlike Baby Girl—who not only sought out the fringe-dwellers, but then became one for a while before restlessly reverting back to the ordinary—Tallasee would have maintained an essential gravity about her. She would have changed others; they would not have changed her.

She doubtless had known, on the very first day of physical-education class, that Turner Smallwood was a fool. She also had known that she wouldn't be able to ignore the sight of a fat girl being harangued and belittled as she thudded her way around a track once a week. So, she had helped one by making a subtle mockery of the other.

Lost in this reverie, Charley didn't hear her question at first. He now had a permanent image of Tallasee, lovely in schoolgirl shorts and with hair loosely gathered at her neck, making sure that a friendless fat girl had someone at her side at her neediest time. It made him happy to be with Tallasee that moment, grinding up hills in his old truck and doing a favor for an old woman.

"What I said was, you never really explained what happened that caused you to get kicked out of school," she repeated.

So he told her about Leander. When he finished, he noticed she seemed lost in her own reverie.

●

Tallasee found herself thinking about Nigel as Charley talked. Rather, she found herself thinking about the differences between them. Nigel had been plucked from obscurity and made famous. He'd had a hit record, gotten to go on tour, been cheered by thousands of people, and been given a tidy pile of money. Also, he got Tallasee, perhaps the best prize of all. But when life evened the score a bit, he fell apart. Tallasee was convinced that the magazine article was never the tragedy that he thought it to be. It was a setback, but what did he have before that? He was a porter in a fish market, hating every minute of the day and dreaming that someone would notice him when he sang in clubs at night. Well, someone did notice, and he became that rare person who gets to live a dream. Yet when the dream ended, as it had to because no dream lasts forever, he wouldn't take stock. He couldn't see what he had acquired and how, even after a sour finish, he was still left with so much more than he could have expected. He could have recovered. But, instead, he'd wallowed in petulance and self-pity, and when he died he left Tallasee with a great wad of unhappiness and guilt. Even worse, there was much anger layered over the top of those things: she was angry at him for not being a man, for not standing up to adversity, and she was angry at herself for mistaking his weakness for tenderness.

Then there was Charley. She knew, of course, what had happened with his little brother. Everyone knew. He'd had to grow up with that, and somehow come to grips with the knowledge that a moment of neglect had helped cause his brother's death. Then, later, he finds himself kicked out of school after he administers a dose of schoolyard justice to a deserving punk, and his reward is to be rejected by the girlfriend who all but suggested he do it in the first place. But does he complain about any of this? No. Tallasee practically had to badger the story out of him.

In fact, she reflected, not only did Charley not whine, but his only apparent response to these recent unhappy events was to go out and get a job, and then launch a search for a runaway teenager because a strange old woman asked for help and because he seemed to think he could somehow provide that help.

As he talked, Tallasee felt as if she had pried the face off a rather simple, ordinary watch and been awestruck at the complexity of the mechanism underneath. There was much going on inside Charley. During the drive, Tallasee realized she had stopped thinking of him as a boy. It also was the moment she realized, in some visceral way, that manhood was going to be no easier for him than boyhood had been.

●

Like the turn to Mrs. Bullock's, the road to the commune made a well-camouflaged declaration of independence from the highway. It was another bare gap in the brush, but this time without even the benefit of a tin can winking from atop a branch to signal its existence. But Tallasee, in an unacknowledged homage to Charley's nagging, was alert for it, and he had slowed to a crawl when the time came to steer off the highway. Again, branches fondled both sides of the truck as they turned, and again, the underbrush thinned moments later when he drove under the forest canopy. Yet where nothing on the drive to Mrs. Bullock's had suggested that they were on the right road, this time they were assured almost immediately by a hand-painted sign affixed to a tree that read:

RAINBOW NATION
ahead 4 miles
love is your passport

Charley looked at Tallasee and she smirked. "You're going to need a name, you know," she said.

"I've got a name," he replied. "Three of them, actually."

"That's too many. The Rainbows prefer one name, and it's usually something like Sundance or Autumn. If you decide to stay, they have you select your own name, because when you're discarding the vestiges of middle-class life, the name goes, too. What's your middle name, by the way?"

"Farley," he said. "It was my mother's family name."

She cocked an eyebrow at him. "So you're a Charley Farley?"

"Yeah, but I'm warming up to this idea of changing it. How does Killer sound?"

"Oh, the Rainbows will love that. Right in step with their love-will-save-the-world philosophy."

"Something more subtle? How about Bayonet?"

Before she could answer, however, Bayonet himself suddenly appeared on the side of the road and waved them to a stop.

●

Actually, it wasn't a wave so much as it was a command. They had just come around a big turn when a man materialized in front of Charley's truck, stepping from behind a tree and raising his arm, palm out, in the classic policeman's order to halt. And, as it turned out, he wasn't actually called Bayonet; his name was Lucas, just as it was printed above the right breast pocket of the army-issue camouflage shirt that he wore. But his appearance at that precise moment, along with the way he looked—a lean figure dressed in a fatigue shirt, blue jeans hacked off at midthigh, red bandanna wrapped around his head Aunt Jemima–style, and combat boots worn without socks—made it seem that Charley had somehow conjured up this wraithlike creature just by uttering the name.

"Jesus. Who is that?" Tallasee whispered as Charley skidded to a stop. Braking wasn't much of a choice, really, but it wasn't a problem, either: the man had practically stepped in front of the truck, so Charley'd had to hit the brake, but the truck was coming around the curve so slowly that it only slid a foot or so on the road's loose rock. The plume of dust that had followed them ever since they'd turned off the paved highway caught up and surrounded the truck.

"It looks like we're going to find out," Charley said as the man stepped up to his window.

The man had to duck his head to see into the truck, making Charley realize how tall he was. He looked at Charley for a moment before shifting his eyes to Tallasee and giving her the same examination. Only then did he speak.

"State your business," he said, sounding like a sentry at a military outpost.

Charley didn't know what to say, but Tallasee didn't hesitate. "Listen, Hitler," she replied, sliding over on the seat to make sure he heard, "every minute we spend here is one more minute I have to wait before dropping myself in Blue Hole."

"You've been here before, then?" the man asked. Tallasee nodded.

Charley was mystified as to what she meant, but the man seemed to understand. "I'll ride with you," he said, walking around the front of the truck to Tallasee's side as she slid to the middle of the seat.

The man said nothing else after getting in, neither explaining who he was nor seeking an explanation—which would have gotten Charley's vote—about Blue Hole. After a minute or two of driving in silence, Tallasee finally asked the obvious question.

"So, who are you?" she said, judiciously passing up the chance to tag him with another tyrant's name. "Are you living at the commune?"

"Lucas," he said, ignoring her second question. There was another long period of silence.

"I'm Tallasee," she said after a few moments. "This is"—she hesitated, and Charley could sense she was pondering whether to introduce him as Bayonet—"this is Charley Farley."

Lucas ducked his head to acknowledge the introductions. "So what are you doing up here?" he asked. "If you know about Blue Hole, you must have been up here to visit."

"I've been here two or three times. They'll know me," Tallasee confirmed, then tried another version of her original question. "You're new, though. How do you like it here?"

"So what are you doing up here?" he repeated. He was as artless in his pursuit of answers as Tallasee was subtle. There was a sudden flavor of interrogation to the whole conversation, and Charley realized there was something amiss here: Lucas was edgy and coiled, his eyes constantly darting from one side of the road to the other, as if he expected to see something dangerous in the woods. Had Mrs. Bullock been there, she doubtless would have said the tension just dripped off that man.

"We're doing someone a favor," Tallasee said. "This old gal I know thinks her grandson is living at the commune. She asked if we'd see if he's here."

"We ain't got any kids living here," Lucas responded abruptly.

"Actually, he was here the last time I visited," Tallasee said. "I took a picture of him." Then she gave Lucas one of those mocking smiles Charley had gotten used to seeing. "Besides, I just said 'grandson.' How do you know I'm talking about a child?"

For the first time, Lucas took his gaze away from the windshield and fixed it on Charley and Tallasee. When Charley saw the expression on the man's face, and the calculation going on behind his eyes, it made him wish that he hadn't looked.

●

The commune was a small bit of squalor set in a generous dollop of paradise.

There were hills all around, as there are everywhere in that part of the world, but thanks to some accident of geology, there also was an unusually large flat area nestled in between, which is where the commune sat. The area had been cleared years before, so long ago that even the stumps had rotted into invisibility, likely the work of a settler whose hopes of cultivating the land had not evaporated until the rocky ground finally had bent his plow beyond the help of a smith's hammer. No one ever successfully grazed or farmed in those hills. While agriculture had taken its first root at the coast three hundred years before, in swampy settlements like Savannah and Brunswick where the ground was lush and forgiving and invitingly flat, and had marched steadily inland over the years, its progress had stopped in places like Barrington, where the hills began to lift—not so steeply that they couldn't accommodate man and his tools and beasts, but enough so that they turned into barriers just beyond. You traveled around or over those hills. You took lumber out of them. Perhaps you even hid in them. But you didn't live off them.

What the hills lacked in the ability to nurture food, however, was offset by the brooding calm they instilled in visitors. These hills, richly forested and nearly impenetrable, seemed to capture secrets and hold them close—you could come to believe that whatever happened there stayed there. Once you arrived at that belief, the governor on your behavior usually put out the off-duty sign. The hills were too vast and many, the woods too thick, and the inhabitants too few for everyday rules to apply.

So, if the commune was a jarring sight to Charley and Tallasee, it could be explained that way. Who said that a tribe of mountain-dwellers dedicated to love, beauty, and brotherhood had to live by twentieth-century building codes and modern standards of hygiene?

In short, the place was a mess. What structures there were had been built of plywood and tar paper, with crude framing and rough floors when there was a floor at all. Two enormous tents, the kind bought from the Sears catalogue by fathers who'd decided family camping was the perfect vacation but then used only once before being permanently packed away in a garage, were pitched in random spots. Their zip-up screen doors were in tatters, and the pole lines were wrapped around any available branch or held down by rocks. There also was a teepee, but when Charley and Tallasee later got close, they saw it was made of the same synthetic material as the tents and that its lodgepoles were badly cut pine saplings with the bark still attached and sap oozing in countless places. A blue tarp had been nailed over the roof of one of the buildings, presumably to keep out whatever rain the tar paper couldn't, while various implements and tools littered the ground. A broken-down station wagon with a missing side window completed the hobo-village ambiance.

Charley slowed the truck as they approached, unsure where to park, then finally stopped altogether. For a moment, no one said anything.

"I do perimeter security," Lucas eventually said. It was an odd statement, seeming to answer a question from a few minutes before that in actuality no one had posed. So, this declaration gave the impression that Lucas had some desire to separate himself from the sight before them: I only take care of the edges. And again, it had a military echo.

"Who do you need to be secure from?" Tallasee asked. "Do you think somebody's going to steal your building secrets?"

She got another version of the same look Lucas had fixed on the two of them a few moments before. Charley made a mental note to explain the value of discreet silence to her later.

"The sheriff's been up here once or twice," he said. "It's best to not let yourself be surprised when company comes."

It dawned on Charley that he wasn't even sure which county they were in. "Whose sheriff?" he asked. "Is this still Soque County?"

"There ain't but one sheriff, man," Lucas said cryptically.

"Why is he visiting up here?" Charley pushed on. "This ain't exactly a place that'd be on his regular rounds."

"If it's Johnny Carver, it's a wonder he hasn't established a permanent office at Blue Hole," Tallasee said.

Johnny Carver was the Soque County sheriff, a fellow whose size and long-established ability to wrestle evildoers and troublemakers to the ground in just a few moments should have made him fearsome, except that he also had a reputation for having a happy taste for liquor and women, which softened his image a bit. He'd been sheriff for as long as Charley had been alive, and he ruled in a manner consistent with his own alleged lifestyle: he tended to go easy on the sins of the flesh and excesses of drink, but God help you if you committed what he considered a real crime or even were so foolish as to backtalk him when he suggested that the next beer would be too many or that your dalliance with someone else's wife might be properly concluded in an actual bed and not in your parked car, however well hidden it may be. Whatever his own appetites may have included, they never were satisfied near home, as far as anyone knew, but his reputation was so firmly rooted that it was taken as gospel. Still, no actual scandal ever was attached to his name, so he'd been reelected several times, each time by a larger majority.

Apparently, no one was going to explain unless Charley asked, so he did. "Will somebody please tell me what a Blue Hole is?"

Tallasee pointed to one edge of the clearing. "If you walk down a path there a little ways, you'll find a stream. There's a spot where the water collects in a deep pool. That's Blue Hole. Everybody goes swimming there." She hesitated for a moment, then added, "Usually naked swimming."

"Yeah, I guess Johnny Carver would like that," Charley said, sounding even to himself like a child trying to affect an adult's worldliness. What did he actually know about the sheriff?

"Sure enough," Lucas said, seeming to agree with something, although it wasn't clear what.

●

The population of the place had changed since Tallasee's last visit. She recognized a few faces, but most of them only smiled noncommittally or ignored her altogether. After Charley parked the truck and got out, Lucas departed without a word and made his way to one of the tents, disappearing inside. Charley and Tallasee stood by the truck, Charley waiting for Tallasee and Tallasee waiting for her memory to retrieve the name of the commune's shaman or guide or whatever non-hierarchical title that the Rainbows preferred.

"There's something going on with that man," Charley said after Lucas had ducked into the tent.

"You'll find guys like him in places like this," Tallasee answered. "Kiwanis Club members tend to stick closer to home."

She hadn't yet realized how good Charley's radar was—that wouldn't happen until they returned to Mrs. Bullock's home in a few days—so she attributed his unease to the general weirdness of the place. She paid Lucas no mind. After a few moments, Tallasee stopped trying to dredge up a name and instead suggested that they just start asking people if they'd recently seen the boy. She'd made two prints of the photograph, so she and Charley each had a copy to show. They divided the settlement into rough halves and agreed to meet back at the truck in a half hour.

Tallasee had taken no more than twenty steps toward the teepee when the man whose name had eluded her stepped out into the sunlight. Seeing him gave her memory the nudge it needed: Osage. He spotted her as she walked toward him, and she could see his mind shuffling through its own deck of face cards until the moment it found hers and recognition registered on his face.

"Hey there," he said, then apparently noticed that Tallasee carried no camera. "No pictures today?"

"No pictures today," she confirmed.

He kept patiently quiet, waiting for an explanation. Tallasee remembered that about him: he'd learned at some point that most people cannot tolerate a conversational void; they'll fill a silence. He would maintain eye contact, put a slightly expectant look on his face and wait for other people to forget that they're not required to elaborate on whatever they've just said. Cops and reporters master this trick early in their careers. Tallasee knew that—she'd talked to enough of both after Nigel died. She decided to wait him out.

"Well, it's good to see you again," he finally said. This was his fallback position: a meaningless utterance is almost as good as silence.

Tallasee was washed with the realization that she deeply disliked him. On her previous visits to the commune, it had been easy to reduce its inhabitants to their essential characters. There was a handful of radicals, whose zealotry was fueled by the escalation of the war in Vietnam and by their suspicion that Richard Nixon would stop at nothing to squash dissent, a suspicion Nixon obligingly confirmed as well founded in coming years; some apolitical hedonists who were happy to have the cloak of counterculturalism to pull over their enthusiastic embrace of dope, beer, and sex; a few sheep, there because someone had led them there, and who would be there until someone else led them away; and a scattering of loners, men usually, who in another time would have drifted into frontier towns and been buried in unmarked graves after misadventure or mishap struck. Then there was Osage.

He had some vague connection to the land itself—ownership of those hills was a confusing jumble of private and public interests, with an even more bewildering quilt of leases and timber rights laid over the top—which gave him an aura of permanency among the many transients. He also was the lone member of the commune to eschew drugs, preferring to skip the almost ceaseless dope smoking and, especially, the full-moon trips that celebrated the end of each lunar cycle with the wholesale ingestion of hallucinogenics. But his wasn't the happy sobriety of a fitness freak, or the maudlin self-denial of a reformed doper. It instead had the unhealthy flavor of manipulation and control.

Tallasee had seen that evident one night during a previous visit. A group of five people had settled in at the commune at some point, two couples and a young woman who obviously was friends with the other women but was with no man herself. She seemed to have assigned herself the job of being the group's conscience, and her disapproval was constant. She fretted about their diet, about this interruption of their college educations, and about the fact that she hadn't seen a dentist in a long time. She warned of the consequences of unpredictable sleep cycles and worried about the unidentified and unseen parasites that surely would crawl into their private crevices as they bathed in the stream. Every rash was the first indication of horrible, exotic afflictions deep in the body, and every cut was a welcome mat to tetanus and lockjaw. She was a combination of hovering, protective mother and class informant, the child who's left in charge of the room when the teacher is called to the office and whose job it is to keep track of which of her fellow students failed in those few minutes to meet her exacting standards of behavior. She was, in other words, the least likely person to have joined a hippie commune. But she was there, Tallasee concluded, only because her friends were there, and however unhappy this life made her, it was better than being left behind. This is what Osage must have sensed as well.

Everyone had gathered in the largest building that night, for the calendar promised a full moon. Tallasee was admitted with her camera only on the pledge that faces not be shown clearly, a promise made easy to keep by the dozen or so candles that provided the only light and thus ensured that any picture would be shadowy and impressionistic. When everyone was seated and still, Osage began cutting small squares from a large sheet of heavy paper imprinted with the cartoonish design of a robed hippie widely known as Mr. Natural. The sheet—

a large blotter, actually—held hundreds of the small squares, outlined in cut-here markings printed on the paper, and each square held one dose of acid mixed by some counterculture chemist and placed with an eyedropper. This was the preferred trip of the day, a hallucinogen so allegedly free of impurities that it borrowed its name from the fellow it stained. A dose of Mr. Natural was a valued commodity, indeed.

"I don't think you"—Osage jabbed his scissors in the woman's direction to make certain he had her attention—"should have any."

"Why not?" she asked. It was clear that she had expected to be offered a dose, even encouraged and cajoled to take it; her prissiness and disapproval flourished in those moments. So, to be denied that which she expected to be thrust upon her was confusing.

"Because you can't handle it," he said.

"I didn't want it anyway, but I could, too," she replied, not realizing how silly she sounded or how easily she was being maneuvered.

"Some people just aren't equipped for this," Osage continued, as if he hadn't heard her. "You need a certain mental flexibility. A willingness to consider other realities. I don't think you have that."

No child of the Sixties, even one with all the instincts of Cotton Mather, could tolerate this. It was like being patted on the head and told to go back to your Nancy Drew mysteries while the rest of the reading club settled in with Hermann Hesse's *Siddhartha*. To accede to his judgment now would be to confirm it. Still, she stood gamely.

"A lot of people have managed to be mentally flexible without this," she said.

"You misunderstood me," Osage said, pressing in with a semanticist's precision. "I didn't say this brings mental flexibility. In fact, it's just the opposite. If you don't have mental flexibility going into it, it can be a very bad ride." There were murmurs of agreement from those whose mental flexibility had been tested so often they seemed permanently dazed.

"This whole discussion is silly," she said dismissively. That only gave him another opening.

"You're proving my point. Not only are you unwilling to believe I may be right, you're unwilling to even talk about it."

Tallasee saw that the group's patience was being tested. Even after they'd washed down the tab with a swallow of beer, it would be a half hour or so before Mr. Natural began working his magic. They were ready to move the evening along. "Forget her, man," someone advised Osage.

Suddenly, the woman held her hand out. "I can do this," she said.

A great cheer went up, prompting Osage to drop a tab in her hand even as he shook his head doubtfully. As it turned out, he was right: she had a very bad time of it. And that, Tallasee understood, was exactly what he wanted.

●

Osage had just turned to leave when Tallasee said, "I'm looking for someone, actually."

"Oh?" he said, and she was sure there would follow another silence for her to fill. But he seemed uncharacteristically curious. "Who?"

"A fellow I saw when I was visiting back in the fall. A teenager, really. He was living here at the time." Tallasee touched her finger to the appropriate spot on the photograph. "Him."

Osage took the picture and examined it. After a moment, he handed it back. "Yeah, I sort of remember him. But I don't know what happened to him. He's been gone for a while."

"When did he leave?"

He shrugged. "I don't remember. It's been at least a month or two, though."

"Where did he go?"

"I don't ask people where they've been, I don't ask where they're going." Judging by the way he said it, almost by rote, it was a phrase that he'd used before.

"But this was a child. Or at least he was young enough to still be in school. What the devil was he doing here in the first place?"

He reached for the photograph again and studied it. "He seemed older, as I remember," Osage said. "Sort of serious and somber. Besides, you never know what people have left behind. This"—he waved his hand toward the ragged collection of buildings and tents—"could have been an improvement for him."

Tallasee noted that his memory had improved remarkably in just a few moments. "Serious and somber? How do you mean?"

"He was quiet. Hardly ever said anything. He seemed sad, too. But he always pitched in and never complained about things like garbage hauling. In fact, I think he took that on pretty much permanently while he was here." Osage looked around ruefully. "You can tell he left."

"Garbage in paradise? I wouldn't have thought it."

He grinned suddenly, a warm and merry smile that invited Tallasee in on the joke and helped her understand how people came under his sway. "Oh, there's lots of garbage in paradise. Whatever burns, we'll just burn here. But other things are dumped in a pile about a mile away. It's our own little landfill. It causes some unhappiness, as you might imagine. We had a big meeting about it once and decided to secede from the consumer society. We would produce no garbage." He gave her another grin. "We didn't reduce consumption, though. We just drove it underground. People began having lots of reasons to drive into town."

"Why is the dump so far away?" she asked.

"Critters," he said simply.

They had strayed, so she brought the conversation back to the matter at hand. "So you don't know where he went? Or why he left?"

Osage's memory suddenly became faulty again. "I'm sorry. I just don't recall."

●

Lucas was scary, no doubt, but Charley speculated that it might have had something to do with Tallasee, who seemed to set off his alarm system. So he figured that if he visited Lucas alone, and showed him the photograph right up front so he wouldn't feel trapped the way he must have felt with Tallasee, then perhaps he would reconsider his declaration that no child had been there. If you give people a graceful exit, they'll take it.

Charley noted which tent Lucas had ducked into, but he circled around and talked to a few other people first, getting shakes of the head and shrugs of the shoulders when he asked about the boy. No one expressed surprise at the idea of a missing person, which made Charley surmise that searches for young people must have been a common occurrence there, that no one really plunges down the rabbit hole without someone following behind to see where they've gone and how they're doing. It's the rare person who's completely detached from those who made him.

When he finally arrived at Lucas's tent, Charley didn't know exactly how to declare his presence—how do you knock on a tent door?—and nothing he'd seen suggested that Lucas was the sort who would react happily to people inviting themselves in. Charley didn't even want to peer in through the windowlike piece of mesh screen that had been sewn into the tent wall. For all their commitment to brotherhood, the Rainbows didn't make it easy to engage in it.

Lucas solved Charley's problem by suddenly appearing at his elbow. Charley had just opened his mouth to call out a greeting when Lucas said: "What did you say your name was?"

Charley hadn't heard him come up behind and didn't know how Lucas had gotten out of the tent without being noticed. He was badly startled.

"Charley Selkirk," he said.

"Where's your girlfriend?"

"She's talking to some guy over yonder," Charley said, waving his arm in the direction where he'd last seen her. "She's not my girlfriend. She's my boss."

"Even worse for you."

"Actually, I like her. But she is a little bossy."

He hadn't meant to be funny—his nerves hadn't settled yet and he was practically stammering—but Lucas snorted. "Bosses usually are. What do you want?"

"Remember we said we were looking for somebody? This is him. His grandmother's looking for him," Charley said, showing Lucas the boy's image in the photograph. "She's real upset. We're hoping someone may know where he's gone."

Lucas neither looked at the picture nor answered the implicit question. Instead, he posed his own: "Charley, how old are you?"

"Seventeen. Eighteen next month."

"So you'll be registering for the draft then, right?"

"Just like I'm supposed to," Charley said, nodding but confused by the question. It wasn't possible for anyone to pretend that they weren't aware of the draft requirements. Even if you'd somehow avoided stepping into any post office and seeing one of those bullying announcements from the Selective Service System reminding every young man he had to register, you couldn't have missed the news reports about draft cards being burned at antiwar rallies and the new underground railroad that shipped evaders to Canada.

"Are you going to college? Going to get a student deferment?"

"I don't think so," Charley said. "I got kicked out of high school." Even as he said it, Charley realized how successful he'd been in refusing to think about the future.

"Are you going to enlist?" Lucas asked, with the patient exasperation of a teacher walking a dull child through a lesson. "You can pick your duty that way."

"I haven't thought much about it," he confessed.

"You're an asshole, Charley," Lucas said cheerfully. "You'll think about it a lot when you're kneeling in a ditch in Vietnam wondering if that's the day you get greased."

"Yes, sir, I suspect that's true," Charley said, wondering how to steer the discussion back to the photograph. For the second time, Lucas solved the dilemma for him.

"I told him that, too," he said, pointing to the picture. "And don't call me 'sir.' You only call officers 'sir.' "

"Told him what?"

"Told him to avoid the service if he could. Bad things happen when people put on uniforms. That's what I'm trying to tell you, too."

"What bad things?" Charley asked.

"I don't know where he is, Charley. He's gone. Now I want you and your girlfriend"—it didn't seem wise to Charley to correct him a second time—"to go back to town and forget about it. You need to worry about staying alive."

Charley was unsure what he was talking about. "You mean the draft?"

"Yeah," Lucas said as he stepped into the tent, "that, too."

Chapter Seven

Tallasee found Charley by his truck. Her efforts had been fruitless, and she could see from his face that he'd fared no better. She couldn't think of anything to say that wouldn't carry an I-told-you-so tone, so she said nothing.

It was Charley, then, who spoke first. "This place gives me the creeps."

"No, these people give you the creeps," Tallasee said. "The place is actually pretty nice."

He looked toward the ragged cluster of structures and seemed inclined to argue, but only shook his head. He leaned against the truck fender next to Tallasee and they let the late-morning warmth wash over them. They were fewer than a dozen miles from the state's highest peak, and the hills surrendered the night's coolness grudgingly and only gradually. A billowy cloud overhead gave the sky a benign look, but it already was apparent that the cloud would find some of its cousins later in the day and that their family reunion would leave the road to the highway muddy and treacherous. Tallasee and Charley still had a couple of hours, though.

"Who'd you talk to?" Tallasee asked.

"Lucas. The guy we picked up on the road."

"It's no wonder you've got the willies. Why did you go see him?"

Charley shrugged. "I thought he might have more to say."

She waited for him to elaborate, but he just jammed his hands in his pockets and stared into the wooded hillside. "Did he?" she asked, the impatience apparent in her voice. Still, it was several moments before he answered.

"He's not supposed to be here," Charley finally said. Tallasee wasn't sure he was talking to her.

"Who? Lucas?"

Suddenly animated, as if he'd just thought of something, Charley turned his attention back to her. "Yeah, Lucas. Think about it a minute. Here's a guy who watches the road to see who's coming, who's apparently had some previous encounter with the sheriff, and who denies that a runaway boy was ever here. What does that suggest to you?"

"That you're never going to let this go," Tallasee said wearily. "It's the only obvious thing to me."

Charley wouldn't be shaken off the scent. "No, it means he doesn't want official visitors. And a runaway might bring official visitors."

"Or, even worse, me and you."

He gave her a look of exasperation. "So who did you talk to?"

"A guy named Osage. He's the leader of the place, if they have such a thing here. At first, he didn't remember the boy. Then he remembered him quite well. Then, when I started asking more questions, he didn't remember him again." Tallasee became aware of how her words sounded.

Charley didn't even try to keep a triumphant tone from his voice. "That's just like Lucas. First he lies about whether the boy was here, then he admits he was here, then he refuses to say anything else about him."

He was right, but Tallasee didn't want to say so. They had asked a simple question of two people—Do you know where this boy went?—and gotten two nakedly evasive responses. There clearly was something going on here, but she just didn't wish to be involved in sorting it out. It was an entanglement, and Tallasee had a wariness of entanglements. She felt that she and Charley had discharged their only duty: Mrs. Bullock had asked them to see if her grandson was here, and they had determined he wasn't. It was a reasonable favor to do for the old gal, but Tallasee didn't think it was reasonable to be expected to follow his track further. They weren't detectives. She had a book to finish. Moreover, she worried that Charley wasn't facing up to the truth that if he didn't do something with his life soon, he'd end up as third knife on the chicken-gutting line at the poultry plant. His vigorous embrace of this whole adventure, which she wrote off as boyish enthusiasm at first, now seemed like procrastination, a way to avoid confronting the unhappy turn his life had taken. And Tallasee wasn't sure that her employment of him was helping matters. She'd been so happy to have someone to do her filing and remodeling that she'd convinced herself it was as worthwhile for him as it was for her. In the grip of a sudden guilt, she vowed to nudge him out the door in a couple of weeks.

"Yeah, it's a puzzle, sure enough," she said mildly. "Listen, detective, we need to get down the mountain before it rains. Do you want to take a quick look at Blue Hole?"

"Sure," he said. Tallasee could see a flush rising in his face.

"Just looking," she said. "No swimming."

●

The trail was old and well traveled; any branch so foolish as to grow in its path had long ago been broken away or hacked off. The path itself had been worn down to the underlying rock, the thin soil having been washed away because no growth helped hold it there and no protective cover of leaves could avoid being ground into dust under the daily foot traffic. The thickness of the forest and the incline of the slope invited no shortcuts; a hiker stayed on the trail not as a matter of faith that it led efficiently to its destination, but as a matter of good sense. At a few places, where the path negotiated a particularly steep patch of hillside or a cumbersome turn, someone had maneuvered stones into rough steps. And at a spot where the path crossed a deep wash in the slope, a drainage ditch of nature's own construction, someone had spanned it with two logs laid side by side, then thoughtfully nailed a dozen footlong sections of flat board across the logs so that hikers didn't have to test each step against the logs' rounded flanks. But those were the few bits of evidence that this was anything but an animal trail a hundred generations old.

Tallasee walked ahead of Charley, because the sense of hiking order all people subconsciously acknowledge requires the person who has been along a path previously to lead the way, even when the route is unmistakable. It was a long walk, a mile or so along a trail that was rarely level and always narrow, which meant that aside from the moments when Charley realized his staring had been prolonged and he deliberately swiveled his gaze into the woods on either side, he spent fifteen minutes watching Tallasee's hips and bottom flex as she walked.

Like everyone else in Barrington, he knew her story vaguely. Her father, a prominent attorney and well-liked man, had died in a car accident just days before she was born. She and her older brother, Tolliver, had been raised by their mother with wildly different results. Tolliver had grown into a rakehell young man, then apparently reformed himself and become the minister for Barrington's largest Baptist church. After the church was destroyed in a fire, however, it was discovered that Tolliver—evidently not quite as reformed as everyone believed—had defrauded the congregation by looting its insurance fund. He did time in prison and then spent a dissolute exile in Atlanta. Conversely, where Tolliver was proven to be an essentially corrupt man with a skin of rectitude and acceptability stretched over him, Tallasee was the inverse image of that: she was a fundamentally kind and decent person with a reputation for impulsive and careless behavior.

The more Charley got to know her, the more he became certain she had not earned that reputation. He'd noticed there seemed to be a certain order and deliberation to everything she did. If her life had taken an untidy turn or two, it wasn't because she was careless; she had a commodity trader's taste for high-risk, high-reward ventures, and the fact that some of them soured could be explained more by the simple law of averages than by declaring the choices were ill considered. She'd abandoned a modeling career at the top of her game for the life of a photographer, but that wasn't as risky as it might seem: she'd prepared for it by learning from professionals, and instinctively had known it's a smart woman who stops answering calls before the calls stop coming. She'd married a touring singer she'd known for only a matter of weeks, but even that was perverse proof of deliberation rather than impulse: everyone wants to live a fairy tale, but when the moment comes to step into the fantasy, most people cannot break free of the gravity of ordinary lives and modest expectations. Tallasee had gambled on an interesting career and a magical marriage, and had won one of those bets.

Her problem, though, was that extraordinarily attractive people aren't credited with brains. She was a sumptuous sight the morning she sought to wrestle the box from the seat of her car, and, like any young man with a surge tide of hormones, Charley was happy for the chance to be in her company for a while. But because everyone honors the principle of balance in nature—that God, in his wisdom and fairness, doles out intelligence to some and beauty to some, but not both to a single being—he didn't realize until later that she also was clever and capable. As did most people in Barrington, Charley had tended to think of her as one would a racehorse: great lines, shows well, sometimes runs right into the rail.

Funny thing, though. Once he understood this wasn't true, he lost sight of her. He stopped paying heed to the body that carried Tallasee around. He noticed she invested no special attention in its appearance, and, in fact, seemed to treat it in much the way a man treats his own. In the morning, when she first arrived at her studio, it would be clear she'd spent a few minutes brushing her hair and pinning it back, or maybe even passing an iron over her clothes, but her apparent concern with such things deteriorated quickly, and by midday her sleeves would be pushed up or she'd have a smudge somewhere on her face or neck. Only her hands, with carefully trimmed nails and almost compulsive applications of lotion, showed evidence of sustained care. But then, her hands were the only part of her she regularly saw—Tallasee didn't avoid mirrors, but Charley had seen she didn't exactly seek them out, either.

Now, however, as she walked ahead of Charley on the trail, he couldn't help but pay heed to the body that carried Tallasee around.

They were in the shade of the forest, of course, but the humidity that builds ahead of a thunderstorm made for a sweaty hike. There was a dinner plate–sized circle of dampness on her lower back that looped down to include the top of her shorts, and Charley's eyes kept coming back to that spot as they walked. It enchanted him. It somehow was both consistent with and contrary to her being—confirmation of her disinterest in improving what nature had done for her, but also a literal soft spot in that armor of disinterest. Heat and exertion and cotton cloth had come together in that moment to form a small, wet oval of desirability.

How could he not see her now? Her fine legs and hips were at eye level for much of the hike, with the parts of them that weren't bare covered only by damp, clingy cloth. Once or twice she turned at the waist to make sure Charley was keeping up, and in those moments he could see that a similar circle of sweat had formed on her belly, holding the shirt close against her breasts. As he had been on that first day, he was struck by how pretty she was; unlike on that first day, he now was also struck by the person this body carried around.

Inexplicably, the image of Baby Girl came to Charley's mind. He suddenly understood that she and Tallasee had been coined at the same mint. Baby Girl was a newer issue, still uncertain and floundering a bit, but her instincts were true: she had a taste for crusades and gambles, and was happily but not destructively impulsive. Someday, a few years hence, another man would dwell on Baby Girl's form and being, and ask himself—as Charley had asked himself about Tallasee just moments before—what fool let this treasure slip away?

Such thoughts tend to limit a young man's attention. So, in one of the infrequent sweeps his gaze took of the forest around them, Charley only got a momentary glimpse of the red bandanna, hidden deep in the woods but moving parallel to the trail. Lucas wasn't done with perimeter security.

●

Tallasee was privately happy to see that Blue Hole was deserted. On her two previous visits, it had been ringed with happily naked Rainbows, who perched on rocks and low tree limbs and took turns lowering themselves into the bubbling fissure or floated in the pool just below the hole. This time, there was a menacing stillness about the place, and as she and Charley stood next to the stream, she realized the commune itself had been depopulated. There seemed to be in residence perhaps half the number of people that there had been just a few months earlier. She wished she had noticed sooner and asked Osage about it.

Charley had said little during the hike, and now kept craning his head to peer back into the woods. "What are you looking for?" Tallasee finally asked.

"Aw, nothing," he said, then turned his attention to the pool of water before them. "How deep is it?"

"I don't know if anybody knows. You can't feel the bottom when you're in it, but you can't go down very far, anyway. The force of the water pushes you back up."

"So you've been in it?" he asked.

She had. The Rainbows had led her to this place on her first visit, but upon arriving had decided that no more pictures were allowed unless she, too, was naked. And when she'd met that demand, another was imposed: she had to lower herself into Blue Hole, which evidently had become a rite of passage at the commune. So Tallasee had set her camera on top of her clothes and stepped gingerly across the smooth, slippery rocks in the stream. The hole was about six feet from the bank, and when she got close, she could see why the name was appropriate. The mountain stream had long ago washed all silt from its bed, and through the clear water she saw the blacks, grays, and browns of the stones that lined its path. But where the water filled the deep cleave in the earth at this spot, it took on an aquamarine shade, a vivid hue that somehow resulted from the depth of the water and the penetration of sunlight to that place.

She had lowered herself into the water, which was so bracingly cold that she wondered if there wasn't also a spring far beneath her feet. The stream fell into the hole from a ledge just above it, a foot or so high, and the constant force of water being dropped into the fissure had the effect of pushing the existing water up and out. That movement made Tallasee feel as if she was being cold-boiled in a giant saucepan, gently but relentlessly pushed to the surface by the water bubbling up around her. She felt supremely buoyant, bobbing freely in the deep, endless hole. When she finally climbed out, and as she sunned herself on the rocks with the Rainbows, all of them naked and stuporous—they from their smoke, she from an unexpected but not unwelcome lassitude—Tallasee realized it was the first time since Nigel's death that she hadn't felt like smashing something.

But now as she stood with Charley on the stream bank, she understood that that had been a fleeting moment of peace. Today there seemed to be something brooding and unhappy about the place, the sense that whatever previous calm had been found there was in fact fraudulent and deceptive. Tallasee had lost her ability to control things; she didn't know what they were doing at the commune or what end would come of this search for a lost boy. She couldn't fathom why she had been so quick to become a wife or how it had turned sour with even greater speed. And she didn't understand why she fretted so much about Charley, why she worried for the future of someone who a few weeks before she'd only vaguely known.

The name of this place suddenly seemed apt. Tallasee felt the only thing she understood was that she'd fallen into her own deep blue hole and couldn't seem to lift herself out.

"Yeah, I've been in it," she said

●

They returned to the truck just as the clouds knitted together and darkened. The first few drops hit the windshield as they turned on to the highway, and before they'd gone a quarter mile it was pouring. Tallasee leaned forward and looked up, as if she could somehow discern the storm's intentions or lifespan.

"I was going to suggest we go see Mrs. Bullock, while we're up here," she said. "But I don't relish trying to get up her hill in this rain."

It would have been a treacherous drive indeed, but had they known then what they would later discover, they would have done it gladly.

Chapter Eight

Before I tell you what I'm going to tell you, let me ask you boys a question: Have either one of you ever been in combat? I don't mean being around some shooting, or hearing some shooting. I'm talking about laying in a ditch, being mortared and knowing you were going to die that day. I'm talking about seeing a whole piece of flesh, a hunk of meat the size of a pork roast, come off a buddy's leg. Having so many rounds shot at you that there's just one, long whizzing sound in your ear. Situation like that, you don't even aim. You just put your rifle over your head and empty the clip. You know your range instructor would holler at you if he was there, tell you you're wasting ammunition and to squeeze off rounds just three or four at a time, but to hell with him. You're going to die that day, and you couldn't care less about the god-damn ammunition. You're going to empty every clip you've got as fast as you can, and then you're going to grab clips off the belts of your dead buddies. And after you empty every clip you can jam into your rifle, you realize there ain't nobody shooting anymore except you, anyway. It's over, and you're just about the only one who ain't dead.

No? Well, let me tell you what something like that does for you. It makes you understand that nothing else in life is going to be that bad.

The point I'm trying to make to you boys is that I'm not talking to you about all this because I'm afraid of what's going to happen to me if I don't. Don't take this personally, but you two don't scare me. You're used to having people sit in here and be all sweaty and nervous. I know that. But I ain't sweaty and I ain't nervous. I'm just acknowledging reality. There's no point in not telling you what happened, because it won't do me any good. So I'll just tell you.

Yeah, I killed that boy. You already know that. Otherwise, why would I be here? I don't even know who he was. About the only thing I know about him is he didn't seem to have good sense. There was something just plain weird about him. I mean, here's your proof: Everyone else up there thinks my uniform is the symbol of something bad, and he thought it was interesting. Just like a little kid would. That's why he followed me up toward Blue Hole. He must have thought he was playing army or something.

Goddamn uniform. I don't have to wear it anymore. I don't know why I do. But it ain't like I've got lots of other clothes. Sometimes it's the only thing available to put on, so that's why I was wearing it that day. Jesus, if I'd known all this was going to happen, I'd have gone bareass, I swear.

Chapter Nine

The storm was faster than Tallasee and Charley were. It moved into Barrington ahead of them, drenching the city with an impressive ten-minute downpour and knocking down an ancient oak tree in a park, just to show off, before departing the far limits as they arrived. It was late afternoon, but the sun still had sufficient vigor to make steam rise from newly wet streets once the clouds had roiled their way out of town. Barrington's local landmarks—the monument to the Confederate war dead; the steeple of the Episcopalian church where Franklin Roosevelt inexplicably had appeared one Sunday morning although Warm Springs was at least a three-hour car ride away; the old-fashioned, neon-laced sign perched above the Krispy Kreme doughnut shop; the de Soto rock, into which the Spanish explorer had seen fit to chisel his mark and the year he'd passed this spot where the Precambrian shield jutted through the earth's dirt skin; the showcase row of antebellum homes that sheltered a dwindling number of Barrington's founding families and a growing number of antique emporiums, tearoom-style restaurants, and law offices; and the masonry arch that sat at the edge of the lawn which protected Barrington Baptist College from the secular temptations that any downtown area, even one nestled in the pious embrace of an officially dry county, nonetheless offers—these landmarks all gleamed wet and clean as Charley wove his way through the city toward Tallasee's studio.

He parked the truck and let it idle, uncertain of whether she expected just to be dropped off or to have him come in. She hadn't said much on the drive home, and she just sat silently as the truck murmured. Finally, she spoke.

"I think we should see Johnny Carver about this," she said.

She seemed to expect an argument, so Charley turned the truck off. But he had a surprise for her. "You're probably right," he responded.

She continued as if she hadn't heard. "I just don't know what else we're supposed to do. The boy was there, but he's not there now and no one knows, or will tell us, where he's gone. And I'm not even sure he's young enough to be considered a runaway. What do you figure he is? Seventeen? Eighteen?"

Charley remembered Lucas's tale of giving the boy advice about the military draft. "Yeah, that sounds right," he said.

"So do we even bother the sheriff with this? I mean, he may just end up telling us people are free to live wherever they want when they get old enough to leave home."

There was no doubting where this was going, which made Charley glad he'd already agreed it was now a matter for the sheriff: he would sound consistent and reasonable, rather than zealous. "Well, why don't we let him decide if he's interested? He's the expert."

"This is Saturday. I doubt we'll even find him."

"It can wait 'til Monday," Charley said, shrugging agreeably, but Tallasee seemed to be involved in some private argument with herself.

"Oh, hell. C'mon in, and I'll call over there now," she said.

Tallasee made placing this phone call a complicated production, in the way of people who find themselves doing something that they don't want to do and need to make known how much trouble they're going to on someone else's behalf. She fished the phone book out of a drawer, dropped it noisily on the desk, and riffled through the pages too quickly, overshooting the county government listings once in each direction before finding them. She asked for the sheriff in a tone of voice that guaranteed no one would want to be helpful, was transferred twice—which only reinforced her imperiousness—and finally listened to a long explanation before hanging up.

"He's out," she said, happy to have her point proven, if only to herself. "In fact, we were closer to him this morning. He's up in the hills, taking care of something."

"So, like I said—we see him Monday."

She nodded, but there was more challenge than agreement in the gesture. "And then we'll be done with this."

●

Charley's mother was sitting at the table in the kitchen when he arrived. She often worked on Saturday; in addition to her regular job at the stone-company office near the quarry, she also worked occasionally on weekends and evenings at Corey's department store, shoring up the staff on holidays or filling in for whichever sales clerk was absent. At the end of almost every week, this is how Charley would find her: sitting with cigarette in hand, as if she'd made it to the kitchen only through force of instinct but lost her steam once she'd gotten there.

Years later, Charley would come to understand how hard she'd had to work to keep them in their home. She'd had no education beyond high school and, because she'd married young and borne children early, almost no work history. Charley's father hadn't been the type to save money, and Shay's funeral had consumed everything she managed to tuck away. So, when Lee Roy Selkirk fled, she was left with a mortgage, a cupboard empty enough to send mice looking for more fruitful grounds, a car with a leaking transmission, and a son who tried to never be in the same room with her, lest he again feel her guilt lashing against his own.

Frances could fix some of those problems. She found work, then extra work. She stayed a little behind the bills for a while, then stayed even, and, finally, stayed ahead. When Charley got old enough to work during the summer, he added what he could, keeping back only enough to buy an old pickup truck that farted a cloud of blue smoke every time it started, prompting his friends to offer their confident opinions on what caused it and then argue with each other over the differing diagnoses. Frances was careful with things like clothes and food—invoking her Corey's employee discount as often as possible and filling her lunch break with nothing but a cup of coffee and a cigarette—and iron-willed in her priorities, which Charley learned when their broken television set went unrepaired for a year before she decided that they could afford to fix it.

What didn't get fixed, however, was the rift between Frances and Charley. What Charley later concluded was exhaustion at the time seemed like a deliberate distance. She was at her best in the mornings, when they would talk a bit over breakfast and Charley could depend on getting a hug as he set off for school, and at her worst in the evenings, when working and fretting and regretting kept her silent. It was in those moments that Charley was most sure she neither liked nor wanted him.

They talked whenever necessary and occasionally when it wasn't necessary, when Frances's gloom and Charley's sense of unlikeability lifted simultaneously. But more and more they had become like boarders, two people sharing a common bathroom and taking their meals together, but otherwise existing in separate spheres. Charley wasn't even certain his mother knew he had a girlfriend. If Frances did know it, Charley was doubtful she knew the girl's name. Also, a year or two back, Charley had stopped showing Frances his report cards, instead just leaving them for her to see on the kitchen counter. Later, he didn't even do that, yet she never asked about his grades. She knew he'd gotten kicked out of school—he'd had to account for his sudden time at home—but she had only given him a flat stare, her eyes half-closed against the cigarette smoke that drifted up to her face. Charley found himself wanting her to be angry, if only for the evidence of caring that anger would provide, but she wasn't.

"Your life," she'd finally said, and that was all.

But then, there was much Charley didn't know about her, either: her friends' names and even whether she had any, her title at work, her favorite movie star and television shows, or what private thoughts winged through her mind as she knelt before a file cabinet at the stone company or passed a dress into a fitting room at Corey's. He didn't know how she'd met his father, because by the time Charley was old enough to be interested in such things, Lee Roy was gone and the topic closed. Charley wasn't even sure of her age, knowing only that she'd been born sometime in the early 1930s.

And they certainly never talked about Shay, nor anything that could lead a conversation back to the day he died. As he'd gotten older, Charley often pondered where his mother was that afternoon. He understood it didn't matter, ultimately, because nothing she could say would erase the reality that he'd left his little brother alone in the house. But the fact that she'd never explained it, and actually had worked hard to put the topic off limits even to police investigators, suggested there was something weighty and cumbersome that only she could see. If Frances never saw fit to acknowledge her own culpability in Shay's death, however, at least she never again, after that one moment in the hospital, pushed Charley away.

Tragedy had not made them closer, but neither had it driven them apart. They were suspended in an odd, silent orbit, both bound and repelled by their respective guilt. So Charley didn't understand why he had the sudden need to talk.

"I've got to register for the draft pretty soon," Charley said, settling into the other chair at the kitchen table.

She looked at him sharply. "You mean the military draft?"

Charley nodded.

"When are you supposed to do that?" she asked.

"When I turn eighteen, I think."

Alarm showed in her eyes. It was as much feeling as he'd seen in her in years. "They can make you go in the service when you're eighteen?"

"I'm not sure about any of this. Some guy"—Charley considered mentioning Lucas, but it didn't seem appropriate to admit his adviser in these matters was a possibly unhinged tent-dweller who guarded a road hardly anyone used—"was telling me about it."

"Telling you what?"

Charley realized that the things Lucas had said couldn't be reduced to an easy summary. The whole conversation seemed to have been a series of sinister and vague warnings: Don't let yourself be drafted, don't continue looking for the boy, don't hang around the commune too long. "Well, telling me that I shouldn't just let it happen, that I should start thinking about it," he said vaguely. "So I guess that's what I'm doing now. Thinking about it."

"We'd both better think about it," Frances said.

It was the longest conversation they'd had in a long time.

●

Tallasee's house was a mess. The living room was full of boxes and furniture that Charley had hauled from the studio in anticipation of pulling up its carpet. The photo negatives were piled on the dining-room table, arranged by year but still awaiting the cataloging she'd hired him to do. He was making progress on both tasks, but he hadn't focused on either of them, which annoyed Tallasee and fueled the sense of unease she had about this third, extracurricular chore they'd taken on.

The kitchen was little better, and she couldn't blame its untidiness on Charley. She made herself a peanut butter sandwich—mostly because it was the only meal she could think of that didn't require her to confront the aging contents of the refrigerator—and walked around the house, taking inventory, as she ate. Tallasee couldn't remember the last time she'd made her bed. The bathroom sink showed dribbles of toothpaste, and the hamper overflowed with clothes that dated to another season. In a corner of the bedroom window, there was a cobweb of sufficient size and design to be considered architecture. The cellophane wrapping of a convenience-store sandwich peeked from underneath a chair in the living room.

Tallasee refused to believe this was her doing—it had to be the handiwork of a doppelganger. She thought of herself as orderly and tidy; she did not let soiled clothes and dirty dishes accumulate. She did not allow things to fall into chaos. She did not let herself sink, slowly and almost indiscernibly, into lassitude and listlessness. She did not get stalled on projects and then hire a teenage boy to untangle a couple of minor knots that in her desperation she had identified as the cause of her problems. She didn't do those things, because those were the actions of a profoundly depressed individual. And she was afraid to acknowledge she was depressed.

She ate as she wandered, eventually finding herself in the dining room again. The contact sheet containing the picture of Mrs. Bullock's grandson sat on top of one of the piles of negatives, and she idly picked it up. She saw what she hadn't seen before.

●

She didn't have a motor drive on her camera because she didn't want gadgets in her life. Besides, she'd grown weary of hearing them in her fashion days, when the sound of a shutter being tripped three times a second and a motor whirring as it pulled the film eventually came to seem like the whisper of a seducer who no longer charmed. So, she advanced her film the old-fashioned way, with her thumb against the lever, which is why a second or so elapsed between each of the three photographs. And that, in turn, is why a perfect sequence of action was obvious in them.

Because the contact sheet was clear enough only to show Tallasee that there was something worth seeing, she made a print of each image that had caught her eye. Then, after shoving a few piles of prints and negatives out of the way to make space on the dining-room table, she set the pictures in a row and examined them.

Tallasee had taken the photographs during one of her previous visits to the commune. That day, before she had gathered everyone together for a group shot, she'd spent the morning wandering about, both studying possible locations for a family portrait and shooting the occasional picture. At one point, she'd seen a nice image—two of the Rainbows, a man and a woman, bent over a large cast-iron pot that was hung over a small fire and presumably contained the day's lunch stew—and decided to capture it. When she looked through the viewfinder, however, it seemed wrong: the scene had the quaint sense of another era, but nostalgia is no particular challenge; what she needed was the accompanying sense of the modern, which would lend an element of the surreal.

Fortunately, there was no shortage of contemporary litter at the commune. On the ground near the couple was a crumpled box that had contained a large battery-operated radio and tape player, its presence the inevitable result of the collision between the Rainbows' commitment to a life untethered to power-company barons and their need for rock 'n' roll. The radio's brand name, bright and large, was clearly visible, and although Tallasee assumed the box had been earmarked as fuel for the fire, the blaze was doing well on its own and the box just sat, purposeless and jarring. Even better, beyond the couple was a vehicle owned by one of the Rainbows, its hood open as it awaited a repair that seemingly had begun and then been delayed. This—the counterculture pioneers surrounded yet unbothered by the spoor of the life they wanted to leave behind—was the tableau to be framed.

Thus inspired, Tallasee had taken three pictures, only vaguely noticing the movement in the background, before her subjects became aware of the camera and began to adjust their bodies and profiles in that way of people who want to look good on film but also want to pretend they don't know a photograph is being taken. But because only movie stars and politicians can do that successfully, they suddenly seemed awkward, and Tallasee stopped shooting. Still, it didn't matter: when she'd later examined the contact sheet with her loupe to select which pictures to print, she'd been disappointed with what she saw. The image in the background was more substantial than it had seemed through the viewfinder, looming larger in the frame than she thought it would and insisting that it be looked at. Tallasee wouldn't have been able to use any of the three pictures anyway, with this figure inexplicably hovering in the background.

He was emerging from the forest in the first frame, coming through the gap in the trees that marked the start of the trail that Charley and Tallasee themselves had followed just that day. He presumably was returning from his own hike, and in that frame he had not yet seen Tallasee; his face was visible, but his eyes were focused with either care or weariness on the ground before him.

He spotted her in the second frame. He had lifted his head and was looking directly into the camera. There was alarm on his face, the look of someone who may not have been caught in the act, but has finished the act so recently that he still carries the whiff of it on him, rendering him unsure how obvious it is to others. An observer can already sense the instinctive search for cover building in him.

The moment Tallasee had spent advancing the film for the last picture was all the time he needed. He was turned away in the final frame, his head already obscured by a branch as he stepped off the trail into the forest. It was pure flight, the unmistakable need to not be seen. Were the last one the only photograph available, his identity would have been a mystery. Did he ever wonder if he'd been quick enough to avoid Tallasee's capture? Or were his instincts so primitive that he'd forgotten the whole event as soon as his alarm faded?

Grudgingly, Tallasee admitted to herself that Charley was right. Lucas certainly acted like a man with something to hide.

●

Charley hadn't had many jobs before that summer, which gave him no point of comparison, but he nonetheless understood that his employment by Tallasee was a strange arrangement.

He had no real schedule, for one thing. He went to work when he wanted, and declared it a day with no regard to the actual time of day. Also, there was an odd flow between his two projects. He would work in the studio until he could do no more without moving some of the clutter to her house; once he got there, he would find himself hovering over the dining-room table, sorting through negatives and cataloguing them by subject and date. Then he would remember that Tallasee had come across a box of negatives under the desk or in a cabinet and told him to add it to the pile, so Charley would return to the studio and end up working on the floor again.

Stranger yet, he never seemed to get paid.

"So, when is payday, exactly?" he asked the Monday morning after they'd visited the commune.

"When are you going to be done, exactly?" she replied.

Lord, she could be scratchy. Sometimes she was a big sister, naggy and condescending; sometimes a mother, careful and helpful; sometimes a girl, sitting on her side of the truck and bantering easily; and sometimes a woman, vivid and glorious and capable of making Charley aware of the unlikelihood that someone like him would ever lay claim to someone like her.

"Hard to say, exactly. Do I have all the negatives, or are you going to keep finding little stashes of them here and there?" Sometimes Charley felt the need to become scratchy himself, lest he be overwhelmed by her.

"Let's assume you have them all. Exactly how much longer is this going to take?" She seemed to be in the mood for a straight answer.

"A week or so," he said. "And figure a couple of more days to get the rest of the carpet out and the floor cleaned up."

"You'd better be thinking about new career opportunities, then, because that'll be the end of your time at Tallasee's Photo Shop and Fun House."

"Boy, that's a shame. I'm going to miss those fat paychecks."

He must have sounded bitter, because Tallasee softened her tone. "Charley, I'm sorry. I don't mean to be so abrupt. I was planning to just pay you once, when everything was finished. Is that okay?" Charley nodded, and she continued. "Look, I don't really need a helper. I was feeling pressure on my book deadline and when this thing with Mrs. Bullock came up, I panicked. It suddenly seemed like I had too much to do, and you were there. But I can push back my deadline and we'll be done with this thing for Mrs. Bullock today when we see the sheriff. So let's wrap up the things you started and we'll move on." She paused, then added, "Besides, I'm a little worried about you."

"Why?" Charley asked. He suspected the answer, and wasn't disappointed.

"Because it doesn't seem as if you're thinking about your future."

First Lucas, then his mother, and now Tallasee. "I'd just be duplicating the efforts of lots of other people," he said, but the remark sailed by her. She'd moved on to another subject, anyway.

"Remember, we're supposed to see Johnny Carver at one o'clock," she said.

●

When Charley went outside, he found Baby Girl leaning against the fender of his truck.

"Hey, sailor," she said, "you want to buy a girl a cup of coffee?"

It had been two months since he'd seen her, aside from the occasional moment when he'd spotted her in her car as he lingered at a traffic light and contrived the sudden need to consult a map or adjust the radio in order to keep from catching her eye. Seeing her now was jarring, and made Charley understand how much his world had both narrowed and expanded: he'd traded the aimless, restless wandering that occupies much of a teenager's life for days that shifted no further than his home, Tallasee's home, and her studio, but he'd also become netted in the affairs of adults, as well as made to face the thoroughly grown-up notion that people his age were considered by the government to be top-grade bullet-stoppers.

Baby Girl looked magnificent. She was somehow fuller and rounder, with the look and the clothes of someone who has become comfortable with her charms. She wore cutoff jeans, with so much tanned leg showing that Charley wondered how she'd gotten out of the house without her mother noticing, and a blue denim work shirt, unbuttoned but with the shirttails knotted at her waist. Underneath was a man's sleeveless undershirt, presumably liberated from her father's drawer, and Charley could plainly see she wore no bra. Her hair was loose and long, and the way she leaned against the truck—one ankle crossed over the other, and hands tucked insouciantly into the pockets of her jeans—was so confidently provocative as to be almost brazen. This was no accidental meeting—she was waiting for Charley and wanted his attention.

He wondered for a second if this wasn't yet another personality she'd draped over herself—hippie chick to cheerleader to sex kitten—before suddenly realizing how fundamentally unfair he'd been to her all along. Her only sin was to be happily visible in her evolution as she grew into a woman. His own evolution to manhood, of course, was sullen and private.

"When did you start drinking coffee?" he asked.

She grinned. "Two days ago. I used to pester Daddy for a drink of his, and he always told me it wasn't for children. So I got up Saturday morning and decided I'd have a cup of coffee, now that I'm an adult." She made a funny, sour face. "It's not so good, really. I have to put a lot of sugar and cream in it."

Catching the puzzled look on Charley's face, she squinched her face up in concern. "Oh, Charley, I'm sorry," she said, marking the second time in just a few minutes that someone had apologized to him. "You see, everybody graduated Friday night. That's what I meant about being a grown-up. I guess we're all adults now."

Charley gave what he hoped was a nonchalant shrug. "So how was it?"

"About what you'd expect. The gym was too hot and the speeches were too long."

"Was there any trouble?"

"Nope. The colored kids sat together and the white kids sat together and everyone went to different parties."

Neither of them said anything for a moment. They had just exhausted the one topic they could have discussed casually over coffee, and anything else that needed to be said probably shouldn't be said in a restaurant with people all around. Besides, Charley was distracted by the conflicting impulses roiling around inside him. Baby Girl looked fabulous, she was being chatty and friendly, and his realization just two days prior that she would be a rare treasure as a grown woman still was fresh in his mind. But equally fresh was his memory of how alone he'd felt when he'd been dismissed from school. Baby Girl had been the second woman, after Charley's mother, who'd seemed to push him away. Today, Tallasee was making it three. Enduring pain is one thing, Charley thought, but courting it is quite another.

"Listen, I've got to go," he said.

"Donny Chambers has been asking me out," Baby Girl said abruptly. With that, they evidently arrived at the topic of the day. "I keep saying no, but I feel guilty about what happened to him."

"You mean, what I did to him."

"Well, I feel bad about that, too. I guess I put you in an impossible spot."

"So your cure for all this is to go out with Donny?"

Charley could see a flush rising on her chest, a place that only a few months before would have been primly buttoned over. "Thinking about it, yeah," she said defiantly.

Just then, Tallasee came out the door and stepped down the sidewalk in their direction. As she passed, apparently heading off on some small errand, she said conspicuously and coquettishly to Charley, "Don't forget our date."

She meant, of course, their appointment with Johnny Carver, but she seemed to want Baby Girl to take it differently. In fact, she emphasized it by saying "Hi there" to her in a cool, other-woman tone as she walked by. When Tallasee got a few steps beyond and out of Baby Girl's vision, she turned and gave Charley a merry, mischievous smile.

He couldn't have orchestrated it any better. "Well, a girl's got to do what a girl's got to do," he said, with a nonchalance he didn't actually feel but could persuasively pretend, thanks to Tallasee.

To her credit, Baby Girl was poised. She gave a pointed glance toward Tallasee's departing form, and then turned back to her former boyfriend and said, "Our little Charley, all grown up."

•

Tallasee never thought of herself as having any gift for denying the obvious, but she developed a sudden, temporary talent for it that summer. Later, she could see that it was self-protection: She had closed down her sensors, which were dangerously overloaded. She felt like a raw, gaping wound, so she'd swaddled herself in the dressing and surgical tape of disengagement. She had made herself willfully oblivious. She didn't care that her pictures of Lucas seemed to confirm Charley's sense that something at the commune was amiss. She just shrugged at what they later discovered at Mrs. Bullock's home. She paid little heed to the amount of time that she spent with Charley, fretting about Charley, or arguing with Charley in silent conversations she held in her head.

It wasn't until things literally fell into a smoking ruin that she finally started paying attention.

Chapter Ten

T allasee wondered if science ever would be able to explain why police stations and sheriff's offices make everyone in them feel like trailer park–living, side meat–eating, underwear-tugging, polyester-wearing members of the underclass. It doesn't matter who you are— the queen of England could walk into a police station and within minutes find herself humming the latest from Merle Haggard and marveling how she ever got along without one of those hamburger-patty stackers that are advertised on late-night television. It must be the light. No one looks good under fluorescent bulbs.

She and Charley arrived promptly at one o'clock and spent several subsequent minutes being ignored by the two people working in the main office. The room was divided by a long counter, with government-issue metal desks and file cabinets on one side and nothing but a half dozen uncushioned wooden chairs on the other, and the two staffers were listlessly plodding through tasks on either end of their side of the room: the man typing a report, stabbing the keys with one finger as he gripped the edge of the typewriter with the other hand, as if to keep it from fleeing; the woman squatted down in front of a file cabinet with a pile of papers on the floor beside her. Both wore brown deputy's uniforms—although only the man carried a gun—and both had an aggressive not-my-job air about them. Neither would even look up as Tallasee and Charley stood at the counter.

"We're here to see Sheriff Carver," Tallasee finally said. Both of them continued to ignore her.

"It's nice of Johnny to hire the handicapped," she said to Charley. "But how do you figure deaf people hear the emergency calls?"

She got a poisonous look from the woman just as the muffled sound of a toilet being flushed somewhere wafted into the room. A moment later, another uniformed woman bustled up the counter and said chirpily, "May I help you?"

"If this is still Monday, we have an appointment to see Sheriff Carver," Tallasee said.

It went right by her. "It's Monday," she said in earnest confirmation, nodding happily as she did. "I'll see if he's in."

She came back a few moments later. "Johnny said for y'all to go right on back," she said, pointing them to a door that wore a sign declaring STAFF ONLY. Her head bobbed once again. "He's at the end of the hall. You can't miss it."

The hallway was painted the same faint green as the waiting area, and the handful of rooms they passed were furnished with the same desks and cabinets. Only the sheriff's office was different.

Johnny Carver sat at one end of what originally was two rooms, behind an enormous wood desk that held several untidy piles of paper, a police scanner that monitored his dispatcher's conversations and calls, a telephone with several lighted buttons—all blinking—and a paperweight that seemed to be a huge bullet of some kind and which would, Tallasee thought, prompt most men to happily start talking about guns and calibers and such. The walls were a jumble of inscribed photographs—one of them from Lester Maddox, the segregationist restaurant owner who'd threatened to drive black diners off with a mattock handle and been elected governor of Georgia as a result; another from J. Edgar Hoover, whose bulldog visage seemed to glower approvingly toward the bullet paperweight—as well as citations from various civic groups and charitable organizations. Hung or tacked in other places were things the sheriff had apparently collected during two decades of restoring order in odd and remote places: a rusted animal foot trap, a four-foot-long rattlesnake skin, a gray, papery hornets' nest still attached to a broken-off bit of tree branch, a half dozen or so homemade knives with taped handles, a car steering wheel bent into an oval during what must have been a memorably bad wreck, and a pocket-sized copy of the Holy Bible with what appeared to be a bullet hole gaping on its cover just an inch below the gold-lettered title and continuing through all the following pages.

The sheriff stood grinning as Charley and Tallasee looked around.

He liked the effect this bizarre museum had on first-time visitors. It was like an adult's version of a boy's secret clubhouse, the place where forbidden items and the things his mother had banned from the house could be stored. Experience must have told him that a visitor's eyes eventually would settle on one item or another, which would provide his cue to begin explaining his treasures. So he waited quietly until Tallasee's eyes lingered on the Bible.

"You know that roadhouse out on the Atlanta Highway, right on the county line? Billy's Place?" Tallasee nodded. It was a notorious honky-tonk, snug up against the Soque County line, from whence it offered Barrington residents the closest place for a legal drink. It also was well known for not being particularly scrupulous about asking for proof of age before selling beer or deciding that a patron had had enough to drink, which meant an almost equal number of inadvertent conceptions and drunken car accidents could be traced back to Billy's. Although going there was a rite of passage among high schoolers, Tallasee was the only one nodding to Johnny's question; Charley was the picture of studied innocence. Johnny may have been a friendly sort and widely called by his first name, but he was still the sheriff. Charley had decided that even a nod would be admitting to too much.

"I took that out of some old boy's shirt pocket after he'd been shot there one night. He'd had a scuffle with somebody and they'd gone outside. The county line runs right through the middle of Billy's parking lot, and this fool manages to stumble over to my side before he dies. Only homicide I had that year." He gave a rueful shake of his head. "Guy shot him right in his Bible, but unfortunately it was just one of those New Testaments the Gideons give out. I guess if they printed the whole Bible, they couldn't make it small enough to put in your pocket. So it wasn't thick enough to save him." He savored the image for a moment, then added: "If that boy'd had any interest in the Old Testament, he'd be alive today."

"What was he doing in Billy's with a Bible?" Tallasee asked. "Was he there to preach or drink?"

"Both, apparently," Johnny said cheerfully. "That's what upset the regular customers. They don't mind being told they're sinners, as long as you don't have a drink in your hand when you're doing it."

He gave a huge smile and waved them toward a pair of chairs facing his desk. Johnny was a large man with a face that seemed to grin naturally and short, bristly hair the color and look of iron filings. He settled into his own chair, pulled out a lower drawer from one side of the desk, then leaned back and propped his foot on it, as comfortable as any farmer wasting a winter morning stoveside at a crossroads store. "So what can I help you with?" he prompted.

For a moment, neither Charley nor Tallasee said anything—evidence, she realized, of the tension between them on this matter. It had become Charley's crusade, so she thought he should do the explaining. But they were there at her arrangement, with her desire to hand this off to Johnny being the reason they now sat in this odd museum of crime arcana. Finally, Tallasee spoke.

"A friend of mine—" she began, and immediately had the sensation of stepping off badly with her first words. She started over. "This woman I know has a grandson who she thinks may have run away from home. She asked me to look for him." Charley shifted in his chair, and she found herself correcting her words again. "Asked us to look for him. She thought he'd joined up with the hippies, and, sure enough, we discovered he'd been at that commune up in the hills. The Rainbow Nation. But he'd already left by the time we visited, so we thought we'd better just tell you about all this." It was a limp ending even to her ears, so she added: "I mean, it seems like a police matter. We really don't know how to look for him."

Charley spoke up for the first time. "Actually, it's pretty strange. Everyone up there tried to deny he'd even been there. But after they saw the photos, it was clear they just wanted us to go away."

Damn Charley. All Tallasee wanted to do was get out of here and be done with this. Johnny must have noticed a shadow of irritation on her face. "Did you two forget to rehearse this earlier?" he asked, a bemused look on his face.

"Well, yeah, we got an odd reaction," Tallasee acknowledged. "But it's probably just because they thought he was younger than he was and when we showed up they thought there was going to be trouble."

"Except that he wasn't that young," Charley interjected again. "I think he was about my age."

"Which is why we probably shouldn't be bothering with this at all," Tallasee said pointedly. "It's not like he's a child."

By this point, Johnny was clearly confused. "Look, I've already lost track of this. What photos are you talking about? And how exactly did the two of you get together on this?"

"Charley works for me," Tallasee said, addressing the second question first. "Temporarily," she added, mostly because Charley had annoyed her.

Something seemed to register with Johnny. "Tell me your name once again," he said to Charley. When he got the reply, he asked, "That thing at the football practice a while back, at the high school, that was you, right?"

Charley nodded unhappily.

"You know, that boy's daddy was in here to see me after you laid that lick on him," Johnny continued. "He was pretty upset. Asking me about filing charges and all. I didn't make him too happy when I said that if his son couldn't take a tough hit, then maybe he ought to find another sport." He hesitated a moment, then added meaningfully: "Along with that colored boy."

"Yes, sir, it all got sort of tangled up together," Charley said.

"I know what happened, son," Johnny said kindly. "People never credit me for knowing the things I do. They think I only know what they tell me, and that if they only tell me what they want me to know, that I'll see things their way." He looked at Tallasee. "Hardly ever works."

She understood she'd made a mistake. She'd been lulled by Johnny's easy nature and japery, been distracted by the odd treasures he displayed with an almost childlike enthusiasm. She wondered how many other people had sat in his office and blundered into revelations or even confessions before they'd understood how clever he was. He was warning her—presumably as a courtesy, after deciding they were hapless but innocent citizens who'd made a few tentative steps into his world and then regretted it—to tell the story, straight up.

"I'd taken some photos at the commune a few months back—" Tallasee began, then hesitated, wondering if she should explain what she did for a living, but he nodded, telling her that he already knew—"and the old gal's grandson showed up in one of them. So we took copies of the picture up there and showed them around, asking people if they knew where the boy was. Charley's right. Even though he was right there in the photo, a couple of people acted like that boy'd never even been there."

"Do you have the picture with you?" Johnny asked.

Tallasee retrieved it from her bag and handed it to him. She also pulled copies of the photos that showed Lucas ducking for cover, holding them inconspicuously in her lap. Johnny was studying the picture she'd given him and didn't notice, but Charley saw them and gave her a quizzical look. Tallasee ignored him.

Johnny set the photo on the desk and planted his finger on the boy's face. "I'm guessing this is who you're searching for," he said. His cop sense had kicked in. "He's got the look of someone who doesn't belong."

"That's him," Tallasee confirmed.

"I know him, too," Johnny added, tapping his finger on Osage's face. "I've been up there two or three times, always ended up talking to him. He's got a funny name."

"Osage."

"That's it. I'm guessing he's one of the people who denied seeing the boy at first."

If Tallasee hadn't already concluded that Johnny was a lot smarter than he let on, this would have cinched it for her. "That's right," she said.

"Who was the other?"

"A guy Charley talked to. He's not in the photo. His name is Lucas. He seems to be the only person up there who hasn't taken a hippie name."

Johnny looked surprised. "Tall, skinny guy?" he asked. "Sort of a wild look in his eye?"

"This guy," Tallasee said, lifting the pictures from her lap and spreading them on the desk. "The one ducking into the bushes."

Johnny examined them while she explained, more for Charley's benefit than for the sheriff's: "I found these in a file a day or two ago. Actually, I came across them before then. But after we'd been up there and seen how strange he acted, they caught my eye. I wouldn't have paid attention to them otherwise." She spoke directly to Charley. "You're right. That guy's got something to hide."

Johnny looked up from the picture he held. "Goddamn," he said with sudden vehemence. "I thought I ran this guy off two months ago."

●

Not for the first time, Charley marveled at how thoroughly confounded he was by women generally and Tallasee specifically. All along, she'd made it clear she thought this whole exercise was frivolous. She'd treated him like a precocious child, patting him on the head and indulging his whims with a labored patience. Sometimes she was sharply or even maliciously sarcastic, while other times she was merely remote and distracted. But every once in a while, Charley would find her looking at him with an odd, searching expression on her face. And when he caught her eye, she wouldn't look away quickly, as the girls his own age were prone to do, as if they'd been found doing something wrong or had revealed too much. Instead, Tallasee would keep looking at him until he turned away in his own unease. Then there was that moment just that morning, when she'd taken some trouble to encourage Baby Girl to believe there was something going on between them, then given Charley a smile a moment later that would have stopped his heart if he hadn't known she was pretending.

As they sat there in Johnny's office, Charley remembered a comic moment in school a couple of years before when an earnest young language-arts teacher, falling prey to the elegantly random bad luck that life sometimes metes out, asked the precisely wrong student for a definition of the word "enigma." She was freshly graduated from a college up North and had arrived in Barrington practically aquiver with a sense of mission and opportunity. She was a believer in what she often referred to as the "Socratic method of teaching," which despite its highfalutin sound seemed to Charley to consist merely of the teacher asking questions of the students, instead of the other way around. At the start of each class, she would settle into an empty desk in the classroom—abandoning her own desk to sit among the masses, following some modern teaching philosophy that held that students would learn more from a friend than from an authority figure—open the textbook in front of her and begin peppering students with questions about the lesson they were supposed to have read the night before.

But because she had made clear during the first week of school that she didn't have much truck with tests and such, that education wasn't competitive and that learning would flower when students no longer felt the stress of performance, she rarely got anything other than a mumbled response or a smart-alecky answer. She met the first with a cloying helpfulness, usually exclaiming "Good!" or "Well put!" and then repeating the answer but paraphrasing it in a way that turned the typically mindless responses of Charley's classmates into the deft bits of insight she'd hoped for all along; she met the second with good-natured exasperation, giving the offender a mock frown but letting everyone know she tolerated a little fun because they were all pals, although by the third or fourth time it happened in a class period she would begin saying things like "Okay, we need to get serious now," as if all the levity had been her idea, but it was now time to let a little learning occur.

One morning as she sat among Charley and the other students, the class came across what must have seemed to her to be a particularly interesting word in the text. "Who can tell me what 'enigma' means?" she chirped. "Lee Ann?"

Lee Ann was a timid, large-bodied girl born of backwoods stock, and if it's true that the world demands that a certain number of people live in mobile homes all their lives and in time grow melon-sized tumors in their gut, Charley believed Lee Ann to be one of the leading candidates. She never volunteered an answer, and clearly didn't want to answer now. She just shook her head.

But the teacher wouldn't let it go. "I know you've read the lesson," she said. "Break the sentence down and focus on its context."

Although Lee Ann's family surely deconstructed literature over hominy and side meat every evening, she still demurred. "I just don't know," she said, her face reddening at the attention.

"Just take a guess at it," the teacher cajoled, working hard for this little blossom of learning.

Her face now thoroughly flushed, Lee Ann blurted out her answer: "It means squirting water up your bottom to make you go to the bathroom."

The class exploded in laughter so raucous and prolonged that it prompted the teachers from classrooms on either side to check on the commotion. Charley's teacher's face took on its own flush as an uncertain smile came and went, while Lee Ann sat lumpily humiliated. Her answer became instant legend, told and retold countless times in the following week.

Not surprisingly, the class never got back to the definition. Charley looked it up later in the dictionary, but never quite got his mind wrapped around its meaning until it suddenly became clear as he sat in Johnny's office that day. It was pointless to try to make sense of Tallasee's moods and reactions. She was Charley's enigma.

As Johnny laid the photo back down on his desk, Charley inexplicably felt happy that they had come to see him on this matter. It was the right thing to do after all.

●

"He's a bad one," Johnny said. "I stopped him on the highway once. Just between us girls"—he gave Charley a sly wink, to include him in the joke—"I really didn't have reason to pull him over. He was sitting right on the speed limit and driving fine. But you do this job long enough, you get an instinct for things, and a lot of bells went off when he drove by. So I pulled in behind him and hit the lights, and we had ourselves a little talk."

"So is Lucas his real name?" Tallasee asked, a question that sounded inane even as she uttered it. What did it matter whether that was his name? Oddly, however, Johnny looked embarrassed.

"You know, I don't remember. You get so caught up being John Wayne you forget to do the simple stuff. I asked to see his driver's license, but didn't write down his name or date of birth. You can find out a lot if you know those two things." He shook his head ruefully. "But I was too busy being a hardass."

Tallasee couldn't resist the question. "Did you give him until sundown, or was he supposed to get out of town right away?"

It had a snottier edge than she meant for it to, but Johnny didn't seem to notice. "Well, I'll tell you," he said. "I'd be happy if I never had to arrest anyone again in my life. Maybe I didn't have reason to stop him, and once I stopped him I sure didn't have reason to detain him. But you know what? That guy was trouble. I knew it, and he knew that I knew it, which is why he didn't squawk about his rights like everyone else seems to do these days. I asked him where he lived, he said he was staying in that commune, so I invited him to find somewhere else to live." A look of exasperation passed his face. "I'm sorry, but I just don't see the sense in letting trouble develop. If I can nudge a guy like that down the road, it's better for everybody."

"Well, he didn't stay nudged," Tallasee said.

"See what I mean? Everybody's a lawyer these days. He knew I couldn't really make him leave."

They seemed to be done, so Tallasee stood up to leave. "Keep the pictures if you need them," she said.

Johnny wasn't finished with the topic of Lucas, however. "I've got something specific to ask him about now," he said happily. "I believe I'll make a visit up there this afternoon. What's this boy's name, by the way?"

Charley and Tallasee looked blankly at each other for a moment. Realizing neither of them knew, Tallasee said, "I guess we never asked."

"Like I said, everybody forgets the basics sometimes," Johnny said. "What's his grandmother's name?"

"Pearlie Bullock. Lives up in the north part of the county, way off the highway."

An odd look came to Johnny's face before she'd even finished speaking. "Real old place? Looks like it's going to melt into the ground any day now?" Tallasee nodded.

"That old gal died last week," he said. "I had to go up there Saturday when her son found her body."

●

Charley had experienced it once before, this combination of seeing into the past and the future simultaneously, on the day Shay died. The first time, he'd realized not only what had happened to Shay but where he would find him just a few minutes hence. He had seen with a horrible clarity exactly where in the pond Shay would be. Sitting in Johnny's office, he had a similar sensation. He suddenly knew what had happened to that boy; not the specifics, exactly, but knew the boy wouldn't be found, and why. Charley also understood that there was something to be found in Mrs. Bullock's home. His tuning-fork gut told him these things.

It also told him that Johnny wouldn't find Lucas. That man would know it was time to get out of town, after all.

•

Tallasee sat back down and a long moment passed silently. "What happened?" she finally asked.

"I won't know for sure until later today," Johnny said. "Coroner will be done then. But it's pretty clear she just died. You get old, your parts start wearing out."

"Her son found her?"

He nodded. "He usually stopped in once a week or so, to carry her to the store or bring medicine or something. But it doesn't seem like he really had much contact with her. She lived up there without a phone, so she couldn't call if there was a problem. And far back as it is up there, it's not like he could look in on her every day. He says he asked her a few times to move closer to town, but she wouldn't do it." He hesitated a second. "I gather she was a peculiar old gal."

Tallasee found herself nodding in agreement. "Is he still up there? The son?" she asked.

"I believe so," Johnny answered. "Or at least he said he'd come back and go through her things." A thought crossed his mind, and he picked up the photograph with the boy in it. "You know, I guess this is his son. When I took down all the information, he said he was her only child. You'd think he would have mentioned something about his boy being missing and all."

Tallasee pondered this for a moment. "Yeah, you'd think so," she said. "So maybe that means our boy has returned home by now." She gave Charley what she hoped he understood was a meaningful look. "Maybe that means by the time we started looking for him, he wasn't even missing any longer."

"Maybe we should go find out," Charley said, damn him.

●

"I think I'll just get out of the photography business," Tallasee said an hour later. "I don't have the time for it, considering my other career and all."

It was the first thing she said since leaving Johnny's office and climbing into Charley's truck for yet another drive into the hills. She seemed mad and wanted to fight. Charley wasn't mad, but couldn't resist the temptation to counterpunch.

"I wouldn't give up photography just yet," he said. "You're really not too good at this other thing."

Her response was to hit him on the arm. It wasn't a girl punch, either. It got him just below the point of the shoulder and she swung through the punch like a boxer would, rather than just popping her fist. It hurt a lot, but she just smirked when he yelped.

"You're fired, too," she added.

"You already fired me," he said as he massaged the feeling back into his arm.

"I mean today. As soon as we get back from this pointless, time-consuming visit to someone who's not even alive anymore."

"Why are you blaming me? You're the one who insisted we go see Johnny Carver."

"Yes, I did," she confirmed. "The whole point was to turn this over to him. But you just won't let this thing go."

"Hang on a minute," Charley said, feeling his outrage build. "I'm not the one who suggested we come up here."

"Were, too. Your exact words were, 'Maybe we should find out.' "

"And Johnny's exact words were, 'Yeah, that would help out.' "

He indeed had seemed happy to have them make this trip. He was in a dilemma: his cop sense told him that something was wrong, but whatever time he spent returning to Mrs. Bullock's home to question

her son would be time better spent questioning Lucas before he disappeared. So Johnny preferred to find Lucas while Charley and Tallasee
were deputized to determine whether the runaway boy still was missing. Simply leaving town was no longer an option for Lucas, as far as
Johnny was concerned.

"He wouldn't have asked if you hadn't said anything. Why couldn't
you just keep quiet and let me tell the story?" she said.

"You weren't telling the story right."

"I was telling the story just fine," she said peevishly. For Charley,
the whole conversation suddenly carried an echo of the innumerable
and chronic low-grade arguments between his parents before Shay's
death. They had rarely talked, but quibbled constantly—no remark
ever was innocent, and the ground underneath could part at any moment to reveal great pools of pent-up unhappiness and resentment.

Tallasee also must have recognized the absurdly domestic tone, too.
"And I hate the way you just read the paper in the morning and ignore
me," she added, mocking her own petulance.

●

There was an old, dented car sitting in Mrs. Bullock's yard when they
arrived. But where Charley on their previous visit had taken care to
stop a respectful distance from the door, declining to drive on what
would have been a front yard had the soil not been so flinty, this visitor
displayed no such qualm. The car had been driven right up to the
steps of the porch and parked at a careless angle, with one tire in a
flowerbed, in the way of people whose homes are rented and temporary, and therefore not worth maintaining. It occurred to Charley that
this was the fate that awaited boys who got kicked out of high school—
you ended up living in places where you parked randomly. Life would
have no front yard, literal or figurative.

A man walked out of the house as they approached and waited on
the porch. Like his car, he showed signs of wear and hard use. There
was a straight scar, of the kind that can only be made by something
keenly sharp, down one side of his face, nicking his eye, and when he
turned his head to spit as they got closer, Charley could see there was

a tooth missing, one of the big ones from in front. The man gave them a wary look, but said nothing.

"Good afternoon, sir," Tallasee said. "We were sorry to hear about Mrs. Bullock. She was a fine lady. I was fond of her." She could be a polite soul when she needed to, Charley noted, although not above a little white lie.

The man looked incredulous. "Who are you? A friend?"

Tallasee nodded, then introduced herself and Charley. "I took some pictures of her once," she said. "It was a year or two back, but we were up here again a couple of weeks ago. She was worried about her grandson and asked us to help. I hope he's okay."

The man looked confused for a moment, then something apparently clicked. "Are you the one that did that picture book?" Tallasee nodded again.

"Well, you want it back? I found it in here."

"No, you keep it," she replied, misjudging his disinterest.

"What am I going to do with it?" he said. "It's just something else for me to tend to." He waved an arm back toward the house. "I'm tempted to just set a match to this place. I don't think that old woman ever threw anything away."

"I'll take it, then," Tallasee said. She sounded much less polite by now.

"Why would anyone be interested in a bunch of pictures of old ladies?" the man asked, seeming to be genuinely curious.

She ignored him. "Actually, we wanted to see if your son has come back home. She'd asked us to look for him."

The puzzled look returned to his face. "I don't know what you're talking about."

"I understand that this is a private matter," Tallasee said. "Everybody's got family problems. But Mrs. Bullock asked us to look for him and when we couldn't find him—"

"Look for who?" he interrupted.

"Your son," she replied, not bothering to disguise her exasperation.

"I ain't got a son," he said.

The three of them stood for a moment, motionless and silent. Then Tallasee turned and looked at Charley. He just shrugged.

Tallasee turned back toward the man. "You don't have a son," she repeated.

He shook his head. "Been married twice, but it didn't take root either time. No kids, neither, unless there's one somebody forgot to tell me about." He gave a gap-toothed, leering grin.

"You're Mrs. Bullock's son, right?" Tallasee asked, apparently hoping this whole matter could be revealed as a simple case of mistaken identity. After all, they had simply assumed that this man was Mrs. Bullock's boy; they hadn't bothered to actually check.

He dashed Tallasee's hope right away. "Sure enough am. Only child she had."

"Well, I'm completely confused," she said, and sat dejectedly on the porch steps.

The man walked down into the yard to face her, clearly enjoying this. "That old gal didn't spin you some story, did she?"

When she didn't respond, he continued: "She wasn't in her right mind. Most folks didn't see it, but she left the normal world years ago. She was always telling me crazy things." He made a show of looking around, craning his neck to take in the relentless forest. "Living up here alone would do it to anybody. I left as soon as I could."

Tallasee remained quiet, so Charley answered. "She told us her grandson had run away from home. She asked us to look for him. Thought he'd maybe gone to live at the hippie commune a few miles away."

The man nodded. "I know that place. It's closer than you think, though. It's just on the other side of the hill here, but you come at it from a whole 'nother direction. So you'd never know how close it really is."

Charley wasn't sure what he was supposed to say at this point. Was there a graceful way to acknowledge they'd spent a month wandering around half the county at the beck of a demented old woman? "That's what she told us," he said lamely.

"Shame you didn't talk to me before you went to all this trouble," the man said, as if Tallasee and Charley had foolishly neglected to check his listing in the Yellow Pages. Their travail seemed to have made him happy and hospitable. "You all come on in and let me get that picture book for you."

They trooped into the house. Charley had wanted to get back inside, and was glad to not have to invent an excuse to do so. There was something he needed to see. And within a minute of entering, he saw it.

●

It was Tallasee, however, who saw the shirt.

They were standing in the front room, listening as the man noisily rummaged through boxes stacked on the back porch. He seemed like the sort who would just heave everything on to the back of a truck and drive to the dump, but he was surprisingly careful and tidy: clothes had been neatly folded, dishes were wrapped in newspaper, and the few braided rugs that had covered the floor were rolled and tied with twine. That this was the work of the same man who could drive thoughtlessly into his mother's flowerbed struck Charley as inconsistent until he realized that household goods could be sold, while flowers had no value.

"Charley, look," Tallasee said as she nudged him with her elbow. They were the first words she'd spoken in several minutes. She lifted her head in the direction of a pile of clothes on the couch. "Is that what I think it is?"

The surrounding forest kept the house in a perpetual twilight, so it took Charley a moment to focus on what she'd seen. Sitting atop the clothes was a shirt, and although the fold left only half its crest and the letters TRE DA visible, there was no mistaking what it was: a faded Notre Dame T-shirt, just like the one the boy wore in the photograph.

They stepped over to the couch and Charley picked up the shirt, holding it by the shoulders. Underneath it was a pair of denim jeans, faded and frayed but clean, with a rip in the seat neatly patched.

"Apparently she was only half-crazy," Tallasee whispered.

The man returned carrying the book, which he handed to Tallasee. Charley was still holding the shirt. "Take that if you want it," he said. "God only knows where it came from."

"I believe I will, if you don't mind," Charley said.

Chapter Eleven

He was a puppy. He would trail along behind me as I went about my business, asking me about a thousand questions but never really listening to the answers. Like I said, I think he was a little slow. Not retarded or anything. Maybe it's just that he acted a lot younger than he actually was. That's what I mean about him being a puppy. You know how dogs are at a certain point? They get as big as they're going to get after a few months, but they've still got a puppy brain. All goofy and all.

I never did quite figure out where he'd come from. They found him sleeping one morning in the shed where most of the cooking gets done. A lot of people are coming and going up there, visiting for the day or just staying a night or two. And, of course, there was the festival of peace and love—a bunch of people came up from Atlanta for that. So maybe he came with a group that was visiting, and just didn't leave when everybody else did. But that's how a lot of people end up there. Aside from Osage and a couple of others, I don't believe anyone stays more than a few months. It's one thing to talk about getting back to nature, but once you actually get there you remember how much you like indoor toilets.

Osage was nervous about having him there, at first. He thought he was a runaway, and he didn't want to give the police any reason to come around. But that boy kept insisting he was eighteen, and after a while everybody relaxed. If he was a runaway, nobody was looking for him. Until Tallasee and that kid showed up. What's his name again? Charley. I'm going to remember him for a long time.

Goddamn Osage. He and I had a good thing going up there. I'd give him the stuff I'd gotten and he'd sell it to the overnighters from Atlanta. Now, before you ask, no, I never took any of that stuff. I saw all the crazy things I ever want to see in the military. I don't need to watch somebody's face melt or pictures slide off the wall or whatever it is you're supposed to see when you eat that shit. I supplied it and he sold it. It was a nice business arrangement. And that's all it was. I wasn't his pal or anything.

But that boy queered everything, of course.

I swear, it was the uniform that did it. He was fascinated with any uniform. The army, too. Somebody had told him about the draft, and I sort of mentioned it one time, so it became the only thing he talked about. You'd think he hadn't heard of it before. Maybe he hadn't. I got the impression he came from one of those poor families you find way up in the hills. I think that's why he was such a puppy. Everything was new to him.

Anyway, he'd always ask me, Were you in the army? I'd say, Yeah. Then he'd say, Did you ever kill anybody? I'd say, Yeah. Then he'd say, Were you ever scared? I'd say, More than you can know, partner.

I guess I should have figured out what he'd do. It ain't like he made a secret of it. He was always following me around the commune, but sometimes he'd pretend he was tracking me or something. You know, hang back and follow me from a distance, peeking around corners and such. God knows what he was doing. Pretending to be a secret agent or something. Like I said—a puppy.

Osage always wanted to conduct our business at Blue Hole. I think he just liked the walk, but he acted like it was important to do things privately. I appreciated that. I wanted it to be private, too. But I don't think he understood that sometimes, the harder you work to keep something private, the more public it becomes. So I don't think we were fooling anybody. Still, things were fine until the day that boy followed me up there.

Just a big game to him. Tracking me through the woods and watching as Osage and I did our business. He probably wouldn't have told anybody. Hell, he probably didn't even know what we were doing. But I couldn't take that chance.

Chapter Twelve

Tallasee envied stupid people. She suspected that when they had a troubling or confusing thought, it simply pushed any previously existing troubling or confusing thought right out the door and took its place, that their mental capacity for accommodating such things was exactly one. But with her, any fresh troubling thought just piled upon all the other ones that already had taken up residence in her mind. Then they started mating, knitting themselves together into murky, unpleasant creatures and giving birth to even murkier offspring. At some point, mostly as a matter of self-preservation, her mind would post the OFF-DUTY sign for a while, until the inventory of troubling thoughts was depleted.

It had been that way in the end with Nigel. She had awakened each morning with the knowledge that everything she did would be profoundly, utterly wrong. No action or suggestion—no trip to the store, no recommendation for dinner, no selection of a television show to help fill the many hours that passed as no one called him back—was safe from criticism. Every choice was a bad one, and even her inevitable decision to make no choice at all was wrong. Her silence became just another entry on his bill of particulars.

Tallasee had the same feeling now. Every step was a misstep, every guess was a miscalculation. The further she and Charley got into this exercise, the more convoluted it became. Even her attempt to simply hand it off to someone else had become mired in mystery. Was there no detaching herself from this?

Charley didn't say much on the ride home, but that was little surprise to her. After all, she had fired him and hit him just a couple of hours before. If things had been reversed, Tallasee would have told him to find his own way home and left him on the side of the road. But there he was, dutifully driving her around. With a twitch of guilt, she also realized that he probably needed the money he'd asked about earlier. She summarized events in her mind: she'd assaulted him, dismissed him abruptly, and not yet compensated him for his work. She felt sure she was out of the running to be named employer of the year.

Finally, though, she became annoyed with her own sullenness. "So what do you figure is going on?" she asked.

She only wanted to make conversation, but Charley obviously had been thinking about it. He answered right away. "Do you believe that guy when he says he had no son? That there is no grandson?" he said. She nodded.

"So do I," Charley said. "Because if he was lying, he was doing a better job of it than I'd figure he'd do. Besides, I can't see why he'd want to lie about it. So as best I can see, he's telling the truth."

"But why would Mrs. Bullock tell us she had a grandson?"

He shrugged. "Because she was crazy. Just like he said."

"I don't think she was, though," Tallasee said. "I think her wiring was bad in a few places, but I don't think she was crazy. Hey, sometimes I wonder about my own wiring." That last part was meant to be context—as in, we've all got problems—but it hung in the air between them for a long, revealing moment. Tallasee felt herself redden.

Charley, however, seemed to ignore it. "I'll tell you what. Let's figure out the things we know and then make some guesses about the things we don't know. Maybe it'll start to make sense." Tallasee nodded.

"Okay—first, there is a boy," Charley continued. "We have a photograph of him. And the picture was taken at the commune. So, whoever he was, he spent time there."

"We also know he visited Mrs. Bullock at least once," Tallasee said. "Maybe that falls into the guess category, but if his clothes were there, it seems reasonable to believe he was there."

Charley mulled it for a moment, then said, "Yeah, I suppose we could say we know that. Especially since she identified him in the picture right away."

"And we know Lucas and Osage both acted strangely when we first asked them about the boy. Like they had something to hide."

"That's a guess," Charley said.

"What? That they acted strangely?"

"No," he answered. "That they had something to hide."

"Why else would they act that way?"

"I don't know. Maybe I'm splitting hairs."

"Yeah, don't make it too complicated. Let's just deal with the obvious for now." Tallasee was beginning to get interested in this exercise. "Here's another thing we know: Mrs. Bullock's home is a lot closer to the commune than we thought."

"That's how he was able to visit her," Charley said.

"That's what I'm thinking. Osage said the commune's garbage dump was about a mile away, and that our boy had sort of appointed himself as the garbage hauler. Maybe he went exploring one day and came upon her house. She used to run hot and cold—you know, be friendly one moment and not so friendly the next—and he could have caught her on one of her friendly days and become her pal."

Charley nodded. "I can see it. He could have become a regular visitor. Walking through the woods every few days or so to visit for a while, maybe doing some chores for her and getting something to eat in return."

"And getting his clothes patched," Tallasee added.

"She gets used to having him around, looks forward to his visits. Then he stops showing up," Charley said. "After a while, she calls you to ask for help. But why does she tell us it was her grandson?"

"Because she doesn't know how else to explain it? Because she thinks we won't help her otherwise?"

"Or because she eventually comes to believe he is her grandson," Charley said. He then glanced over at Tallasee. "It doesn't really matter, though, does it? She may be full crazy or just half crazy. But, the fact is, that boy is gone."

Much as she had earlier at the old woman's house, Tallasee suddenly felt very tired. Yes, the fact was, the boy was gone. Another fact was that Tallasee still had a rock-hard reluctance to be involved in this matter. Something told her there was no benign explanation to all this. They wouldn't learn that this mysterious young man simply had decamped for another haven of peace and love. His presence hung in the air like a malignant spirit, pervasive and constant. Tallasee had the feeling that this would end badly, which was an alarming prospect on its own; worse yet, it would be another thing in her life that ended badly, which gave it the flavor of something to be avoided at all costs. She kept circling back to her original opinion of this search: they shouldn't have started it, and they certainly shouldn't finish it.

But Charley's desire matched Tallasee's reluctance. He sought some salvation in this effort, she suspected. Perhaps there was some unhappiness deep within him that he thought could be cured by this, just as there was an unhappiness deep within her that she was sure would be fueled by it. But Tallasee understood that Charley's desire ultimately would overwhelm her reluctance, because passion always triumphs over do-nothingness. Besides, however deeply it might be buried at the moment, Tallasee knew she'd always had a taste for underdogs.

From all this did her weariness spring. "That's the problem with the world," she said. "There are too many facts."

●

Tallasee offered to buy dinner. The sun had settled into the crest of the largest hill behind them, putting some parts of the road into a deep shadow, as if its setting somehow drew the gloom out of the forest. At the point where the road escaped the steepest hills, it made a long sinuous curve around one end of Howard's Lake, which once had boasted an outdoor dance pavilion and a collection of rustic cabins. It had enjoyed a heyday as a resort, attracting well-known swing bands from Atlanta for the Saturday-night dances held all summer, and it was commonly reported that when actress Susan Hayward—who, along with other stars and a whole crew, arrived in Barrington to film the 1951 movie *I'd Climb the Highest Mountain*—had visited the lake, she'd pronounced it the prettiest place she'd ever seen. The citizens of Barrington returned the compliment, declaring to one another that she was the most fetching star in the film galaxy and for years after referred to her on a first-name-only basis among themselves—whenever

anyone mentioned "Susan" in the context of movies, no further identi-
fication was necessary. In fact, her passing approval of the lake—if
there even had been any such utterance, considering the license taken
by the film studio's public-relations office—eventually grew to embrace Barrington itself, so that for a generation afterwards a visitor in-
evitably would hear someone assert, "Well, you know, Susan Hayward
said this town was the prettiest place she'd ever seen."

But now, almost twenty years later, the cabins were boarded up and
moldering, and the pavilion had been enclosed and turned into Gil's
Fish Camp. You could rent a motorboat and buy night crawlers there,
although as often as not the worms would be dead and the boat's engine would expire in the middle of the lake, leaving you to shout and
wave until the old fellow who ran the rental concession noticed your
distress and puttered out to tow you back to the dock. So people generally didn't visit to fish; they went to Gil's to eat.

It specialized in what is called "family-style dining," which
Charley sourly noted would have meant, in his family, a mother and
son eating a silent meal in a kitchen haunted by a dead child and
missing father. At Gil's, however, it meant that you sat at a long table
with strangers and bumped elbows as you helped yourself to whatever
food had been prepared that day and set out in large bowls.

But Gil had a nice touch with lard, so no one minded the arrangement. Fried chicken and catfish were available every night, with the
occasional country-fried steak thrown in when Gil was feeling fancy.
The vegetables always were fresh, the pie crusts never showed the
dark-brown evidence of having been left in the oven too long, and the
pitchers of iced tea always were properly sweetened. Legend had it
that a visitor—somebody's relative from up North, according to the
story—once had asked for unsweetened tea, apparently the first time
such a request ever had been made. When it came, the customer was
given a glass of ice water with a tea bag jammed into it. As the tea bag
slowly leaked a brown stain into the water, the customer, assuming he
was being mocked, had asked to see the manager. When Gil emerged
from the kitchen, the man held up the glass and asked in a haughty
tone how he was expected to drink this.

"You mean you were going to *drink* it?" Gil replied in amazement.
"We were wondering why you wanted it."

Because country folk tend to eat early, the restaurant was nearly empty by now, at summer sundown. Tallasee and Charley sat at the end of a table overlooking the lake, shifting their chairs toward the window in the way of people who, as they wait for food to arrive, are anxious for the distraction of a view. Tallasee was depressed and Charley was wary, and the combination didn't make for lively dinner talk.

"She's really pretty," Tallasee finally said.

Charley, having no idea who she was talking about, felt as if he'd missed the first half of the conversation. "Who is?" he asked.

"Your girlfriend."

"She's not my girlfriend," he said. "We broke up. I already told you that."

"Did you break up with her?"

"No."

"Did she break up with you?" Tallasee continued.

"Yeah."

"Do you think it's common for women to doll themselves up to see former sweethearts?"

"I wouldn't know. I've never been a former sweetheart until now," he answered.

"So what did she have to say?"

"She came to tell me she was thinking about going out with a guy I don't like very much. Not that it's any of your business."

Tallasee ignored the second half of his reply. "Let me make sure I understand. Your ex-girlfriend gets dressed up in her best check-me-out clothes, finds your truck, leans against it until you appear, then proceeds to tell you she's being wooed by another guy. And you don't think this means anything?"

Charley felt a flush in his face. "It means she's a tease."

Tallasee shook her head pitiably. "Men ain't worth teasing. Women understand this. There's not much sport in it, 'cause it's too easy to do. And you poor fools become so distraught."

"Are you supposed to be revealing these secrets of womanhood?" Charley asked.

"Probably not. But then again, I do a lot of things I'm not supposed to do." She switched subjects abruptly. "Shouldn't you call your mother and tell her you won't be home for dinner?"

He shook his head. "We don't eat together much."

"That wasn't exactly what I was asking. Doesn't she worry when you don't come home at night?"

"She doesn't seem to," Charley said. It was a simple and truthful answer, but harsher than he meant it to be. "I mean, I guess I've gotten old enough to come and go on my own." That was softer, yet it veered into fiction: Their relationship was too complicated for Charley to grasp, much less explain. Frances may not have been as attentive as a mother should, but neither had she turned herself over to the vices and carousing that inattentive mothers generally did. Charley had a home and a mother who always was there. It's just that neither was very comfortable.

"How long has it been just the two of you?" Tallasee asked.

"My brother died when I was nine, and my daddy left shortly after. He's also dead now." He mulled that thought for a moment. "So I suppose history's sort of running against me."

She didn't say much after that. She just looked at Charley for a long time.

●

Tallasee later understood that it couldn't actually have happened, because Gil's is five miles from Barrington and even the slightest breeze would have scattered the smoke before it reached her. But in the immediate aftermath, she came to believe that she had smelled it. She came to believe that as she and Charley left the restaurant and walked to his truck, she detected smoke in the air. So vivid was this memory that she could see herself lifting her face and pointing her nose toward Barrington, wrinkling it a bit as she wondered what was burning.

But then, that's what people do—they retrofit their memories. A woman whose husband suddenly leaves will think back to the days immediately before his departure and dredge up a dozen new memories that, in hindsight, seem to have been clear signals of his intent. A man in battle will remember that just before his position was overrun and his comrades slain, the insects went quiet and the fine hairs on his neck raised themselves.

It's all fanciful, of course, a device by which people can avoid confronting their ignorance. No one wants to look back on a traumatic event and concede that they were utterly insensate to its beginnings. Instead, they will rewrite history. They will adjust their recollections, breathing life into whatever number of clues are necessary for them to construct an after-the-fact framework of indicators and hints that in hindsight prove at least a subliminal awareness of the coming trauma. Then they will marvel at their instinct, taking comfort in the notion that deep in their gut they had known all along that something was amiss.

Tallasee was no different. Even long after, she was loathe to admit she missed the many things Charley saw. In candid moments she could acknowledge she was willfully blind; but other times, she found herself remembering things like a whiff of smoke in the air or tickles of alarm as their search for the boy became more and more bizarre. Those memories were to her fantastic, as vaporous and unreal as the promise of love until death.

Here's the simple fact of the matter: Charley was alert and smart, while Tallasee was lumpy and self-pitying. He figured out what had happened, but she had to be led to the truth.

Chapter Thirteen

Later, in the weeks after Lucas was charged with murder, Charley learned much about the operations of police agencies. He'd pictured it as one large brotherhood, tens of thousands of men and women who, even though they worked in different towns and states, swapped information freely, could make immediate contact with one another with radios and special teletype devices, and had access to a mammoth central file from which any fingerprint could be produced and where any suspect's prior collisions with the law were detailed. The reality, however, was much different, as Charley observed when Lucas was formally charged with murder.

The sheriff's department first phone call to the state bureau of investigation wasn't returned. A second, more insistent call was placed the next day, with the result being that a state investigator scribbled a few notes, promised to see what he could find on Lucas, then promptly used his notepad as a resting place for the cheese Danish which, thanks to twenty years of consumption, he'd been conditioned to crave every morning at ten o'clock. It was only when a third call was made on the third day—this one luckily catching the state investigator in midafternoon, late enough so that his postlunch drowsiness had begun to recede but early enough so that he could still get something done—that the background and history of Durwood Kingman Lucas began to emerge.

Even then, it came grudgingly. The trail led first to the Marine Corps, then to the Defense Department, and finally to the Federal Bureau of Investigation. None of the three seemed interested in providing information; they wanted only to receive it. So, in the aftermath, there was a long period during which one investigator after another traveled to Barrington, summoned Tallasee and Charley to a borrowed office, asked the same set of questions as the investigator before him had asked on behalf of a different agency, took careful note of the answers even as he instinctively and unconsciously let doubt register on his face, then apparently filed his report carefully so that no other rival investigator could have access to it.

Still, Tallasee and Charley managed to piece together the story. They weren't suspects, so the various investigators tended to be chattier than they otherwise would have been, sharing bits of information and filling in the gaps of Lucas's history almost as readily as Tallasee and Charley rounded out the investigators' understanding of what had happened in Barrington. The investigators were candid in the way of people who know that a full confession had been made. They knew there was little concern that the memories of witnesses could be tainted; even if there were a trial, it would be a perfunctory, one-day affair requiring neither Tallasee's nor Charley's participation. But it was certain that there would be no trial.

It turned out Lucas wasn't much different from Charley—a fact not lost on Charley. He'd grown up in the same hills, in another town, albeit one smaller than Barrington and placed beyond a sufficient number of ridgelines as to actually put it in North Carolina. He'd also been reared in a home with one parent, although in his case it was a mother who was absent, and Lucas likewise had made an abrupt and diplomaless exit from high school. He'd spent an idle year working at ill-paid jobs—a career track that Charley seemed to have launched into that summer—until the Selective Service System made him one of the lucky winners in its annual sweepstakes to see who would get to join the army and visit an exotic, little-known corner of the world called Vietnam. There were a couple of hundred thousand winners that year, as it turned out. Many of them won a permanent stay.

As often happens, Lucas thrived in the beginning. He was one of those classically disordered young men who benefit from the firmness of mind and body that comes with basic training. He'd reported for duty at Fort Jackson, South Carolina, on his assigned date, arriving by bus in the middle of the night in the company of several dozen other young men who'd been collected from several other points during the long, slow drive. Only Lucas among them didn't seem to mind when—

as they stood in a single line just outside Fort Jackson's gate, where there was only enough light to make everything seem strange and otherworldly—a sergeant dressed in the uniform of a Marine Corps drill instructor had walked along the line and tapped every second man on the chest, chanting "You . . . you . . . you" as he did. When he reached the end of the line, the sergeant ordered those men he'd selected onto another nearby bus.

"Ladies," the sergeant announced, "you've just volunteered to become marines. Next stop, Parris Island."

Lucas didn't see that it made much difference where they trained, but his comrades hadn't taken the news as gracefully. Hung for a moment in that murky zone between the civilian and military worlds, they shifted their feet uneasily and looked at one another, wondering if in fact they could be forced to board the bus. Being drafted into the army was one thing; being shanghaied off to the country's most infamous boot camp was quite another. That it was happening in the middle of the night, outside the fort's gate, and with no officers in sight gave it just enough flavor of the illicit to embolden one recruit to voice his unhappiness.

"Wait a minute," he said. "We're supposed to be going into the army. You can't do this."

The sergeant walked toward the recruit, moving with a menacing slowness. When he was directly in front of him, the sergeant leaned forward at the waist until the brim of his drill instructor's hat grazed the recruit's forehead.

"GET ON THE BUS, MOTHERFUCKER!" the sergeant yelled directly into the recruit's face.

The investigator who told this story to Charley and Tallasee grinned as he recalled Lucas's memory of the effect of the sergeant's order. "He said you'd have thought this was the last ride to paradise, considering the way those boys ran for that bus. Here was their worst damn nightmare—Marine Corps boot camp, for Christ's sake—and they acted like they couldn't wait to get there."

Lucas became the man the Corps wants to think all its recruits ultimately become: someone who finds tough fiber underneath the soft flesh and sloppy thought of civilian life, who comes to truly believe in the ideals of honor, duty, and discipline. There's a certain raw hardness that seems to be bred into some people, and Lucas had it. The marines distilled and focused that hardness, making him into someone with not only a refined sense of righteousness, but the ability to wreak quick and terrible violence on anyone who offended it.

Of course, the Marine Corps preferred that Lucas save his avenging sensibilities for the nation's enemies. But, as it turned out, he had his own idea who the enemy was that summer at the Rainbow Nation.

●

Tallasee had to admit that she'd never comprehended the structure of the military. Whenever anyone started talking about battalions, brigades, regiments, and platoons, she was lost. Sometimes she thought it was kept deliberately confusing so that only insiders would understand how it worked. Men twit women for their apparent need to belong to garden clubs and organize home-shopping parties and such, but Tallasee felt that that could be put to rest, for she had yet to meet any Junior Leaguers who felt the need to wear a uniform, decorate it with patches, form themselves into a strict hierarchy, and give one another all sorts of impressive titles. Men just didn't have the moral high ground on this matter.

She also didn't have a great grasp of the geography of Vietnam. She knew where Saigon and Hanoi were located, and roughly where the line was that once divided the country in separate halves. But when people who had been started naming the specific towns and hamlets where they served, she was lost. She recognized some of the names, of course: she knew of the siege at Khe Sanh, and knew the whole mess had its roots in a place called Dien Bien Phu, where the French lost a key battle. But, in private moments, she would confess that for a long time she'd thought that the Tet offensive had taken place in a city called Tet.

So when they told her that Lucas had been assigned to the Second Battalion, First Marine Division in a place called Dong Ha, Tallasee had no idea what that meant. The only thing she clearly understood was that that's where he became unhinged.

●

The story had a benign beginning. Lucas and his pals became big brothers to a Vietnamese boy. He was maybe ten years old and an apparent orphan, a grinning scoundrel who just showed up one day and resisted all attempts to shoo him away. He spent the first day or so pilfering items from the soldiers, but the fact he never actually got away with anything made it clear it was a game. He liked the attention he got from these big, rough-looking men, who had quickly understood there was no real risk that they'd lose anything, and, as a result, had given their threats of recrimination a good-humored tone. After a while, the boy tired of the game and just began hanging around, prompting the soldiers to give him the occasional chore to do or errand to run. At first, the only words of English he seemed to know were "You number one," but he was clever and a good listener, and as the soldiers already had the common scattering of Vietnamese words, in quick order a sort of pidgin dialect evolved. Within a week of his first appearance, the boy was the squad mascot. The soldiers called him Shorty.

He accompanied them everywhere except, of course, on patrol. When Shorty had grown confident that he'd earned a place among them, he seemed to ease up on his scampering and badgering, which had been his way of keeping their attention. He learned to sit easily with them and stay alert for a summons to fetch or deliver something. Some of the men tried to teach him how to clean weapons, or expected him to keep the bivouac tidy, but he didn't prove particularly adept at these tasks. He was, after all, just a child, with a child's attention span.

Mostly, Shorty was their good-luck charm. The men got in the habit of rubbing his head each time they set off on patrol, or when it was their turn to drop themselves into one of the many holes that had been dug beyond the encampment's lines and spend the night listening for the approach of the enemy. It started out casually, but soon became a ritual: every man in the unit would make it a point to run his hand over Shorty's head. For several weeks after the boy's arrival, the men suffered not a single casualty, which reinforced the notion that he was a talisman. At some point, the men even began forming themselves into a single line to rub Shorty's head as they filed past, thus ensuring that no one forgot and brought bad luck upon them. Shorty understood the ritual and would stand still as the men went by, grinning as each palm made its circumnavigation of his scalp.

One day, Shorty accompanied the men on a twenty-four-hour trip to Danang. It never became clear why they took him or how they got him on the helicopter, which wasn't supposed to carry civilians; everyone who was interviewed about what happened a few nights later was vague in the way of people who know that mild infractions of the rules only remain mild if nothing happens as a result. But the fact was, Shorty was with the men. And he sported a new tattoo to prove it.

That Lucas, a straight arrow to the other men, let him get a tattoo surprised them. Technically, they'd been sent to the sprawling airbase on a mission, but in reality it was a half-phony task created by their commanding officer for the sole purpose of getting them there to get drunk and get laid. Well aware of this, when they'd clambered out of the helicopter and been instructed to return to that spot at twelve hundred hours the following day, the men all assumed Shorty would be in Lucas's custody while the rest of them set out to see what damage they could inflict on themselves. While they respected Lucas's discipline and skill, the other men thought that he was wrapped too tightly. He drank sparingly and without vigor, and had little apparent interest in the Vietnamese women whose charms were so easily acquired. Also, he had scolded them once when one of the men had given Shorty a cigarette, and had wagged his finger in the boy's face and made threatening noises when he'd caught him draining a few sudsy drops from an empty can of beer that had just been discarded by one of the soldiers. So, it was understood that Shorty would stay with Lucas. The two of them would eat a few lazy meals, wander around the city, and spend long, deliberate hours buying the comic books and transistor radio that Shorty had been promised was his reward for his faithful service over the prior few weeks.

It was with a sheepish look, then, that Lucas climbed into the helicopter the next day. The other men, haggard from the night's debauchery, stirred a little, but whatever questions they might have had about

Lucas's expression went unasked. Besides, it was explained a moment later, when Shorty clambered into the helicopter behind Lucas and declared cheerfully, "Tattoo number one!"

He proudly held out his right hand for the men to see. On the back of the hand, where the little-boy flesh still hid the veins and tendons that would rise as he got older, there was a fresh tattoo of an American flag. It was a small design, because there simply isn't much skin on a child's hand to work with, and the flesh remained swollen from the needle, but it clearly was Old Glory—albeit an Old Glory with only four stripes and a half dozen stars.

"Tattoo number one!" Shorty exclaimed again, then saluted. He turned his hand so it almost cupped his right eye, and when he did it became apparent this patch of flesh had not been chosen for decoration randomly: Shorty wanted to fly the flag every time he saluted.

"Goddamn," one of the men said, more in wonder of Lucas's uncharacteristic permissiveness than of the tattoo itself.

"Well, it was his idea," Lucas explained. "It was what he said he wanted. I was going to buy him a radio, but he insisted on this."

"Radio number ten," Shorty confirmed.

"Did he get some pussy, too?" another of the men asked. The others smirked.

Lucas didn't respond, but the sheepish look disappeared from his face. He squatted next to Shorty during the short flight back to Dong Ha, hovering even more protectively than usual. In the following day or so, it became apparent to the other men that Shorty had picked Lucas to be a special friend, and that Lucas was happy with the role. As Shorty's pockets kept producing new items—a pocketknife, a key chain, a shark's tooth hung from a silver chain—the picture of how the two of them had spent their night in Danang emerged: they simply had wandered, with Lucas buying whatever Shorty wanted. They'd reached that perfectly balanced joy that comes only when one person is happy with anything he gets and another is happy to buy whatever the other wants.

The other men, through some osmosis of understanding, realized that they no longer could expect Shorty to do their bidding. He and Lucas had become a unit, a Caucasian big brother and Asian little brother, which meant that rather than just pointing to some bit of housekeeping or giving instructions on an errand in their pidgin language, the men now needed to ask Lucas before recruiting Shorty to do a chore. That is how Shorty came to be sent to the dump the day after the men returned from Danang.

They'd left for the trip on short notice, and had had no time to police their camp before departing. Also, like Shorty, they'd indulged in a bit of binge shopping themselves, meaning the camp soon became littered with boxes and wrappings, not to mention the things that were discarded because the men now had newer, better versions of the same items. At some point, after the trash had grown into an impressive mound, one of the men approached Lucas and said, "Hey, how 'bout if Shorty hauls this stuff away?"

"Do it yourself," Lucas replied. "He ain't the camp nigger."

It was the wrong thing for a white soldier from the South to say to a black soldier from the North. Martin Luther King Jr. had been murdered earlier that year, race riots had broken out in many American cities the year before, and the almost exclusively white face of the antiwar movement made many black folks wonder if the real issue wasn't so much that American boys were getting killed in Vietnam, but that white boys were getting killed.

"Yeah, well, I do it myself, then I guess I'm the camp nigger, huh?" the other soldier said with challenge in his voice. For a moment, the two men just stared at each other.

Lucas finally relented. "Hey, man, I'm sorry. I didn't mean nothing. Let me go find him. A little work will do him good."

A few minutes later, Lucas returned with Shorty. They'd found a discarded rain poncho somewhere, which Shorty spread on the ground. He piled the trash in the middle of the poncho, pulled the edges up to form a sack, then threw it over his shoulder and went trudging away.

The dump was on the other side of the airstrip, perhaps a half mile away. Given that distance, plus the combination of any child's distractibility and Shorty's habit of showing off his new tattoo by ostentatiously saluting everyone he encountered, no one wondered why the afternoon passed with no sight of him. But as dusk arrived, Lucas grew uneasy. Shorty was afraid of the dark; only in Danang, among the lights and movement of the city, had Shorty not grown nervous about the onset of night.

"I'm going to look for him," Lucas eventually declared.

"We got to go out tonight," one of the men warned. It was their squad's night to man the holes dug beyond the airstrip's perimeter, meaning that a pair of them would pass the night hours listening and watching for movement by the enemy.

"I won't be long," Lucas replied. "Besides, we'll need our charm."

But he was back in a half hour, alone. The other men suddenly were uneasy, too. No one had been hurt since Shorty arrived, and the thought of two of them spending the night in a vulnerable spot outside the lines without first rubbing the boy's head was unnerving.

"I wish the squirt would show up," said the black soldier who'd originally wanted Shorty to haul away the garbage. He then added something of an apology to Lucas: "We're cool, man, but don't be talking that talk."

"We'll be all right," Lucas said vaguely. "Let's saddle up."

Lucas and the black soldier filed through the great coils of razor wire that surrounded the airstrip and walked a quarter mile beyond, settling into one of the holes and arranging their gear so it was both accessible and out of the way as they shifted about in endless and hopeless attempts to get comfortable in the dirt. Their job was to be nervous and twitchy, to jump at every shadow and small movement, and it was a skill that came naturally as the night closed in. Most times, dawn arrived with no violence to precede it. Occasionally, though—often enough to require men from one of the squads in the holes every night—a lone enemy would crawl close to the wire to snipe a few rounds in hopes that a stray shot would bring someone down. Or a pair of them would drag a mortar close and send explosives deep into the airstrip compound. It was the task of the men in the holes, then, to watch for this.

It was all wickedly foreign to Tallasee. She understood that it happened; she knew men hunted one another in the dark, and killed without hesitating. She grasped the fear that surely lived in them just beneath their skin, something so palpable and alive that it was almost a separate organism, parasitic and draining. But what she didn't understand is why men are drawn to it. What is it about fear and terror that somehow also feeds them? Even the investigator who told Tallasee and Charley the story became lost in it. The simple act of speaking it made him animated. Whereas before, he'd been perfunctory and uninflected in his questions to them, he later brought skill and vigor to his storytelling.

●

"You're supposed to keep quiet, of course. You can't hear and talk at the same time. You're not even supposed to smoke. Maybe the gooks can't see your cigarette, because you're squatted down in a hole, but they'll sure get the smell of it in the air. Some people swear they can smell Americans, anyway. They say we smell like decay.

"So it can make you crazy, sitting there listening and watching. You hear things all night long, but nothing's ever clearly, unmistakably the enemy. I mean, it's not like they have bells around their necks. You think you hear something, but when you start listening hard for it, there's nothing. Another time, you don't hear anything, except the silence itself then becomes something. This was a small airstrip, nothing moved in or out of there at night, so things got very, very quiet when you were outside the wire. And this was NVA territory. I mean, there were Vietcong, too, of course, but being so far north, you knew the North Vietnamese regulars were always real close by. The VC were one thing. You know, shoot one or two mortar rounds, then run like hell. But the NVAs were something else. They were real soldiers, and if they came there'd be lots of them. So you'd sit in that hole all night, wondering if this was going to be the moment when the NVAs decide to put that airstrip out of commission once and for all.

"You've got a radio with you. Every half hour, you're supposed to check in, so what you do is pick up the handset and push the talk button twice, holding it down a second or so each time. That comes across as two long, buzzing clicks to the radio operator back at the airstrip. It's sort of an all's-well signal. But they also have this code worked out. Suppose you were looking the wrong way or somehow got surprised, and all of a sudden there are guys crawling toward the wire, just thirty feet from your hole. You could open up on them, but that's just committing suicide. Who knows how many there are? Somebody's going to drop a grenade in on you. And you can't just get on the radio and send up an alert. They'll hear you even if you're whispering. So you pick up the handset and key it three quick times, wait a moment, then do three more. You count off ten seconds, then do it again. Then, in case the radio operator is off taking a leak or something, you wait a minute or so and do it again. When they hear that, they're supposed to send in the cavalry.

"So here's what happened that night. The radio operator's sitting there when he hears three fast clicks, then another three. He waves an officer over, and sure enough a few seconds later they hear it again. Three and three. Okay, they've got some action outside the wire. The officer turns to leave, you know, to sound the alarm, but before he takes a step, they hear Lucas screaming.

"He's a quarter mile away, remember, but the screaming is so loud it causes both the radio operator and the officer to jump. They said it was just bloodcurdling. Then all hell breaks out. Somebody's shooting out there beyond the wire, I mean just emptying their clip, and then of course a bunch of guys inside the wire open up, shooting in the direction of the noise. The other grunt who was in the hole with Lucas is shouting into the radio, but he's yelling right into the handset and there's so much noise otherwise that nobody can tell what he's saying for a minute. And he sounds freaked out, too. Finally, they figure out he's telling them Lucas is out of the hole, that he's the one doing all the shooting and that our guys are about to kill him, which they probably would have except they're just shooting into the dark and you always end up going high when you can't see what you're shooting at. So they finally get everyone inside the wire to stop shooting, and Lucas had emptied his clip and dropped his weapon at that point, but he's still out there somewhere screaming.

"They get the other grunt back on the radio, which takes a while because he's so freaked out he's got the key held down. See, you can talk or you can listen, but you can't do both. So all they can hear is him panting right into the radio, until he figures out he's got it keyed, which is why no one is talking to him. But even when he releases it and they get through, he's not much help. Apparently something has completely spooked him, but he's scared of leaving. Which, of course, shows good sense, because not only is the VC probably out there somewhere but Lucas is raving in the darkness and who knows when the guys inside the wire are going to open up again? So he's squatted down in the hole, with the handset jammed against his ear so the VC won't hear it when the officer comes on.

"The officer doesn't know what the hell to do. He'd like to send up a flare so he can see if anyone's coming, but all that's going to do is make Lucas an easy target. He's tempted to tell the other grunt to crawl back to the wire, but the guy is calming down a little and the officer is nervous about not having somebody out there while all this weirdness is happening, especially since he can't light up the area. Finally, he decides to send a couple of guys out there. He gets the grunt on the radio, tells him two men are coming out for him. Tells him to keep his weapon down, that these guys are gonna be coming from the direction of the wire and he shouldn't be shooting at anybody. He tells him to click the handset twice if he understands. A moment later, it clicks twice. But the officer later said there was a long pause between those clicks, like the guy's hand was shaking so bad he could barely do it.

"So two grunts set out for the hole, which must have taken bigger balls than I've got. Pardon my language. I mean, something very weird has happened out there, you've still got Lucas wandering around yelling at the VC, you've got a bunch of guys behind the wire all jacked up and jumpy, and you're moving toward a guy who may or may not be able to resist the temptation to open up on any strange noise he hears. It must be true that marines look after each other. I guess it's nice to know somebody's going to come after you in a situation like that.

"Anyway, the two guys get out there without a problem. This hole ain't roomy, only big enough for a couple of guys, so the three of them in there makes it tight. But that one grunt is squeezed against one side, they later said, like he was trying to stay as far away from something as he could. Turned out, he was.

"One of them puts the handset against his ear, then clicks it a couple of times. The officer's right there, been waiting for them to check in. They worked out a plan, the officer talking and the grunt clicking yes or no in response. Later on, they realized they hadn't needed to be so quiet. Hell, the VC knew where they were. They'd crawled right up to the hole and tossed something in it. They were long gone. But the grunts didn't know that, of course. They didn't know anything. It was all just darkness and weirdness out there.

"We're not talking complicated strategy here. What they did was, they'd noticed Lucas seemed to be circling the area, which was easy to tell because God knows you could hear him all over the place. So they simply waited until he'd circled close, then the two grunts put the butt of a rifle against his head and dragged him back to the hole. They hated doing it, but that wasn't the moment to try to talk him into coming back. They just knocked him senseless, then sat on him after he came to. It probably helped to be packed in together like that. Fortunately, it was only another hour or two 'til dawn by then, and once they got everyone back in the hole they gave the officer the signal and he began sending a flare up every once in a while to illuminate the area. But like I said, there was nothing to see. The VC were gone. They'd done what they set out to do.

"When it got light, the officer sent a patrol to sweep the area and bring those guys back inside the wire. Lucas had quieted down some, and they'd tied his arms behind him anyway to help keep him still, but he started hollering again as soon as they had him up and walking. As soon as he could, the officer put Lucas on a helicopter and had him taken to Danang. He never came back.

"Of course, the soldier who'd been out there with Lucas knew what had happened, but he hadn't said anything to the other two grunts 'cause he was afraid it would set Lucas off all over again. But as soon as everyone was back inside the wire, he told the story. The officer went out to the hole to see for himself. It was right there, in the bottom of the hole where those guys had sat on it all night, but the officer didn't want to touch it, much less bring it back. So he just had some men fill in the hole. Nobody else was going to want to use it again.

"Those VC had cut off Shorty's hand, the one with the tattoo on it. You have to believe they knew Lucas was his buddy, and they probably even knew he was in the hole that night. They hit him right in the face with it. Thing smacked right against his cheek when they tossed it in. When Lucas figured out what it was, that's when he started screaming."

The investigator, happy with his telling of this story, leaned back in his chair. There was an energetic vicariousness in him, an appreciation of detail, that made clear he'd mulled this tale a long time. Charley and Tallasee likely were the only people he'd get to tell it to, unless he was the type who haunted bars and was prone to talk to strangers. His fellow investigators knew about Lucas—in fact, they'd likely gathered many of the details this fellow had so lovingly archived—so they weren't interested in a rehashing of the tale. And he had the look of someone whose wife forbade him to talk shop at home. So, Charley and Tallasee were his only audience. He let a few silent moments pass before adding the coda.

"Like I said, he never got back to his unit. He was shipped to a couple of different facilities, finally ended up back in the States. I don't know if the Corps ever meant to send him back, or even take him back, but it doesn't matter 'cause Lucas just walked away one day. Just disappeared off the grounds of this hospital where he was being treated. Somebody like that always turns up somewhere. At home, usually. Like that's not the first place people are going to look for him. But Lucas just dropped off the face of the earth. Until all this foolishness broke out here, he was a ghost. They'd have never run that boy to earth if it hadn't been for you two." He fixed a look of malicious innocence to his face. "By the way, did anyone from the Corps ever thank you?"

Charley ignored the question. "So what happened to Shorty?" he asked.

The investigator pouted for a moment, miffed at this suggestion he'd left out part of the story. "Apparently, nobody saw him again, either."

"You figure he died?" Charley persisted.

"I doubt it," the investigator answered, regaining the high ground of the story. "In fact, the VC would want to keep him alive. He was a lesson. It was one thing to hang around the Americans—God knows enough of them do, selling us stuff all day long and telling the VC where to find us at night—but it's quite another thing to admire the Americans so much you get their flag tattooed on your hand."

"Jesus, he was just a kid," Charley said.

"What are you telling me for?" the investigator replied with mock protest. "Go tell the VC."

●

To everyone else, the analysis was simple: Lucas had become un-hinged in Vietnam, and this explained his subsequent murderous vio-lence. But Tallasee didn't see it that way. Lucas had befriended a young orphan, showed him kindness and generosity, then learned in a graphic and horrible way one night that his friendship had resulted in the deliberate and numbingly cruel maiming of this child. Screaming in horror and rage, and then running away, was not a sign of insanity to Tallasee. In fact, it seemed like a perfectly natural reaction.

She knew, firsthand, that people usually acquire their unhappiness and disillusionment in small increments. The curdling of life typically is mercifully slow, a stealthy process that allows you to adjust to its pace so that the sourness doesn't overwhelm you. But Lucas had been swallowed in one swift moment.

Chapter Fourteen

Charley and Tallasee found the fire through a perverse unfolding of revelations. When they got to the edge of town, they sniffed the air and declared: There's a fire somewhere. As they spotted the smoke after making the few turns that would take them to Tallasee's studio, they concluded: Must be in the middle of town. When they got near enough to see the revolving red lights of the fire trucks reflected in the night sky, they exclaimed: It must be close to the studio. As they made the last turn, Tallasee said, "Oh, dear Jesus."

The street in front of the studio was clogged with trucks and firefighting equipment. Hoses were laid like great, fat snakes across the asphalt. A pair of firefighters directed a stream of water into the studio, through what had been the front window, but because the fire was in the last minutes of its life, other men already were stowing equipment. An enormous fan, mounted on wheels, had been rolled to the front door and placed so as to pull smoke from the building. A power generator mounted on one of the trucks hammered away, and the dispatch radios had been turned up loud in case another call came in; together, they gave the street the jangly, noisy atmosphere of a disaster scene. A knot of spectators stood on the opposite sidewalk, and next to a vehicle that seemed to be the command car Charley and Tallasee saw Johnny Carver talking to the fire chief.

Tallasee was out of the pickup truck before it even stopped. Charley parked haphazardly in the middle of the street, next to one of the fire engines. Even amid the confusion and panic, he found himself momentarily savoring this rare chance to simply leave the truck wherever it rolled to a stop, with no regard to traffic or regulation. Still, even then, the responsible-citizen side of him stayed true: he left his keys in the truck, should it need to be moved in a hurry.

When he caught up to her, Tallasee was trying to wedge herself behind the fan and through the studio door, but was being restrained by a firefighter.

"Let go of me, you big lug," she was saying as Charley approached. It was the only time, aside from a Jimmy Cagney–era movie or two, that he'd ever heard anyone actually use the term "big lug."

"You'll have to give us a few more minutes in here, ma'am," the firefighter answered politely, proving that bad manners don't necessarily come with lugness.

They had shut down the hose and passed it through the broken window to a firefighter who'd suddenly appeared inside, presumably by way of the back door. As he took the hose, another firefighter also loomed out of the darkness of the studio and began pummeling holes in the wall with an ax. Charley always had assumed that firefighters used axes to break down doors and rescue people from fires—another misconception that could only have come from movies—but when he saw a glow behind the wall where the hole had been made, he understood their actual purpose. The man with the hose jammed the nozzle into the hole and let fly with a blast of water, killing whatever fire had hidden itself in that part of the building's frame.

The process was lost on Tallasee, however. "What are you doing in there?" she shouted. "You're making a big mess."

"Honey, it's not going to make a difference," Johnny Carver said. He'd come up behind them. "Everything is ruined anyway."

He had a mournful, apologetic look on his face. Tugging gently on Tallasee's arm and pulling her away from the fan and its roar, he led her to the far side of the street. Charley hadn't been invited along, but he trailed behind anyway. The sheriff seemed to have something to say.

He did. "Listen, I feel terrible about this. I think this is my fault," Johnny stated.

Tallasee lifted her head. "What do you mean, your fault?"

"It's my fault because I'm a dumbass. Lucas did this, I'm pretty sure. The chief"—Johnny nodded vaguely in the direction of the com-

mand car—"says the fire was set. It's real easy to tell that when somebody doesn't care if you know. He took a couple of gallons of gas and
just poured it over everything. They found the burnt-up can sitting
right by the back door."

"Why would he want to burn my studio?"

"Because I'm a dumbass, like I said," Johnny replied. He felt
around his pockets until he found a pack of cigarettes. He tapped one
out, then offered the pack to Tallasee. She shook her head. He hesitated for a moment, then offered the pack to Charley.

"Hell, I guess you're old enough to start killing yourself," he said,
but Charley also declined. Johnny lit his cigarette, then continued.

"I didn't mean for this to happen. I'm sorry. Here's what happened.
I drove up to the commune this afternoon, just like I said I would. Now,
a smart man would have taken a deputy with him to circle the area to
make sure Lucas didn't slip off into the woods. Or at least a smart man
would have been real casual about things, acted like he was just
checking in and then hanging around to see if Lucas showed up. But
because you've got an old fool for a sheriff, I didn't do either one of
those things.

"No, sir. Not me. I go roaring up there and make a big show of
tracking him down. I'm sticking my head in all those teepees and
tents, demanding to know where he is. Hell, I'd have probably kicked
some doors in, except there ain't any doors up there and you look
pretty stupid trying to kick open a tent flap. I can't find him anywhere,
which only makes me madder. Finally, that guy comes along. What's
his name, again? The guy who sort of runs the place?"

He'd directed the question to Tallasee, but she didn't answer. After
a moment, Charley did. "Osage," he said.

"Yeah, him. So he wants to know if he can help me with something.
Kind of smart-mouth about it, in a way. You know how people are when
they put you down by being real polite to you? Well, that's the way he
was. It just sent me over the edge.

"Thing is, I'd let myself get mad as I drove up there today. I've got
the sense something bad has happened with that boy, the grandson,
and maybe I'm feeling guilty about it. I mean, I had Lucas out of his
car one day but then just let him drive away. So if it turns out I'm

right—" He hesitated for a moment, then corrected himself—"I mean, if it turns out we're right and something bad has happened, then I'm going to feel terrible because I maybe could have prevented it."

Charley briefly wondered if this was the right time to tell Johnny what they'd learned on their visit, but decided to wait. He also was mystified by this rambling story, and how it related to the fire, so he sought to nudge the sheriff back on course. "You're pretty sure Lucas is involved in this?" Charley asked, waving a hand toward the ruined studio.

"He's a psycho," Johnny answered confidently. "And a deserter. His stuff was in one of the tents, so I looked through it 'til I found some papers. He's a marine, it turns out, although he's apparently decided he doesn't want to be one anymore. I called the Defense Department when I got back to the office. It took a bunch of calls, actually, but they wouldn't tell me much except that he was involved in some atrocity. And when they decided he was mentally unfit for service, he just up and walked away one day. So, yeah, I suppose we'd have to call him a prime suspect."

Tallasee also didn't understand how this talk of Lucas related to the fire, but she shared none of Charley's diplomacy. "When do we get to the dumbass part?" she asked abruptly.

A sheepish look registered on Johnny's face. "As I was saying, I was mad by the time I got there, mostly at myself but also just mad in general, and when Osage showed up with that mocky attitude, I decided I'd had enough of him and everyone up there. So I told him."

He still walked around it, unwilling to say what he'd done. Finally, Tallasee asked, "Told him what?"

Johnny turned and studied the firefighters, watching as they clamped a floodlight to the sill of the broken front window and turned it on, pouring light into the studio's interior. After a moment, he turned back. "I told him I knew that boy had been there. I told him we had those pictures, which of course he knew, since you two had been up there with them. But the dumb thing was, I also told him there were pictures of Lucas. But I made more of them than there actually is. I sort of suggested they were incriminating. Like we had him by the balls."

He paused, waiting for Tallasee to say something, but she only stared at him.

"So Lucas apparently decided to come destroy the evidence," Johnny concluded.

●

Tallasee had heard it said that there's a blessing in fire; that for every one item a fire takes it hurts to lose, another ten are found to be easily done without—that there's a certain spirituality that comes with suddenly being stripped of the many things you mistakenly thought were critically important to daily life. That you learn to place value in relationships and memories, which are not destroyed by tragedy but magically made stronger. That a fire is, simply, cleansing.

These are the utterances of comfort, however, weighed with same unknowing confidence as the declaration that the newly dead are in a better place. In fact, as Tallasee learned, fire is a trauma. People are taught to contribute something to the world, and if someone's contribution is destroyed forever in a single terrible event, then what is left? Nothing. The world is crowded with people whose accomplishments, for one reason or another, fell short. They were crippled by drink, insecurity, or the bad memories of childhood. Perhaps they lacked talent, discipline, or drive. Sometimes, they were just a step short or a moment late. A fire is just another excuse, and in all cases the result is the same: a zero on the scoreboard.

Everything had been in her studio: every photograph Tallasee had ever taken was gone, along with her equipment, contracts, notes, and files. All was now a sodden, sooty mess. The firefighters continued to search for places where the fire had burrowed, and she could hear a faint crunching as they moved about and ground the remnants of her work under their boots. Occasionally, one would move in front of the light or have his shadow thrown on a far wall, and in their coats and helmets they were faceless and anonymous. Just as the medieval executioner sought to hide from death under a hood, perhaps they thought that fire could not find them in their own homes if they hid in sameness.

She was suddenly and profoundly tired. She needed to sit. They were under the awning of the drugstore across the street from the studio, and even though there was a bench not fifteen feet away—a spot where Tallasee often saw old people sunning themselves as the pharmacist filled their prescriptions—it seemed too far to her. She plopped down on the sidewalk where she stood, so abruptly that Charley and Johnny thought that she'd fallen. They knelt on either side of her.

"Are you all right?" Johnny asked.

She nodded, then looked at Charley. "Can you take me home?" she said.

●

She didn't say whose home. So Charley chose his own.

Tallasee paid little attention during the drive, instead keeping her gaze focused on a spot on the truck's hood, so she was surprised when Charley turned into his driveway. "What are we doing?" she asked.

"It might be smart for you to stay here tonight," he answered. "In case some other fires break out."

"You think he'd burn my house, too?" She didn't seem as alarmed as she was curious, which was Charley's first indication that she didn't remember.

"I doubt it," he said. "But it ain't the kind of thing you want to be wrong about."

"It doesn't matter, anyway," she said. It was his second indication.

Frances was in her usual spot in the kitchen, with a cigarette in her hand and a cup of coffee before her. Charley was holding Tallasee's hand as they came through the side door—she hadn't seemed inclined to even get out of the truck until he'd walked around to her side to open the door, and then she came along only after Charley had taken her arm. When Frances saw them, she stared for a long moment as the smoke from the cigarette curled around her face.

Finally she spoke. "It ain't going to make you as happy as you think," she said. "But I suppose you have to find out for yourself."

●

For a long time afterward, Tallasee was embarrassed about it. When they'd entered the kitchen holding hands like lovers—and after Charley made a perfunctory introduction, then simply announced that Tallasee would be staying overnight—Frances apparently had concluded Tallasee planned on sleeping with her son, in her own house, while she puttered around downstairs. And, as Tallasee later realized, she seemed to give some left-handed approval to the arrangement. This was indeed an odd mother/son relationship.

Tallasee's recollection of that night would always remain fuzzy, as if her memory was a movie into which several strips of white leader film had been spliced at random places. She had never been as tired as she was that evening, not even in those worst days just before and after Nigel's death. She didn't have the energy to argue with Charley about whether it was safe for her to go home, or even to grasp the appearance of the situation when they entered his house. She held his hand for the same simple, elemental reason a child holds a parent's hand: it made her feel safe and comfortable.

The house, with two bedrooms at the top of the staircase and a bathroom in between them, wasn't large. It was the sort of place a young couple buys knowing, and never doubting, that they'll leave someday as the family grows larger and prosperous. But when Charley's family was halved, there had been little need for a larger home. If pain expands to fill an available space, why give it more room?

Charley led her to one of the bedrooms, which had twin beds pushed against opposite walls. Tallasee could see it was Charley's room, but in the light from the hallway, she could also tell that one side of it had been turned over to the memory of a child. There were pages torn from coloring books attached to the wall with tape that had long since turned brown and dry; a bedspread decorated with happy scenes of cowboy life covered the far bed; a small pair of shoes sat on the floor under a chair; and on the dresser was a small collection of jars containing the remains of long-dead bugs.

Still holding her hand, Charley took Tallasee to the other bed and they sat. "Do you want to wash up or anything?" he asked. Tallasee shook her head.

They sat quietly for a moment, then he spoke again. "You've forgotten about your photos, haven't you?"

"You mean the photos I used to have?" she answered, bitterness breaking through her fatigue.

"No, I mean the photos we hauled over to your house," he said. "Actually, the ones I hauled over to your house. And I'm still waiting to get paid, by the way."

Despite the half-light in the room, Tallasee could see him grinning. He was right. She had forgotten. She'd only lost some equipment, which could be replaced in days. All her prints, negatives, and files were safe at her house. What had seemed like a life-altering disaster just moments before was now, at worst, an annoyance. She became almost giddy.

"Oh, Charley, you wonderful man," she said, hugging him. "I'm going to give you a raise and a bonus. And an extra week of vacation. I may even make you a vice president."

The swing in her mood confused him. "I'm not sure it's good to be so successful at my age," he said after a moment. "What goals will I have left when I'm thirty?"

"Yeah, maybe I'll hold off on giving you the key to the executive washroom," she said. "Why didn't you say something earlier? You let me stand there the whole time thinking everything's been ruined. You jerk."

That seemed to remind Charley of something. "What's a big lug?" he asked.

It was Tallasee's turn to be confused. "A what?"

"A big lug. That's what you called that firefighter who was keeping you from going inside the studio. I've heard it before, but I've never known exactly what a big lug is."

She realized he was making fun of her, but she didn't mind. "I don't know the precise definition. I only know 'em when I see 'em." She remembered her original question. "Why didn't you tell me this earlier?"

Tallasee could tell he was grinning again. "It was too much fun watching Johnny Carver apologize. How often do you get to listen while the sheriff tells you what a dumbass he is?"

"I'm glad you enjoyed it," she said.

It was a curious moment. After she'd leaned over to hug him, they somehow never got quite disentangled, so they were touching at any number of places: knees, arms, and thighs, mostly. Also, they were whispering, as if there was someone else in the room trying to rest whom they didn't wish to disturb. Tallasee felt comfortable with Charley close to her, so comfortable that it made her understand how long it had been since she'd had a cluster of minutes when she didn't worry about all the things that recently had gone wrong or soon would. She'd been a happy child, and as a younger adult it seemed she had moved through the world easily, stepping lightly but surely as she made her way. Now, she was given to fretting, snappishness, and bad judgments. Only there with Charley did she have a stirring of her former confidence and calm, the old sense that all previous moments had deliberately arranged themselves to lead to this one. It was lovely and serene, and she wanted to make it last. She still felt tired, but it was a different sort of weariness.

"I'll let you get some sleep," Charley said, making to leave.

"No." She stretched out on the narrow bed, nestling against the wall to make as much room as possible, and pulled Charley down beside her. "Stay for a while."

He arranged himself carefully so that a discreet few inches separated them, but that was not what Tallasee had in mind—she wanted touch and comfort. She wanted his breath on her neck and his arm around her. She'd once had the same uncommon steadiness he possessed, and she wanted it back. She wanted to press herself into him until she absorbed it again.

She hooked her leg over his and wriggled close. She felt him tense; the poor lamb must have been uncertain as to what was happening. "It's all right," she murmured, but he didn't seem to relax. After a minute or two, she squirmed closer against him and felt the cause of his discomfort.

Men are such pitiable creatures sometimes; their desire betrays them. Longing in a woman is never advertised as flagrantly as it was in Charley that moment. A woman's response can be coy, if not disguised altogether, but a man has no such choice. He can never pretend he isn't interested once his hydraulic system has cranked up.

"It's all right," she whispered again, and pushed her hips against him to prove it. She felt deliciously wanton. There she was, lying on a bed with a bashful young man in his childhood room as his mother sat with her coffee in another part of the house. It crossed Tallasee's mind that this could be a more lurid male fantasy only if she'd been wearing a Catholic-school uniform. Without underpants. But she didn't care. Even though some remote part of her brain was scolding her—bleating that the journey from her depressed and listless state of just over an hour ago to this hip-grinding, overheated moment was a wild emotional swing and therefore suggestive of a dangerously unstable mind—it didn't matter. She'd always been careful and thoughtful, and look what it had gotten her: a bad marriage, widowhood, and the role of Sancho Panza to Charley's Don Quixote. So why not indulge in a few minutes of recklessness and irrationality?

She put her arm around him and pulled him close, mashing her breasts into his chest. There still was hesitancy in him, but then his arms came around her and he slowly pushed his knee up between her legs. They kissed for what seemed to be a long time, Charley still hesitant and Tallasee pushing into him. At one point, however, Charley's hand made a tentative exploration of her stomach, rubbing a slow circle through her shirt and giving each loop an incrementally longer arc that finally brought him to her ribcage. But his hand stopped there, his uncertainty once again ruling the moment.

Tallasee took his hand and placed it on her breast. They kissed again as Charley's hand did its duty, gingerly at first, but then with more confidence. When Tallasee's hand began to make an exploration of its own, it was plain that there would be no retreat from this.

"Charley, take off your clothes," she whispered.

She had expected a further touch of hesitancy, but he surprised her. Charley was undressed and had shut the door almost before Tallasee had her own shirt unbuttoned. He started to help her, but the urgency in his hands made him suddenly clumsy. "Easy," Tallasee said, stroking his cheek. "I'm not going anywhere."

He withdrew his hands as she finished getting undressed. "I'm a little new at this," he said as her naked body wriggled close. "You might have to show me a couple of things."

He meant it seriously, not realizing how funny it sounded to Tallasee, who smiled in the dark at the thought that had there been just a peep of light, his request would already have been fulfilled. But she kept the amusement from her voice.

"I will," she said. And she did.

●

Later, when they were finished, and as they sought to extend the moment by murmuring in one another's ear and letting their hands drift randomly, Tallasee waited for remorse to set in. It seemed reluctant to arrive, however. Charley had wanted to do this, and she had needed to. Each had been the other's balm, kneaded deep into that place where it did the most good and where guilt could not flourish. Her only moment of doubt came when Frances discreetly knocked at the bedroom door.

"Charley?" she said. "There's somebody downstairs who wants to talk to you."

Charley hurriedly pulled on his clothes and left the bedroom. "Who is it?" Tallasee heard him ask.

"I don't know. Some man," his mother answered.

"We were just resting a little." His voice had the too-casual tone that comes when people who aren't good at lying try it anyway.

Frances wasn't fooled. "Everybody needs a little rest now and then," she said. "God knows, I've rested a few times myself."

Tallasee's doubt left her. Frances clearly had a finely honed sense of what in life was worth her outrage. And this didn't qualify.

●

Lucas was sitting outside on the steps leading to the side door. Charley opened the screen and went out, stepping around Lucas to lean against the fender of his truck. The light from the kitchen was bright behind Lucas, keeping his face in a shadow and making it hard for Charley to see his eyes. A pair of moths made a diligent examination of the screening, hoping to find their entry to the better, brighter world inside.

"Sheriff's looking for you," Charley said.

"I know," Lucas said impatiently. "Did you send him up there?"

"No, not exactly. But I suppose we gave him enough reason to visit."

"You're just not going to let this rest, are you?"

Charley shook his head. "But I know more than you think, though."

"You don't know anything," Lucas said.

Charley resisted the temptation to show off, to prove he did know some things. "How did you find where I live?"

"Real piece of detective work," Lucas said. "I looked in the phone book. There ain't but one Selkirk there."

Charley remembered that he'd told Lucas his name when they had first visited the commune. "So what are you going to do?" he asked.

"That sort of depends on what the sheriff's going to do," Lucas responded.

"He's not exactly looking to me for advice. But it's certain he's after you. He's pretty sure something bad happened to that boy."

"Nothing happened to that boy," Lucas said vehemently. "Goddamn. Why doesn't everyone just leave this thing alone? I told him to leave. I told him to do whatever it takes to avoid getting drafted. It's the same thing I told you. But the difference is, he listened. He knew good advice when he heard it." He paused a moment, then added: "Which is more than I can say for you."

"You mean he just ran away again?" Charley said.

That earned a contemptuous look. "Are you having a hard time understanding this? Yes. He left. He said he had somewhere to stay where no one would find him. And now he's gone there. And that's the end of the goddamn story."

"Where'd he go? If Johnny Carver knew that, maybe everyone would stop worrying about him."

Lucas stared at Charley as if he was getting dumber by the minute. "The whole point is to keep him away from people like Johnny Carver. Maybe you've heard that evading the draft is against the law."

"So what are you going to do?" Charley asked again.

"Well, I can't stay, thanks to you and your girlfriend. So I figure you owe me a ride. That's why I'm here."

His girlfriend. His enigma. At first, Tallasee had been friendly in a big-sister sort of way, engaging and comfortable even if she was a bit too sure Charley would simply do what she wanted. In his memory, their initial meeting had taken on a magical quality: in a single day, starting with the moment Charley stopped on the sidewalk and offered to help with a package, he'd been propelled into what now seemed like a whole new period of his life. He'd shed something in those few hours. They'd driven deep into the hills on a glorious afternoon, and the journey had had an epic taste to it, as though every turn of both the road and conversation was a foray into new ground. Charley had been enchanted by her casual acceptance of his presence. She apparently believed not only was the world a place which delivered help when she needed it but that Charley understood this as well.

But later, at other times, Tallasee would seem remote and unhappy. She would disappear within herself for long periods, leaving Charley to the tasks she'd assigned and barely acknowledging his arrivals and departures. What conversations they had during those times tended to be prickly and bristling, as if unhappiness was something that came cloaked in the innocent words of others and therefore had to be repelled. Then, as the summer wore on, she had become inexplicably angry, finally announcing her intention to send Charley away. His sin, it seemed, was to become interested in the very thing she'd recruited him to help her with on that first day.

But there had been that afternoon when, while driving, they had told their stories, when he'd captured the vivid image of her as a younger woman who sought out the friendless and helpless. Later, as they walked up the forest path to Blue Hole, yet another image had formed, that of a woman who somehow was desirable without being seductive, fearless without being reckless, equal without being the same. It had filled Charley with a sense of anticipation and loss at the same time, as if he accidentally had learned of a secret passage into the minds of women, but had discovered it too late to make a difference in the one instance that mattered to him.

And now, on the official last day of his employment, he was given what must have been the summer-job equivalent to a gold watch.

"She's not my girlfriend," Charley said, realizing as he did that it wasn't the first time he'd said it.

Lucas ignored him. "You got your keys with you?" he asked, tilting his head toward the truck.

"Let me tell you what I saw today," Charley said, suddenly struck with an idea.

It was mostly speculation, but when added to the things Lucas knew, a plausible idea took form. And as this idea found its shape, Lucas became agitated. Charley was reminded again of why Lucas had made him feel afraid from the very moment he'd stepped into the road in front of them and demanded that they stop—the violence in him was palpable. Tonight, Charley had been lulled by his calm manner, by his seeming lack of anger that he had Charley to thank for the sheriff now seeking him. Almost immediately, Charley regretted that he'd said anything.

His mother had no such qualm. Frances heard everything, standing out of sight just inside the screen door. If Charley had known that she was there, and could have seen her face, the sight of it may have unnerved him as much as Lucas had. Charley's story had brought back too much at once: someone else was describing an evil that she thought she alone knew.

Frances would have liked to know more, would have preferred to talk to this fierce-looking stranger herself. But that wasn't the moment for it. Not with Charley there.

Perhaps life had left her with the sense that one did not trust fate to make all things even. Or maybe Frances decided that she herself was fate, that this was her moment to wield a terrible swift sword. In any event, she was the answer to the question that nagged police in the aftermath, the mystery they never solved.

This also was the beginning of the unraveling of her secret.

Chapter Fifteen

So who rolled over on me? Oh, never mind. I know you ain't gonna tell me. But it had to be Osage. He's the only person who knew. I should have dropped him at the same time. I don't know why I ever got mixed up with that fool.

Nobody's going to believe this now, of course, but it was an accident. Like I said, that boy was a puppy. It was like I'd scratched him behind the ears or rubbed his belly or something, and he decided to become my friend. A dog, though, you can at least chain up when it gets to pestering you. Of course, I couldn't do that with him. You don't do that with people, although if I had he'd still be alive and we wouldn't be having this conversation right now.

Here's what happened. Osage and I were walking up to Blue Hole. Like I told you a minute ago, that's where he liked to do business. It was sort of a long walk, but I didn't mind, usually. Once in a while it was worth the effort. What I mean is, one time we got there and some girls were swimming naked. I kept hoping that would happen again, but it never did. Life just ain't that generous, I guess.

Anyway, I kept getting an odd feeling as we walked that day. A couple of times I stopped to listen, but whenever I was quiet, everything else was quiet. But the farther we went, the more sure I was that somebody was following us. Osage kept saying he didn't hear anything, but he has his head up his butt most of the time anyway. He thinks he's a guru of some kind. Anybody who goes up there ain't going to see nothing but a bunch of dropouts and dopers, but Osage thinks it's some kind of tribe. With him as the leader. Hell, he couldn't lead a rope if he was holding it by one end.

I finally decided to check for sure if we were being followed. There's one spot on the path where the trail bends around this big rock. Actually, it ain't a rock so much as it is a piece of the hill that juts out there by the path. And the trail falls off for a while just beyond that rock, so if you're coming up on it you can't see past to tell if anyone's on the trail ahead of you. So if you step off the path right there and stand quietly, whoever is behind will get right up to you before they know you're there.

Another thing about Osage—he usually had a walking stick with him. Like he was goddamn Moses or something. Anyway, we reached that rock and I said, Hang on a second. Then I said, Give me that stick and just stand right here. And be quiet. He gave me this smirky, superior look, but he handed over the stick. I felt like smacking him with it.

Sure enough, we'd only been standing there a minute or two when I heard someone coming up the trail. Whoever it was, you could tell he was trying to walk quietly. We heard him stop a couple of times, probably trying to figure how far ahead we were. But like I said, that's the point on the trail when you're walking blind. So he was going to have to step around this rock sooner or later, and when he did I was going to take that opportunity to help him understand that he shouldn't be following folks. If you get what I mean.

Now, I suppose if I'd thought about it I would have realized it was that boy. It's not like he hadn't done it before, tiptoe along behind me around the commune, pretending to be in the army. But those other times, it had seemed like he wanted me to see him or catch him. Like the way a little kid does when he wants attention. But whoever this was, he didn't want to be seen. So it just never occurred to me that it would be him.

But of course it was. We heard him come up the trail just the other side of the rock, could even hear him breathing hard, 'cause it's real steep there. I kept my eye on the ground, and as soon as I saw a foot, I stepped onto the trail and hit him with the stick.

Osage had cut himself a big one. Once it dried out, it would have lightened up some, but it was still pretty green that day. It was heavy. Had some heft to it. I was holding it like a baseball bat, and when I saw his foot I swung that stick at waist level. With any luck, I'd get him just below the ribs. You hit somebody there, it'll be a few minutes before they draw a good breath.

In baseball, you learn to swing through the pitch, just like you learn to push through your punch if you're in a fight. It's all the same principle. You get your power in the follow-through. I only wanted to put him on the ground for a few minutes. Even if I'd hit him a little high, the worst it would have done would be to break a rib, which means every time he breathed for the next two weeks it would have felt like somebody was sticking an ice pick in his chest. That's a little cold, I know, but he wouldn't have followed me around no more.

But this fool ducked right into it.

I don't know what he was doing. Maybe he was a little winded, and had bent over to catch his breath. Maybe he dropped something. Maybe he just decided it was a good time to see if he could touch his toes. Who the hell knows? I don't know. But I got him in full swing across the side of the head. Right there on the temple, where your skull ain't too thick.

He dropped the way you would if all your muscles went slack at the same second. He'd sort of fallen on his side, but his face was in the dirt, right facedown into it like he was looking at it up close. In fact, that's the thing I remember best. His tongue was out like he was licking the trail, it was just coated with dirt and stuff, and I was thinking, you know, he's going to have one hell of a case of cotton mouth when he wakes up. I mean, I knew I'd hit him pretty hard, but I figured he'd get up after a while. Everybody's had their head rattled at some point.

But he was real still. After just a couple of seconds, it was clear he wasn't breathing. I knelt down, rolled him over on his back and pressed my finger into his neck. What I felt was this sputtering kind of heartbeat, sort of the way an old car runs on a cold morning. After just a moment or two, though, I didn't even feel that.

Oh hell, I says.

What's the matter? Osage asked. I could tell right then he wasn't going to handle this very well. His voice was kind of . . . watery, I guess you'd call it.

I think I killed him, I says.

I was right. He didn't handle it well. He started breathing real hard and shaking that boy, like he could wake him up or something. C'mon, c'mon, you're all right, he was saying, had that boy by the shoulders, bouncing him up and down.

You ain't doing him any good, I says, right sharp-like.

Then he starts looking at me like I'm going to do him the same way. Which, to be honest, I considered doing. Mr. Superior, running his own little world up there, comes apart the first time something serious happens. Ain't that usually the case, though? It's always the people who act like they've got the world by the balls who are useless when you actually need them for something. For a moment there, I thought, this guy's going to be a problem.

But I'm not a killer. It may be hard to believe, considering what I've just told you, but that was the only time I've ever killed anybody. And it was an accident. I don't go around killing people to solve problems. Hell, setting that fire was stupid enough. So I didn't do anything to Osage. I just gave him his stick back.

What are we going to do? he says.

We're not going to do anything, I says. Except take him into the woods a ways.

So that's what we did. We rolled him off the trail and dragged him a long ways down the hill, 'til we found a spot where I thought we could bury him. We could have just stuck him in one of those gullies and covered him up, of course, but the first rain would have washed everything away and left him exposed. So I told Osage we had to dig a hole and bury him good. I made it sound like I was concerned with burying him decent and everything, but the fact is, I just didn't want animals getting after the body.

We didn't have anything to dig with, of course, but if you can find a spot where the rock's not too close to the surface, the ground's pretty soft. I mean, it ain't nothing but a couple hundred years' worth of rotted leaves. We found a flat rock, about the size of a small plate, and I let Osage do most of the digging. It kept him from just standing around, fretting.

He was better by the time we got that boy covered up. Although he had another bad moment when I picked up the stick to put in the hole, so we could bury it, too. I could see he was wondering whether I was going to come after him, too.

You know, I realize now I didn't even know that boy's name.

We just went straight back to the commune after that. We didn't do our business. In fact, we never did business again. Osage avoided me after that, and I didn't trust him anymore. He wasn't exactly a steady hand in a crisis.

You want to know the thing that bothered me the most that day? As we were coming back down the trail, just as we got to the clearing where the commune is, I see that gal with her camera. Like I really needed my picture taken just then.

Chapter Sixteen

Poor Charley, Tallasee thought. She somehow had infected him with her own confusion while at the same time claiming his clarity as her own. Perhaps wantonness did that for her. Why should only men be made strong by desire? In the moments after he left the bedroom, Tallasee felt as if she were a great ship sailing in the open sea after a long and useless period in port, with every deck and station calling the bridge to report that all systems were functioning remarkably well. The body had checked in first, sending a delicious heat to even the remote stretches of skin, where it lingered for a long time after Charley left. Then the brain cranked up a reasoning process that had malfunctioned all too often in recent months, making a dispassionate inventory of damage and concluding that within just a few days of the arrival of new photo equipment, she could be right back where she was before the fire, and maybe even a little ahead if she was clever about her purchases and ended up with better stuff. Finally, the heart announced its return, revealing that it did in fact care what had happened to Pearlie Bullock's grandson, or whoever he was, and admitting its shame for having pretended otherwise for so long.

The tectonic plates of personality, which had drifted apart for a while, somehow locked together again that night. Tallasee was getting better.

After a minute or so, she sensed Charley's mother still standing in the hall outside the bedroom door. Tallasee sat up in the bed and ran fingers through her hair, then smoothed the bedspread to an unwrinkled innocence.

"Mrs. Selkirk?" she said. "Let me introduce myself."

Frances gave the little-boy side of the room a quick look as she entered, a movement that had the flavor of an almost involuntary reflex. Tallasee also noticed how young she seemed. Earlier that evening, in the kitchen's hard light and with cigarette smoke drifting around her face, Frances had seemed older and heavier. Now, in the less-judgmental twilight of the bedroom, Tallasee saw that her movement was light, and that underneath her clothes she was trim and graceful. She also realized it was likely that Frances had borne Charley at an early age, which would mean that there was a scant few years' difference between them. But even this didn't register as a pang of conscience so much as an interesting fact.

Charley's mother also turned out to be more forthright than Tallasee had suspected. "You're Tallasee, right?" she said before Tallasee could say anything. "Charley has spoken of you."

"Yes, ma'am," Tallasee answered.

"I didn't mean to hover in the hall. But somebody wanted to talk to Charley, so I thought I'd give them a few minutes before I went down and started eavesdropping." Tallasee could see Charley's sardonic grin on her face before she abruptly asked, "Has something bad happened?"

Tallasee didn't know how much Charley had told her, so she confined her answer to the night's events. "There was a fire. My photography studio burned down."

"Oh, dear. How did it start?"

"The sheriff says somebody set it."

Frances was absolutely still. After several long moments, she changed course. "I'm worried about Charley," she said.

"Why?" Tallasee asked. "He's a fine young man." She wanted to steer the conversation back to the fire, but Frances gave her no chance, again switching direction.

"Tallasee is an interesting name. Where does it come from?"

"It's from my mother's family. You know how Southern folk are. Any last name eventually gets used as a first name. We don't waste them."

"That's why I'm worried about him," Frances said. "Tallasee, I've lost one son and I have no marriage. If they take Charley to fight their war, there may be no one to pass family names along to."

She'd been sitting next to Tallasee on the bed, but now she stood and leaned against the door frame. "Are you going to take him from me?" she asked.

"No, ma'am. He's got a girlfriend." Not that I'd bothered to account for that just a few minutes before, Tallasee thought.

Frances didn't seem to hear the answer, instead looking for a long moment at Shay's side of the room before turning back to Tallasee. "I don't mind if you do. I've neglected Charley for a long time. Being unhappy seems to have required all my attention."

"Charley's fine," Tallasee repeated, uncertain as to exactly what this conversation required of her.

"Do they make married men go into the army?" Frances asked.

"I don't know," Tallasee said, then figured out where this was leading. "Charley has a girlfriend, and it's not me. I've just hired him for the summer to work in my studio."

"You've got a mighty friendly management style," Frances said. "Are you a happy woman, Tallasee?" She seemed to have a taste for abrupt shifts in conversation.

It was a question Tallasee often had pondered recently. "I used to be. I haven't been lately, though."

"Have you ever thought much about how someone becomes happy?"

"Yeah, a lot," Tallasee answered. "But it seems like the more you think about it, the more elusive it becomes."

Frances nodded. "I wasted a lot of time trying to figure out how to do it. And you know what I finally realized?"

"What?" Tallasee asked.

"That reducing the number of things that make you unhappy is probably the closest to happiness you're ever going to get."

●

Tallasee slept for a while after Frances left, dreaming of vague things that somehow were both threatening and comforting at the same time. She must have slept lightly, though, because she stirred as soon as Charley came back in the bedroom. She could sense his uncertainty as he wondered whether he should lie down with her or spread out on the other bed.

Again Tallasee sat up, although this time she didn't feel the need to smooth the bedspread. "Hey there," she said.

Charley didn't wait for her to ask. "That was Lucas downstairs," he said.

That brought Tallasee fully awake. "Oh, Lord. We'd better call Johnny Carver."

Charley shook his head. "We'll call him in the morning."

"But Lucas could leave. He might not be here in the morning."

"He's not going anywhere. He's sleeping in the shed out back. There's an old cot there we keep for company . . . when we used to have company."

Tallasee felt as if she was talking to a slow-witted child. "He burned down my studio. He has to know the sheriff is looking for him. Of course he'll leave. It's the first thing you learn at crime school. There's probably a class called Avoiding Capture 101."

Charley sat on the bed next to her. "He knows the sheriff is looking for him, sure enough. But I'm not sure he set that fire."

"Why?" she asked. "Did he deny it?"

"No, not really. He didn't say anything about it at all. When I mentioned it, he just shrugged and said, 'Hey, I've got my own problems.' Besides, if he had set the fire, it wouldn't make sense for him to come here."

He had a point. "So why did he come here?"

"He wanted me to give him a ride out of town," Charley said. "He thinks we owe it to him, since we got the sheriff stirred up about that boy."

"So Johnny was right about him being a deserter?"

"He didn't say, exactly, but it's pretty clear he used to be in the military and now he's not. And he doesn't want to be anywhere around the sheriff. So, yeah, I guess Johnny was right."

"You're not going to drive him somewhere, are you?" Tallasee asked.

Charley looked worried. "Problem is, now he doesn't want to leave."

●

When she was a little girl, Tallasee had a neighbor with a dog that chased cars. It was an annoying little beast, a terrier of some kind, and its murky dog mind had concluded cars were a great menace. It barked at them constantly, and whenever it could slip between the neighbor's legs as she opened the door for some reason, it would race to the street and confront the cars in person, snapping at their tires and running alongside for a half block or so, yapping madly until it was satisfied its territory once again was safe. Then it would trot home and allow itself to be coaxed back inside the house with a dog biscuit.

Of course, the day came when it got tangled up under the wheels of a car. One of its annoying little terrier legs was broken, and the dog was taken to the veterinarian, who set the bone and wrapped the leg in a hard cast. By the next day, the dog was back home, and at the first opportunity it slipped out the door to chase a passing car, thumping across the yard like some canine version of Long John Silver. Whatever agility it once had was gone, naturally, so while the prior day's accident might have been a fluke—the dog had, after all, dodged cars successfully for years until then—the outcome of that morning's encounter was a foregone conclusion: it was dead before it even came to rest against the curb.

Tallasee didn't wish to be that dog.

She would learn from her experience. She had been asked to help an old woman, but let weeks lapse before she actually did anything; then she and Charley had played detective instead of going to Johnny Carver and letting an expert handle the matter. She would not make that mistake again. She would not hobble to the street and place herself before an oncoming car.

She and Charley indeed switched roles that night. He'd begun this adventure with a missionary's confidence in his rightness and seduced by the apparent simplicity of the task. But after visiting Pearlie Bullock's home that day and seeing what sat on her kitchen table, and after his talk with Lucas a few hours later, his certainty had wavered. He'd been sure that something bad had happened to the boy and that Lucas had been involved; now, his grip was less firm.

But Tallasee had the zeal and clarity of the newly converted. She may not have been any more sure than Charley as to what had happened, but she knew how they could find out.

●

Tallasee told him she had a friend who could help.

She spoke of him vaguely yet intimately. When he got older and recalled the conversation, Charley recognized that Tallasee referred to him in the way a person of discretion speaks of a former lover with whom relations have remained cordial. He was confused by it at the time, though. Through the course of the summer, he had come to understand that Tallasee lived within herself more thoroughly than anyone he knew, including his mother, who was something of an expert at it herself. Tallasee seemed to have almost no need for the company of other people. Charley had been with her virtually every day since the morning he'd helped tote the boxes from her car into the studio, and not once in that time did he see Tallasee share a private moment with anyone. Except him.

Her friend's name was Quentin Mackie, and she called him early the next morning. They had slept separately on the two beds in his room, with whatever moment Lucas had interrupted now apparently gone forever. But as he settled into Shay's bed, she had whispered, "Good night, Charley," and he was sure he could hear something sweet and regretful in her words. That night was marked by more longing than Charley had ever felt: for Tallasee, for Baby Girl, for Shay, for his mother. He wondered why it was that he had to live outside the walls of so many other people.

Tallasee telephoned Quentin early from Frances's kitchen, seeking to catch him at home before he went to work and recalling his number from memory, which gave Charley an unexpected pang of jealousy. She had explained that he was with the state attorney general's office in Atlanta, and that if he couldn't help them with their problem himself, he would know people who could.

Quentin Mackie was a good listener, judging from the half of the conversation that Charley overheard. He let Tallasee set out the story in her own fashion, and when she was done, he apparently asked a series of precise questions that helped fill the gaps in her narration. Then he must have recited back to her his understanding of the tale, because Tallasee spent several minutes listening and only offering an occasional "that's right" when he needed confirmation of a particularly fuzzy point in the chronology. She had done a good job in the telling, Charley silently conceded, not skewing the story to give less weight to his suspicions and more to her doubts, and in the end Quentin decided that the full power and majesty of the attorney general's office, in the form of his own person, should be brought to bear on this matter.

"He'll meet us at my house at noon," Tallasee said after she hung up the phone.

She had a sense of happy anticipation about her, which didn't surprise Charley. He had noticed that when she called, she'd introduced herself only by her first name. And she hadn't needed to give him directions to her home.

●

Tallasee knew him from college, it turned out. "We dated for a while," she explained to Charley, with an elaborate casualness. "He's a good fellow. You'll like him."

At her insistence, Charley had driven Tallasee home even before she had anything to eat. As he pulled to the curb in front of her house, she said, "Remember, Quentin said to not mention any of this to Lucas."

"I won't," he answered.

"And be back here at noon," she added. "Maybe even a little before. You can help me pick up a bit."

"It sounds like I'm back on the payroll."

"Hey, you made the big mess, piling boxes everywhere. The least you can do is tidy up when company's coming."

"It's what you told me to do," Charley protested. "And when did this guy become company? This isn't a social call."

Tallasee ignored the question. "Plan to be here at eleven thirty. It won't take long."

Until that moment, she had made no acknowledgment of the events of the night before. But now, as Tallasee reached for the door handle to open it, she hesitated, then shifted in her seat to face Charley. "Listen, I have to confess something. I think you've been a better friend to me than I have to you," she said.

Charley wasn't sure what he should say, or if he should say anything at all. So he shrugged.

"I've been unhappy for a while," she continued. "I think I'm starting to be okay now, and one of the reasons why is because we've spent time together this summer."

Charley started to speak, but Tallasee interrupted him. "Just let me talk here for a moment. I'm not going to pretend that I understand why things seem to be better. I'm just going to accept it as a gift. Like you were. You were a gift to me, and I hope"—Charley could see a faint flush rise in her face—"I was a gift to you."

"You were," Charley said. "It was a great present. Just what I wanted."

Tallasee laughed and stroked his cheek, much as she'd done the night before. "Yeah, it was a regular Christmas, wasn't it? But here's the thing about gifts," she said, serious again. "You can only open them once."

Charley nodded. Even as Tallasee had joined herself to him, he had sensed this. In her had been the abandon of someone leaving things behind, not the measured care of someone with an eye on the future. Still, he wanted that closeness again.

"I've got a birthday coming up, you know," he said.

Tallasee laughed again and got out of the truck. She got halfway up the sidewalk to the door of her house when she noticed her neighbor, who'd apparently stepped outside to get the newspaper, was paying conspicuous attention to them. Tallasee stopped and turned back toward Charley, waving cheerily. "Thanks for a wonderful evening," she called. "What did you say your name was again?"

Charley was halfway home before he remembered that she hadn't actually confirmed that he was still an employee.

●

Despite his instructions, Charley couldn't ignore Lucas. Just because he was an army deserter and alleged arsonist—not to mention the leading suspect in the disappearance of the boy who was somebody's grandson, if not Pearlie Bullock's—didn't mean that good manners could drop by the wayside. You give him a place to sleep and a bite to eat before you arrange his betrayal and capture.

Charley had put him up in a room in the rear of the shed behind the Selkirk home. The room was lined with shelves meant to hold the result of an annual canning effort, but Charley and Shay had turned it into a secret clubhouse years before. Charley had unfolded the old cot and invited Lucas to stretch out for the night. He wasn't as afraid of Lucas as he should have been. Hearing Tallasee's dispassionate explanation to Quentin Mackie of the recent events had made Charley realize his suspicions were built on little more than a hunch. And it was not a hunch Quentin had placed much stock in: his conclusion at the end of the phone call from Tallasee was that circumstances, indeed, suggested that Lucas was at the center of whatever was going on. But the tuning fork in Charley's gut just didn't hum when he was around Lucas.

He was asleep when Charley looked into the room at the back of the shed. Charley went in the house to shower and change clothes, then checked again. Lucas still hadn't awakened, so Charley put an apple and a couple of doughnuts on a plate and set it on the floor next to the cot, then leaned a note against it saying: "I'LL GIVE YOU A RIDE IF YOU STILL WANT IT. BE BACK LATER."

Tallasee had done most of the cleaning by the time he got to her house. It was tidier than Charley had seen it before, with no stray bits of clothing draped over chairs and no dishes piled in the kitchen sink. Magazines and books had been collected into neat piles, curtains had been tied back from the windows, and the carpet bore those odd, swooping tracks that are left by vacuum cleaners. On the kitchen counter were a couple of bags of groceries, crackers and snacks and such, and when Charley peeked into the refrigerator he saw a big pitcher of newly brewed tea that had been set inside to cool. Only the dining room, with its boxes of files from her studio piled on its table and around the floor, remained as it had been.

She had shouted him in when she'd knocked, but had not appeared from her bedroom. When she emerged a few minutes later, pulling a comb through her damp hair, she was wearing a dress for the first time Charley could remember. It was light cotton, cut low enough in the front for him to see a faint sprinkling of freckles across the top of her chest and even lower in the back, where it barely reached halfway up her spine. Her legs and feet were bare, but she carried a pair of sandals, which she dropped by a chair in the living room. She was relaxed, confident, and utterly gorgeous. Charley suddenly felt dowdy and awkward.

"I think you've got that dress on backwards," he said, hoping a little needling would even things up. It didn't faze her at all.

"Nah, you only wear it that way on special occasions," she answered.

"This seems to be turning into a special occasion."

Charley knew he sounded petulant. All this was for the benefit of a visitor from Atlanta, not him. He knew this was a moment for him to be worldly and cavalier, but he couldn't make himself be those things. Tallasee didn't respond, and he could see her smiling to herself as she sat and strapped on her sandals, but when she was done, she gave him a sly wink. "Even I need to be a girl once in a while," she said, then, after a pause, continued. "Charley, you're not going to make me regret anything, are you? I hope not, because that was the least regrettable thing either one of us will ever do. It was a purely sweet moment. And life doesn't give you too many of them."

He began to see. Tallasee didn't behave as if she'd bestowed some great treasure upon him. She was grateful for him, and wanted him to be grateful for her. And that gratefulness suddenly seemed to come easy. "It was sweet, sure enough," he said. "Listen, you look great. This Quentin guy is going to be impressed."

Tallasee performed a model's runway turn, then put Charley to work. He cleared the boxes from the dining room, hauling them to a small enclosed porch off the kitchen, then took a rag and furniture polish and cleaned the table. As he worked, Tallasee fetched an enormous serving plate from a cabinet and arranged slices of cheese and crackers in several large rings around its edge, then decorated the center with a cluster of grapes. Charley could hear her humming quietly, and the sound of it made him terribly sad.

Tallasee was healing herself, and she was leaving him behind. Somehow, she was reclaiming a sense of happiness and purpose at the precise moment that those things seemed irretrievably beyond his reach. Earlier that summer, there had seemed to be a certain kinship of injury, but that was gone. What he sensed from her now was a detached pity. They were like two dogs trying to cross a busy highway, but while she'd successfully navigated the traffic and reached the far side, Charley still stood on the shoulder of the road, feeling heavy and slow and sure that he would never make it across.

Perhaps that's why he came to feel a debt to Quentin Mackie. He stopped traffic long enough for Charley to find his way across the road.

●

Tallasee predicted Quentin would arrive exactly at noon. "He has this mania for being punctual," she said. "If he says he'll be somewhere or do something, it'll happen. It used to annoy me no end."

They had finished preparing for the visit and were sitting on the front porch. "Why?" Charley asked.

"Because I was a foolish girl. But also because he seemed to make a moral issue of it. He'd always arrive right on time for a date, and if I wasn't ready you could almost see him piling on the demerits."

"How awful," Charley said. "Did he abuse you in other ways? Bring you flowers? Hold the door for you?"

She grinned. "Yeah, it was a real nightmare. Those good manners and all that attention. No one should have to endure that."

Sure enough, a car pulled to the curb in front of the house right at noon. From forty feet away, Quentin Mackie was an unremarkable man of average height and weight who, before he left the car, elaborately adjusted each window so that all were cracked open the same one inch for ventilation. From twenty feet away, he looked like someone who invested in expensive clothes but wore them sensibly and casually in the heat, with the shirt open at the collar, tie loosened, and sleeves rolled up two turns to reveal surprisingly large and strong forearms. From handshake distance on the porch, a forceful but friendly character radiated from him. The man who had seemed bland and fussy from the street was, up close, confident and thorough.

"You look fabulous," he said to Tallasee. It was a sincere appraisal: he'd had his eyes locked on her from the moment he was halfway up the sidewalk.

She smiled in acknowledgment. "Hey, Quentin," she greeted him, and they shared a hug. He then turned toward Charley.

"This must be young Mr. Selkirk," he said, putting his hand out for Charley to shake. "I'm Quentin Mackie. I'm from the government and I'm here to help you." He had a merry, self-mocking look on his face.

Charley had resolved to not like him, but he already felt that melting away. Still, he was aggressively formal. "How do you do, sir" Charley responded.

"I'm good," Quentin said, then seemed to examine Charley for a moment. "You play any ball?"

He nodded. "Football, yes, sir."

"Call me Quentin. Defensive back?"

Charley nodded again. "And some wide receiver."

"They ever get things settled down at the school here? They could put one hell of a team on the field if people would stop paying attention to what color everyone else is."

Charley felt himself blush. "I'm out of school now. I haven't been keeping up."

"Are you going to play any college ball?" Quentin asked. "You look like you could run through walls."

"Why don't we go inside and have some tea," Tallasee interrupted. Charley knew that she was trying to steer the conversation around this particular pothole, but he wouldn't let her.

"Actually, things haven't settled down much. I got into the middle of the trouble and was kicked out of school."

Quentin looked at him coolly. "You get in a fight with a black kid?"

Suddenly, it felt good for Charley to explain it. "No, one of the white players deliberately hurt a black kid, so I went after him. I hit him harder than I should have, though. Knocked him cold. He was the starting quarterback. Everybody got real mad."

Quentin nodded approvingly. "You reap what you sow. Sounds like your boy got what he deserved." He gave Charley a speculative look. "You didn't like him anyway, though, did you?"

Charley grinned. "Not much."

"Justice is sweetest when it's personal." Quentin turned back to Tallasee. "Let's go have that tea. I don't know if I can be the same avenging angel Charley is, but we'll see what I can do."

As they walked into the house, a comfortable feeling settled around Charley. Quentin was smart and intuitive. Tallasee had said that he would help them, and now Charley believed he could.

●

Of the two of them, Charley was the neediest. Quentin saw that right away. He paid much attention to him, listening closely when Charley spoke, soliciting his guesses at several points, and giving him a just-us-boys look when the swimming habits at Blue Hole were mentioned. Tallasee could see Charley open up. He sought Quentin as a plant seeks the sun, literally turning his chair at one point to better face the older man as he spoke. There was a natural camaraderie between them that would have made her jealous had she not felt Quentin's eyes lingering on her several times.

An easy woman had taken him from Tallasee. She wondered if there was some inexhaustible supply of them, standing just offstage waiting for women like her to suddenly become priggish and push their men away. Tallasee and Quentin had met a few years before while standing together in line at a fast-food restaurant near campus called the Varsity. He'd ordered the cheapest thing available—a grilled Swiss-cheese sandwich, which at the time cost a quarter and could be embellished with lettuce and tomato for another dime—but when he'd pulled the change from his pocket he was embarrassed to find he didn't have enough money. With her own order stalled behind his, Tallasee had dropped a couple of quarters on the counter in front of him and said, "My treat. And send it through the garden, if you want."

He grinned abashedly, but indeed had the counterman add lettuce and tomato to the sandwich. He'd then waited for Tallasee to collect her lunch, then suggested they sit together. "Although for another quarter I'll go away," he added.

"No, I'll cut my losses," Tallasee had answered. "I'll put up with you."

He was chatty and friendly, and they sat for a long time after finishing their lunch. She learned he was in law school, that he had grown up in an old Atlanta neighborhood called Buckhead, and that he knew Barrington, his family having been in the habit of making an annual fall pilgrimage to the mountains when the leaves changed. Tallasee asked if he'd ever stopped at the packing house; it's cold enough in north Georgia to allow apple growing, and the packing house did a good business each autumn selling bushels of apples to visitors. Its owner typically hired local high school girls to help during the busy season—she had worked there herself a couple of years—and the sight of all those healthy young women had evidently made a lasting impression on the younger Quentin.

"We'd stop by every year," he said. "Apples make me very happy."

Before they left, he asked her for a date. "I don't know if you can afford it," Tallasee said.

He didn't respond right away, instead digging his hand into a pocket. He withdrew two quarters and placed them in her palm. "Here," he said. "I owe you this."

"Why didn't you just pay for your lunch?" she asked, genuinely puzzled.

"I would have, eventually. But I thought I'd give you the chance to jump in first."

"This is how you pick up women?"

"I've never done it before," he said. "I only thought of it when I noticed you behind me in line."

"Why are you even telling me this? Now I'm going to feel like I should search your pockets if we go out."

He kept a deadpan look on his face. "A man can dream, can't he?"

Tallasee had to laugh. They went out that evening, then again several more times. There was an immediate familiarity between them, a relaxed and easy intimacy that had the flavor of an old friendship even as they discovered new things about each other. In some cases, a relationship like that becomes sterile when a man and woman who find they have much in common begin to feel like brother and sister. But Quentin didn't let that happen. He kissed her at the earliest decent opportunity, and when he did, it was clear he had an appetite for it.

But he also was endearingly patient. They savored each small step toward what seemed to be sure to happen.

They never got there, however. For some reason, Tallasee decided she needed to balance his precision and orderliness. She became impulsive and unpredictable, often insisting that their dates be spontaneous affairs free of all planning or schedules. She had concluded he was too rigid, but only by a little, so she thought her mercurial behavior somehow would liberate the free spirit within him.

It didn't. All she did was complicate the already-burdened life of a law student. Also, at a few unfortunate moments, she unconsciously became a Southern belle, deciding Quentin needed to work harder to get her. The effect was predictable: they spent less and less time together, and, fool that she was, Tallasee sought to cure the drift by becoming ever more impulsive and to spark his desire by becoming ever more remote. One day, Quentin told her he needed to burrow into the law library for a whole weekend, to prepare a paper he had due. So they didn't talk for three days, then they missed a couple of telephone connections the following week—and suddenly it was gone.

She saw him only one more time. She was sitting on a bench beneath one of the ancient oaks that shade the yards between the original university buildings when Tallasee noticed Quentin settling into a spot on the library steps. He didn't see her, so she just sat and watched him for a few moments. When he looked at his watch after a minute or so— a gesture so familiar, so typical of him that it made her smile—Tallasee was caught by a sudden desire to talk to him. But as she gathered her things and stood, a woman walked up and they embraced, then set off together toward town. Tallasee recognized her immediately—a flamboyant member of one of the more famously promiscuous sororities on campus. She was right on time.

●

Quentin listened well, as Tallasee knew he would, and had an idea, as she also knew he would. It was simple and elegant, and required only a little preparation. They would have the afternoon free.

There was someone whom Tallasee wanted to see. She suspected that she would find her at one of the three or four places where young women tended to work in the summer, all of them retailers who valued the presence of comely sales associates. But after two fruitless stops, a whim took her to the town's veterinary clinic, where she parked under a tree and waited. Sure enough, the girl came out a few minutes later, carrying a small dog to a car for an elderly woman. Of course she would want to work with animals, stroking their heads to calm them as the vet administered inoculations. Tallasee herself had done it one summer.

She caught up with the young woman before she went back inside. "We've never really met, but I'm Tallasee Tynan," she said. "Charley and I work together."

The woman gave her a smile that was both friendly and puzzled. "Yeah, hi. I'm Dorothy."

"That answers my first question. So you're not really called Baby Girl?"

She turned sheepish. "Well, I always have been. But I'm trying to get everyone to stop. I can't imagine being grown up and going by that name." She lowered her voice as if to take Tallasee into her confidence, although there was no one else outside. "I really hate it, if you want to know the truth."

"Why do people call you that?"

"It's what my daddy called me when I was little, and it just stuck."

"I guess you can be thankful he didn't call you something like Booger," Tallasee said.

Dorothy grinned but said nothing, waiting for Tallasee to state her business. Tallasee knew what she wanted Dorothy to understand, but not quite sure how to say it. It wasn't the sort of advice that decent, Christian Southern women were accustomed to hearing.

"I want to talk to you about Charley," Tallasee began. "I think he's special."

Dorothy regarded her for a long moment before replying. "I've always thought so," she replied coolly.

Tallasee realized what she was thinking. "We're only friends," she explained, and hoped Dorothy could not read her face as a vivid image flashed into her mind of her leg hooked over Charley's. "He's been working for me this summer and he's told me a little about you."

Most women would want to know what had been said about them, but Dorothy didn't ask. "I've missed him," she said.

"Well, he misses you, too."

"Then why doesn't he call or something?" Dorothy asked. "I went to see him one day"—Tallasee, remembering her vamping on the sidewalk while they talked, again wondered if her face betrayed her—"and I thought maybe we could start over. But nothing happened. It made me wonder if he'd found another girlfriend . . . In fact, I wondered if it was you."

Tallasee was tired of feeling furtive. It was time for candor. "I've thought about it. In fact, if I was a little younger, you might not see Charley again. That's sort of why I'm here. Maybe I'm telling you something you already know, but you'd be foolish to let him get away."

"He may already be gone," she said. "Besides, I've got some pride."

"Pride has nothing to do with it. The problem is you've given him a choice. You've made it clear you want to start over, but most men aren't very brave about such things. When they have to make a choice, they'll choose to not get hurt."

"I don't want to get hurt, either," she said with no real conviction. Her natural compassion already was stirring.

"How old are you?" Tallasee asked.

"Eighteen."

"Do you know about birth control?"

She colored, but nodded. Tallasee was beginning to see what Charley saw in her: she was a game girl, pretty and sweet natured but with grit underneath.

"Dorothy, just take him. You know how to do it. Make him yours, because if you don't, somebody else will. And you'll regret that for a long time."

Dorothy nodded again. She was still standing outside the vet's office when Tallasee left. And as Tallasee drove home, she vowed to start taking her own advice.

Chapter Seventeen

Charley's job, according to Quentin's plan, was to offer Lucas the bait. They worked out exactly what Charley would say, then rehearsed it several times, with Quentin playing Lucas's role. Nuance was everything, he said.

"You want to tell him enough so that he'll understand this is the night to act," Quentin instructed, "but not so much as to make him wonder why you're telling him so much."

Charley never had met a more orderly person than Quentin. Virtually everything he and Tallasee would do or utter that afternoon was scripted. They talked about what they should say, then they said it to hear how it sounded. Then Quentin would speculate about what could be misunderstood or misleading, and they would make adjustments and go though it all again. "It's standard preparation for trial," he said, and by the time they were done, Charley understood its value: even though it really only took an hour or so, by the end, he was utterly focused on the task at hand.

Before they went their separate ways for the afternoon, Tallasee mentioned the sheriff. "I suppose I ought to call Johnny Carver now and tell him my negatives and files are safe at the house," she said. "We might as well let him off the hook. He's probably fretted long enough."

Quentin nodded. "Don't tell him I'm here, of course. Most sheriffs tend to be touchy about their territories. I'll deal with any jurisdictional dispute only when I have to. If I have to at all."

"Listen, if you solve his problem for him, he'll probably kiss you," Tallasee said.

"You think I'd come all the way from Atlanta for anything less?" Quentin said. Charley tried to ignore the look that passed between them.

●

Lucas was awake when Charley arrived. The food was gone, but Lucas looked edgy and bored as he sat on the cot. "Where the hell have you been?" he demanded.

"I had to tend to some things," Charley said. "That fire created all kinds of problems."

"What fire?" he said. "You mean that thing last night?"

Charley, thanks to the long rehearsal, knew to be careful to not reveal arson was suspected. "Yeah, remember? Tallasee, that woman I work for, her studio burned down last night. Everything's a big mess.

"It could have been worse, though," he added after a moment.

"Worse how?"

Tie your shoe or something, Quentin had said. It's casual conversation. You can't be obvious about it. We want him to see the bait, not the hook. Charley busied himself with collecting the food remains on the floor by the cot.

"We thought at first all her pictures had been destroyed," he answered. "But as it turns out, everything was at her house. So she didn't really lose much."

Don't watch for his reaction, Quentin had said. Give him a moment.

Charley nudged open the door and threw the apple core into the woods behind the house, then set the plate on the workbench to be collected when he left. "And now it's your job to clean up, right?" Lucas said, making the next step easy.

"Yeah, eventually. Not today, though. We're supposed to meet an insurance adjuster there, but he can't come 'til nine this evening. They told me not to touch anything until he examines the damage. Apparently it's going to take a while."

Finished. Charley's job was to let Lucas know the photos were safe at Tallasee's house—that he'd failed to destroy them after all—and that the house would be empty tonight.

Quentin's theory, of course, was that anyone who takes advantage of a second chance necessarily was involved in the first.

●

Reinforcements had arrived by the time Charley got back to Tallasee's house. Quentin introduced him as Pete and said he was a surveillance expert, but to Charley and Tallasee he clearly was a cop, with the badge of some state agency attached to his belt and a gun in a holster on his hip. Pete didn't say much, only nodding in their direction when introductions were made, but he became chatty when he learned that Tallasee was a photographer. He'd hauled a huge black case from the trunk of his car, and he invited her to hover over it as he detailed its contents: several cameras, special lenses, and a collection of lights that Pete called his "slave units."

Quentin's plan was meticulous yet simple. It rested on a pair of assumptions. Actually, the first of them—that the fire the previous night indeed had been arson—didn't remain an assumption for long. Shortly after Tallasee called him, Johnny Carver called back to say the fire marshal had concluded that it indeed had been set. But the second assumption—that Tallasee's photographs were the arsonist's target—would not be so easily confirmed. They would only know that if he came.

"What we do," Quentin explained, "is let the suspect come to believe his job is unfinished, but that he has another opportunity to wrap it up. Then we let our expert here"—he nodded in Pete's direction—"build a snare for us."

It took Pete a couple of hours, even with Tallasee's help. They spent a long time choosing exactly where to set his cameras, squinting through the lenses as they told Charley—the stand-in for the bad guy—to move this way or that as they made sure the photo would capture him regardless of where in the room he stood. Once the cameras were placed to their satisfaction, and once Quentin and Charley were instructed to keep well clear of their tripods lest even a mild nudge alter the view the lens would see, Pete and Tallasee arranged the lights. They made the room as dark as possible, shutting blinds and draping towels wherever the light leaked through, then set three lights in places chosen only after Pete had tripped the flash mechanism countless times, taking readings on his light meter as he did. When he was satisfied there was not an inadvertent dark corner available—a place, he said, that long experience had taught him that a bad guy will always somehow find—they finally were done. In the meantime, Charley had learned why the lights were called slave units: only one of them was connected directly to the cameras; the other two had sensors built in, and they would be tripped when the light from the first flash reached them.

The cameras would be activated every time someone stepped on the weight-sensitive wires that had been arranged under the braided rug, Pete explained. "We don't put any of the leads near the door," he said. "We want him all the way in the room when he hits one. But I can tell you almost exactly what'll happen then. The first time the lights flash, he won't know what the hell it is. He'll be dead still for a moment. Then he'll take another step, hit another lead, and they'll flash again. Then he'll bolt. He'll probably hit one more on his way out, but we may not get a full flash on the last one. Sometimes it takes the lights a second or so to recharge after they've been tripped, so if he's moving fast we may not get a good shot."

Still, they had two cameras in the room and the prospect of at least two good shots from each. "I'll get you a picture of him," Pete said. "There's no hiding from me."

●

After the trap was set, Quentin and Pete left for a while, saying they wanted to eat. Tallasee still had food in the kitchen, but when they'd finished arranging the lights, the house suddenly felt claustrophobic. She suspected dinner was just their excuse to get out for a while. Besides, Tallasee had seen Pete whispering to Quentin at one point, and he wasn't being as quiet as he thought.

"Are we going to take this guy down if he doesn't come along?" she heard him mutter. Quentin shook his head, but that only meant they'd talk about it later. So, Tallasee thought, the boys are going to go off to check their ammo or whatever it is men do, while she and Charley stayed behind and did what women do: tidy up. She could tell Charley wanted to be with them.

The phone rang a few minutes after they'd left. It was Quentin.

"I'm getting old and feeble," he said. "I forgot about your car."

"What about it?" she asked.

"It has to be wherever you're supposed to be tonight. You have to think like a bad guy. What would you conclude if you saw the car in the driveway?"

"That I was still home."

"That's my girl," he said. "Not only beautiful, but smart, too."

"And talented," she added. "I probably ought to park as close to the studio as I can."

"We'll pick you up there in ten minutes," Quentin said, then hung up.

●

They all had something to eat, as it turned out. Tallasee found a parking spot about a half block from the studio, and as Pete had put his car in Barrington's only municipal parking lot, they crammed into Quentin's government-issue Ford and drove to the edge of town. They ate in the car at a drive-in, parking far enough away from the other cars to give them privacy, but annoying the waitress who had to haul their food an unreasonably long distance.

"You figure a nice tip will make her feel better about things?" Quentin asked as she marched away sullenly with their order.

"How much do you plan on leaving?" Tallasee said. "It's going to take a lot to make her forget she's got fat arms. And she probably lives in a trailer, too."

He pondered for a moment, then said, "Yeah, some things you just don't forget."

She doubted that he was talking only about the waitress. At least, she hoped not.

●

They got back to Tallasee's house about thirty minutes before dark, and parked two blocks away—"think like a bad guy," Quentin repeated when Tallasee cocked a questioning eyebrow at him. They walked the rest of the way, approaching from the rear after tromping over a neighbor's lawn. Going directly to the garage, which sat about forty feet behind the house, they huddled in its middle. The light outside was fading quickly, and it already was gloomy in the garage.

"Now we wait," Quentin said, his voice low. "Do you have any lawn chairs in here?"

Tallasee pointed to a pair of folding, web-seated chairs hanging on a hook on the back wall. Quentin stepped lightly as he eased them off the hook and unfolded them, setting them on the floor in the darkest corner. His caution was infectious; they all had slowed their breathing and begun moving with an exaggerated carefulness. Pete found a crate and moved it to the wall just to the side of the window, from which he could see the back of the house.

There was something by the door that Tallasee didn't notice until her eyes adjusted to the dim light: a large fire extinguisher, like the ones often seen scattered around commercial buildings. She figured it must have been a chemical extinguisher, because instead of a hose it had a great nozzle that looked like a blunderbuss that a Puritan would have carried three hundred years ago. Quentin saw her looking at it.

"We put it there earlier," he whispered, his breath warm in her ear. "We borrowed your clothesline, too." She leaned toward him to ask why he needed it, but before she could speak he pushed his forefinger against his lips. There would be no more talking.

Pete settled onto the crate, putting his elbows on his knees and leaning forward a little. He'd found an old towel in the garage and had folded it carefully several times to make a pad for his seat. It was his only concession to comfort: Tallasee sensed he was a man accustomed to spending long watchful hours in these kinds of situations.

Quentin and Tallasee sat in the lawn chairs. He'd motioned Charley toward one of them, but Charley had only shaken his head. He seemed fretful and morose. He paced around the garage until he felt Quentin staring at him in silent disapproval, then sat on the floor and leaned his back against the wall opposite from Pete. For a long time, the quiet was breached only by the occasional rustle as one of them shifted their weight to get more comfortable as some part of a leg or buttock became numb from sitting. Only Pete seemed capable of remaining totally motionless. At one point, Tallasee felt Quentin moving and suddenly his hand was clasping hers. She smiled for a long time in the dark.

Their man came an hour later.

●

Pete alerted them by tapping a fingernail on the side of the crate three quick times, then raised his hand, palm out, to dissuade any of them from getting up and looking out the window. They had sat in the dark for so long that their eyes had adjusted to a catlike effectiveness.

They stayed absolutely still. A couple of times, Tallasee thought she heard a noise from the other side of the garage wall, but when she listened for the sound, it never was there. Then, suddenly, a shape passed by the window, headed toward the house. She felt Quentin's hand tighten in hers and saw Pete press his head into the wall next to the window, hoping to not be seen if the shadow looked back. A moment later, Pete leaned forward again and peered out the window, then pointed at the front corner of the garage. The shadow was standing there.

Tallasee then heard a familiar noise. It stirred some atavistic memory deep in her brain, but even though she'd heard it before, she couldn't identify it. When she heard it a second time, she got closer but it still eluded her. It wasn't until she heard it the third time—and when the light mounted on a pole in front of the garage, which she had turned on at Quentin's suggestion, suddenly went dark, followed by the tinkling sound of glass falling on the driveway—that she knew what it was. Any Southern girl with a brother would recognize the sound of an air rifle. The shadow had shot out the light.

For what seemed like a long time, but probably was only a few minutes, nothing happened. The shadow waited to see if any neighbor had heard the sound and would seek to investigate. No one came, but still he waited. Tallasee imagined she could feel Quentin's pulse through his hand, but of course it was only her own. Her every sense had been heightened: There was an odd, metallic taste in her mouth, and she could almost feel the design of the lawn chair's webbing through her pants. What would have been considered a quiet night any other time instead seemed like a cacophony. She heard far-off car horns, a train whistle, the whisper of someone's television set, and the slap of a screen door somewhere followed by a mother's shouted instruction to not leave the yard. The slightest breeze that barely would have stirred a curtain in her house that night seemed to be so brisk as to threaten to take the leaves from the trees.

Then—again—there was the sound of glass shattering. This time, Tallasee knew immediately what it was. He'd broken one of the panes in her back door. Pete and Quentin stood at the same instant, although Pete raised his hand once more. Easy. Easy. After a moment, he pointed to the small door adjacent to the garage's car-sized entry. He and Quentin tiptoed to the door and Pete pulled it open an inch or so, peering toward the house.

"Let's go," he whispered suddenly. They pushed their way through the door and ran toward the house. Charley and Tallasee had been told to stay in the garage, but they violated the spirit of that order by pulling open the side door to watch. Tallasee knew she would hear from Quentin about this later, but she didn't care. Still, she grabbed Charley's arm to keep him from going any farther than the doorway.

The plan was almost comically simple. Pete and Quentin ran silently to the back door and crouched on either side of the steps leading down from it. They had uncoiled the clothesline so that each long end of it was draped over the side of the steps, invisible in the dark, and now they each grabbed one end of the line and pulled against it, lifting it about a foot high. They had just gotten set when the flash went off the first time.

He'd left the back door open when he'd gone inside, so in that instant when the light poured from the doorway Tallasee could see Pete and Quentin in silhouette, straining against each other like a tableau painted on an ancient vase. Just as Pete had predicted, the flash went off a second time a couple of moments later, and then again a moment after that.

The man came out the door almost at the same instant the third flash was tripped. Even if he'd seen the clothesline stretched in front of him, he was moving too quickly to stop. But Tallasee didn't think he saw it. The line caught him just above his shin and he went down hard. If he'd been on level ground, he wouldn't have had time to even get his arms in front of him to break the fall, but the fact there were three steps down to the yard was a perverse blessing: he was able to get his hands out, but it also meant he fell farther and hit harder. He was turned toward the garage as he fell, and even in the dark Tallasee noticed that his mouth was pulled open as his face skidded along her brick walkway.

Still, there was flight in him. Although obviously dazed, he was pushing himself up and moving his legs when Pete sprung from his spot next to the steps and planted a knee into the man's back. There was no hesitancy or gentleness in him. Pete had all his weight pressed down between the man's shoulder blades, and with a practiced motion he jerked the man's hands behind him and cuffed them. Only then did he roll off the man's back, remaining on the ground next to him with a hand on his shoulder.

It all happened in just a few seconds. Quentin was ready to help, but Pete had been so quick and efficient that he was left only to stand nearby. Quentin still had his tie on, and he must have been filled with a sudden feeling of being a Boy Scout pretending to be a tough guy.

He looked in Tallasee's direction and she could sense him grinning. "I've got to get out of the office more," he said.

Charley and Tallasee walked over to them. Pete produced a penlight from a pocket and shined it on the man on the ground. For a moment, no one spoke as everyone stared at him in disbelief.

It was Quentin who finally uttered what they all were thinking.

"Well, Charley," he said. "You were right."

Chapter Eighteen

Charley was sure he never would live through another day as profoundly strange as the next twenty-four hours turned out to be. It was to be expected, though. When your sheriff is charged in the death of a runaway boy—with breaking and entering, arson, and drug dealing thrown in for good measure—it's a sure bet that things are going to be unsettled.

Quentin, however, didn't let his surprise paralyze him. He knew exactly what to do. He and Pete took Johnny Carver back inside Tallasee's house and sat him down at the kitchen table, his hands still cuffed behind him. When the lights were turned on, they found a plastic milk jug on its side in the room off the back porch where the cameras had been set up. It had been filled with gasoline, half of which spilled when Johnny had dropped the jug after the flash was fired. Most of the gas had been soaked up by the braided rug near the door, but the smell was overwhelming. Tallasee moved to clean it up.

"Let me do it," Pete said. He stuck his little finger into the jug's opening and carefully tilted it upright, then lifted it a few inches with the crook of his finger. "Toss that rug in the yard," he said to Charley. After Charley had dragged the rug outside, Pete set the jug back down exactly where they'd found it.

"Prop the door open and put a fan on that spot," Pete instructed Charley when he came back in. "We'll be all right in a few minutes. Gas evaporates quick."

When they returned to the kitchen, Quentin was just hanging up the telephone. "Who are you people?" Johnny asked.

"Sheriff, my name is Quentin Mackie. I'm with the state attorney general's office. That fellow whose knee you've recently become acquainted with is Peter Carr, of the state bureau of investigation. I believe you know Miss Tynan and young Mr. Selkirk."

"What'd you boys do? Set a camera up in there?"

Quentin nodded. "I'll bet we have a fine portrait of you. We can make you some wallet-sized prints, if you'd like."

"Nah, I never took a very good picture," Johnny answered. He then looked over at Pete. "It ain't going to be that easy next time. You might want to bring some help."

The way Pete grinned made Charley think that he wouldn't need help.

"There's not likely to be a next time, sheriff," Quentin corrected him. At that moment, the phone rang.

"That'll be the attorney general," Quentin said. "I'd better take it in the next room."

●

Quentin had to get approval from his boss before actually arresting Johnny Carver. But, as he explained to Tallasee and Charley later, he didn't expect a problem, and he didn't get one. "He's a tough old scoundrel," Quentin said. "Likes to mix it up occasionally. And it helps that I've won a couple of cases for him that he didn't expect to win."

Still, the attorney general hated a surprise. "He was pretty unhappy that I'd set this up without his knowledge and approval. He's got this great, rumbling voice, and he says"—Quentin lowered his voice in imitation—" 'Mr. Mackie, first you tell me you've taken into custody the longest-serving sheriff in the state of Georgia without first offering me the courtesy of a little warning. Then you tell me that the only member of your little band of schemers who even suspected the sheriff of any wrongdoing is a high school dropout. Who is this young man? Perhaps I should have him supervising you, considering I don't seem to be doing a very effective job of it myself.' "

"I hope you explained I'm not a dropout," Charley said. "I was kicked out of school."

"Yeah," added Tallasee, "that sounds a lot better. Not stupid, just a juvenile delinquent."

Quentin shook his head ruefully. "Instinct counts for something," he said. "But that was a lot to hang on one simple photograph."

Charley had felt a tickle in the back of his mind the morning they sat in Johnny Carver's office and showed him the picture of the boy. Until that moment, Johnny had been relaxed and normal. After seeing the picture, however, Charley realized that Johnny seemed to choose his words very carefully. Tallasee later claimed that she didn't see any difference in Johnny, but Charley could tell. When you live in a house where not much is said, your hearing gets real good.

Then, after they had driven to Pearlie Bullock's house and Charley saw the same picture on her kitchen table—the copy they'd left with her that first time he and Tallasee had gone there, when she'd asked them to find her grandson—Charley knew that Johnny was caught up in this somehow. He'd been in that same kitchen just a day or two before, probably had sat at the old woman's table while interviewing her son, and surely had seen the picture. Johnny couldn't have missed it. She'd propped it up against the napkin holder, with the salt and pepper shakers parked at each corner to keep it from sliding down. You only had to look at Johnny's office walls, with their collection of odd items, to see he didn't miss much. He'd seen the photograph at Pearlie Bullock's house, then pretended he was seeing it for the first time when Tallasee showed it to him. Why?

Quentin, with the benefit of hindsight, declared that there was a simple answer: Johnny just wasn't too smart. "He walks into this old woman's kitchen, a routine investigation into what was clearly a natural death, and there's a picture of a boy he'd accidentally killed just a couple of months before. It rattles him. Then a couple of days later, you two are in his office, showing him the same picture and telling him you've been nosing around the commune, asking about this same boy. Worse yet, he's been lifting drugs from the evidence bin and selling them to this guy Osage. So he has a typically guilty reaction. He says nothing, because he isn't sure exactly what's going on and he wants to hear more about what you know."

Charley pondered this for a moment, then said, "But it could have been so easy for him. All he would have had to say is, 'You know, I just saw this picture two days ago.' No one would have suspected anything. We still thought Lucas was our guy at that point."

Quentin nodded his agreement. "That's what I mean. A smart person sticks close to the truth. Look at it this way: You're one of four things—dumb and guilty, dumb and innocent, smart and guilty, or smart and innocent. Being any one of three of those things will prompt you to just admit you've seen the picture, because you're either smart enough to know it's not incriminating in and of itself, or because you're innocent and have nothing to hide. But when you're dumb *and* guilty, your first instinct is to cover things up." With a touch of wonder in his voice, Quentin added, "You'd expect better from a cop."

"But why does he burn up all my stuff?" Tallasee asked.

"It's another dumb move. When you showed him the other pictures you had, the ones of Lucas looking guilty and ducking into the bushes—which of course we now know was because he's an army deserter—Johnny begins to wonder what else you've got on film. He wonders if he's going to turn up in a picture he didn't know was taken, and that he'll wish hadn't been taken. So he sends the two of you on the mission to Mrs. Bullock's, and, because he's dumb, he doesn't realize you'll also see the picture there on the table. While you're gone, he burns the studio down to destroy whatever pictures of him may exist."

"Who would have thought Johnny Carver had that in him?" Tallasee mused. "The worst thing ever said about him was that he liked to carry on with women."

"I don't think he does have it in him. Or he didn't at first," Quentin said. "He's a little dumb and a little greedy. He was selling drugs for pocket change. Every once in a while, when the confiscated drugs had accumulated to a certain point and he figured some if it wouldn't be missed, he took them up to the commune and sold them. He only dealt with Osage, so it was a low-risk enterprise. Until, of course, he accidentally killed that boy, when the stakes became a lot higher. Then he was willing to commit arson to protect himself. That's how it happens—corruption is a series of small surrenders. Johnny eventually might have found it necessary to deal with Osage." Quentin's tone turned ironic. "You never know about those hippies—they get hopped up on drugs, resist arrest, and sometimes unfortunate things happen during the struggle to subdue them."

"But fate gave him Lucas instead," Tallasee said.

"Indeed it did," Quentin said. "It must have seemed like a godsend. An army deserter, already known for his erratic behavior. I think Lucas also would have ended up resisting arrest. Everything would have been pinned on him after he was dead."

●

As it turned out, Lucas didn't resist arrest at all. He went along quietly.

Tallasee and Charley stayed at her house after Quentin and Pete had taken Johnny away to be interviewed. They stepped around the jug of gas on the floor—Pete had declared it evidence and instructed them to not touch it—but otherwise straightened up, sweeping broken glass and returning the clothesline to the garage. Charley cut a pane-sized piece of cardboard and taped it into the spot where the window had been set into the door.

"Nice work," Tallasee said. "Could be the start of a whole new look for this place. Maybe I should haul my mattress out and throw it into the yard."

Quentin called around midnight. He told Tallasee that Johnny had admitted to killing the boy, and that he would be taken to court the following morning to be arraigned. Quentin then asked to speak to Charley.

"This is going to be very big news tomorrow," he told Charley. "A lot of people are going to be here. Reporters from Atlanta, TV crews, people like that. I'll be required to explain to the judge how we came to believe the sheriff was involved in criminal activity. And because"—Quentin paused for a moment—"because it wouldn't be right for me to pretend that I even suspected it, your name is going to come up."

Charley could hear the bemusement in his voice. Quentin had been too polite to openly scoff at Charley's suggestion that Johnny was their man, and had even agreed that the sheriff and Lucas should be told the same stories, that each should have the same bait dangled before them. But he had only been humoring Charley—everyone expected Lucas to show up at Tallasee's house. Now, as he'd had to do with the attorney general, he'd have to tell the judge that the trap set for one person snared another.

"So, people are going to want to talk to you," Quentin concluded. "My advice is that you not say anything, because we still have a case to make. But they'll have the cameras on while you're not saying anything. Do you have a suit?"

"No," Charley answered, then explained pointedly: "Can't afford one. I haven't gotten paid yet this summer." Tallasee rolled her eyes.

"Doesn't matter," Quentin said. "Just tuck in your shirttail and make sure you shave. For maybe the only time in your life, you'll be the object of desire in the morning."

"What do I do with Lucas?" Charley asked. "As far as I know, he's still at my house."

"Well, I'm not sure," Quentin admitted. "Technically, he's a fugitive, but that's the federal government's worry, not mine. Still, I probably should let the U.S. attorney's office know where he is." He paused for a moment. "For some reason, that doesn't taste right, though."

"No, it doesn't," Charley said. "But he'll probably be gone by tomorrow."

"Especially if he has a good reason," Quentin said. He didn't elaborate, but Charley knew what he meant.

They hung up and Charley went home. Even this late, he wasn't surprised to find his mother still sitting at the kitchen table. "Is everything all right?" she asked.

"Johnny Carver got arrested tonight. Turns out he's the one who burned Tallasee's studio. He might have killed somebody, too."

Charley expected this to be jaw-dropping news, but she only nodded. "It ain't enough," she said cryptically. Suddenly, Charley understood his mother somehow was involved in this, that she knew things he didn't. He stared at her for a moment, and Frances returned his look with a level gaze of her own. She seemed to expect him to ask something.

"Has something happened I don't know about?" Charley said.

"Honey, it's been a long time since we had a good talk," she said.

"But this ain't the time to have it. I just hope everything turns out all right for you and your girlfriend." There it was again: *girlfriend.*

Lucas didn't even say that much. He, too, was awake, still sitting on the cot with a sense of coiled purpose that suddenly was apparent to Charley. The night before, Charley impulsively had told Lucas of his suspicion that Johnny was somehow at the center of things. Tallasee for weeks had not wanted to be bothered with any of it, and of course Quentin, whose calm and methodical style was so immediately soothing to Charley, wouldn't show up until the next morning. So Charley had confided in the one person who, in a perverse way, seemed to care about what had happened to that boy.

Now Charley just wanted Lucas to forget about it. He told Lucas that he had a half a day's head start before federal officials were told where he was, and offered to drive Lucas to the Atlanta Highway, where a friendly motorist looking for company could have him miles away in minutes. But Lucas wouldn't leave and he wouldn't talk. Charley went to bed with a terrible sense of foreboding.

●

Quentin had told Tallasee and Charley to meet him downtown the next morning for breakfast, but when Charley got to Tallasee's house, he found Quentin there, finishing the meal that she'd obviously just made for him. Quentin's hair was wet and he'd shaved, but he was wearing the same clothes. He evidently had not planned to be in Barrington this long.

"Do you want to hear about it?" he asked as Charley entered the kitchen. "I think we're about to put this one in the win column."

Quentin told them about Johnny's confession, and of the surreal moment when the sheriff was booked into his own jail by one of his own deputies, who was so unnerved by the sudden appearance of his boss in handcuffs that Johnny ended up writing his own name in the jail log, grinning cockily as he did. Pete had been left behind at the jail, Quentin said, "to make sure the sovereignty of the state's law-enforcement apparatus is observed."

"In other words, to remind them there's a bigger dog in the yard now," Tallasee said.

"That's right," Quentin confirmed happily.

He stood and finished his coffee. "Come down to the courthouse in an hour or so. We'll be bringing him in then. It's a sight you're not likely to see again."

"Do you figure anybody's going to know you're wearing women's underpants?" Tallasee asked.

Quentin blushed. "I didn't have any clean underwear," he explained to Charley. "I had to borrow some."

"Try not to stretch them out," Tallasee said.

"My butt's not that big," he said.

"I wasn't talking about your butt," she replied.

Still blushing, he departed. Tallasee and Charley left about forty-five minutes later, and found that the block around the courthouse already had become busy. Just as Quentin predicted, the news had traveled and the Atlanta television stations had responded, setting up their cameras on the sidewalk and interviewing the local citizenry, some of whom were hearing the tale for the first time and giving the surprised reactions the news crews hoped for. At exactly nine o'clock, with Quentin's sense of punctuality apparent only to Charley and Tallasee, a car driven by Pete pulled up to the side door of the courthouse. He and Quentin got out, while two deputies emerged from a car that had followed them to the entrance. Pete opened the back door of the car he'd driven and helped Johnny out. Everyone's attention was focused on the two men, who were standing by the car as Johnny regarded the crowd, which in turn regarded him as they nudged and whispered among themselves. No one saw Lucas. When a second round of television interviews was later done, not a single person could claim they'd seen him lay the rifle across the top of a parked car across the street and fire it.

His Marine Corps training had held. He needed only one round, which hit Johnny square in the chest. Afterward, Lucas just left the rifle sitting on top of the car and waited. He didn't resist arrest.

Chapter Nineteen

Many things changed that day. Some were apparent to Tallasee right away, others unfolded themselves gradually over the next few weeks, and a few weren't revealed for years. But she believed that the changes were all for the good. Somehow, the world became a better place when Johnny Carver departed from it.

It was interesting for her to review the reports of Johnny's death and its aftermath, to track the slow shift of perception through newspaper articles. The first day's reports, as might be expected, focused on the murder, barely acknowledging the fact that Johnny was in custody and about to be charged with crimes. In fact, one early wire-service version of the story thoroughly garbled the facts, asserting that Johnny was working with state officials on an arson investigation when he was killed by a suspect. But the whole event was too profoundly interesting for a one-day treatment, so reporters who had the luxury of spending whatever time it took to separate facts from lore eventually were able to sketch very deft portraits of both Johnny and Lucas. By the time they were finished, careful readers were ready to believe Lucas had performed a service to mankind.

Tallasee realized Quentin had been only half-right about the sheriff. Johnny Carver indeed had not plunged into criminal behavior; he'd descended into it slowly, in small steps that were ultimately laid out in the mercilessly stark pages of the newspaper. But where Quentin had believed it to be an inadvertent descent—a series of bad decisions and small compromises of integrity that had led to a tragic accident—the reality was much darker. As more and more people came forth to reveal things they had hidden away within themselves, to tell how some encounter with the sheriff had left them humiliated and scarred, it became clear this was not an example of how small things can pile up and overwhelm someone. If Johnny's embrace of wickedness was slow and prolonged, it was only because he took care to ensure he'd gotten away with one evil deed before moving on to a more ambitious one.

There were a couple of accounts of late-night traffic stops involving teenage boys who, after making the mistake of not being sufficiently respectful, found the sheriff on them with a sudden, vicious fury. There was the heartbreaking tale of a Mexican man, a fruit picker working illegally in Florida, who kept his life's savings in cash because he didn't trust banks to not turn him in and who had the bad luck to get lost in Johnny's jurisdiction while on his way to see his sister in New York, with the result being that Johnny decided his life's savings would be an appropriate fine to be exacted for turning without signaling. Mostly, though, the stories came from women: Johnny had a taste for what police reports blandly call nonconsensual relations. He had a nose for despair and vulnerability, and was alert for situations in which sex could be coerced from a woman who otherwise would have to choose between paying a traffic ticket or paying the rent. Sometimes, he didn't even bother with coercion; a pair of teenage girls finally came forth separately to report that Johnny had raped them in his car after following them at night for miles before stopping them on an empty stretch of highway. Both girls described identical sensations of growing fear as they became aware that the same set of headlights had been behind them for many long minutes; giddiness when the sheriff's flashing lights came on and they realized they were in for a traffic ticket at worst, and not the drive-in movie–fueled image of horrible death they'd begun to form; unease as Johnny inspected their licenses and then ordered them to pull down a remote dirt lane out of view of any other passing car; and finally horror as he climbed atop them and made reality of their dark fears of just a few minutes before.

"He must have thought he was bulletproof. That nothing would happen to him," Quentin said one evening weeks later, as he and Tallasee picked over the story yet again. "And that was a literal belief, apparently. Did I tell you what I found out? It turns out Johnny was in combat during the Second World War. Serious combat. He took part in the invasion of one of the islands in the South Pacific, and every man in his unit was killed. When they found him, he was coated in the blood and flesh of his buddies. He wasn't hurt, but it affected his head, although not in the way you might think. He became convinced no harm would ever come to him, that no consequence would ever need be paid. Even that night after we caught him in your house and he told us what had happened, he wasn't making a confession." Quentin's face took on a look of wonder. "He seemed to be trying to help us understand how all this didn't amount to much."

Later, Tallasee concluded that it was a measure of the perverse nature of society's judgments that when Lucas reacted to the death of a child in an understandable way, he was declared to be crazy; but when Johnny seemed to simply swallow the horror he'd seen, no one realized it'd made him a monster. It was simply assumed he was made of sterner stuff.

Until his sordid past was uncovered, in fact, the only effect the war seemed to have had on Johnny was to make him averse to uniforms. He hardly ever wore his own. It was just one of life's sour little ironies that he had worn it on the day he visited the commune and caught the eye of Pearlie Bullock's young friend.

●

No one ever learned the boy's name. With the sort of radar his kind always seem to have, Osage—who might have known it—had sensed that things were about to become unpleasant, so he left. Johnny Carver had assumed Osage would testify against him, and in fact thought Osage already had provided evidence, which partially explained Johnny's unusual candor on the night he was captured. But at that moment, Quentin and Pete were hearing about the mysterious boy for the first time. When they visited the Rainbow Nation two days later, however, Osage was gone.

Many of the Rainbows were gone, actually. The few who remained were recent arrivals and didn't know the boy. But they grudgingly pointed out the trail to Blue Hole to Quentin and Pete, who easily found the spot where the path bent around a large rock outcropping. Minutes after that, they spotted an unnatural mound on the forest floor.

They returned the next day with help. The body was uncovered and trundled down the path to a gleaming ambulance, which was parked incongruously next to a rusted Volkswagen van with a peace sign painted on its nose. The autopsy showed the death had happened just as Johnny said it did: the boy had been hit on the head, but there were no other injuries to him.

There was nothing in his pockets to indicate who he was, and no Rainbow came forth with any personal possessions. Various missing-person reports were collected and examined, but none matched, and a thorough search of Pearlie Bullock's near-empty home, grudgingly allowed by her son, turned up nothing. Even dental records would have been of no help because, as the coroner later determined, the boy had apparently never in his short life visited a dentist.

No one ever claimed him. Officials held the body for several months before finally burying him in the municipal cemetery, marking the spot with a temporary metal marker. It was the only proof that the boy had ever existed, and it lasted only until the day a graveyard employee accidentally ran over the marker with a tractor and replaced it with an uncarved stone from the maintenance shed.

●

Tallasee and Charley learned the tale of Lucas and Shorty only later. Like Johnny's story, that story also eventually unfolded itself in the newspaper. But the reporters had trouble with Lucas: he seemed to deserve a little understanding, yet he'd killed a defenseless, unarmed man. Tallasee, having spent time on the edge of the publishing business, understood the problem of trying to write the first draft of history and perform analysis at the same time. You may know enough to explain things, but not so much as to actually understand them.

As time went on and details emerged, however, the appropriate balance of feeling about Lucas was reached. A horrible thing had happened to a Vietnamese child, almost surely but inadvertently as a result of Lucas's friendship with him; then, later, as Lucas found himself feeling protective of another young man—someone who, like Shorty, suddenly appeared one day, apparently without family or support in the world—something horrible happened to him, too. The combination of those things, Lucas's lawyers successfully argued, put him out of his mind. His reaction was to eliminate the thing that had caused such profound unhappiness, and that thing was Johnny Carver.

But, of course, you can't go around shooting the people who make you unhappy, prosecutors responded. However deserving Johnny may have been, and however unhinged Lucas may have been, lawmen could not simply shrug their shoulders and call it even. Thus, Lucas, found unfit to stand trial, was committed to an institution for the criminally insane. What worked for him once, though, didn't work a second time. The fence around the institution slowed him down, made it harder to leave than the military hospital he'd previously fled. And the guard in the tower must have been profoundly unhappy to see Lucas clambering over the wire one afternoon shortly after his arrival.

The rules were different for the guard—it was permissible for him to shoot the thing that made him unhappy. So he did.

●

Still, there was a single enduring mystery out of the whole affair. Lucas somehow had obtained a gun and known where to be that morning. Lucas himself, before he died, claimed that he'd stolen the gun from a house the morning he shot Johnny, but gave only a vague description of the home. Also, no homeowner came forth to report a burglary. And when asked how he'd known the sheriff would be taken to court that morning, Lucas had only shrugged. Just guessed, he said.

Only Quentin and Tallasee knew Lucas had been in Charley's care the night before Johnny was killed. Quentin had a long, private talk about it with Charley, and after that no investigator felt the need to pursue the subject.

But Tallasee did. "Did Charley give him the gun?" she asked Quentin later.

"He says he didn't," Quentin answered.

"Do you believe him?"

"Yes."

"Does he know who did?" she persisted.

"He says he doesn't."

"Do you believe him?"

"What I believe is that there's a point where no more justice can be served," Quentin said. "The official record of this case shows Charley knows nothing about the gun."

"So that's it? It just remains a mystery?"

"Life isn't always as tidy as we'd like it to be."

"A few years ago, you'd have had a note written on your calendar that said, 'Solve gun mystery, one-thirty to two-thirty,' " Tallasee said.

"Yeah," he replied, "and a few years ago you'd have told me to stop obsessing on it. So we seem to have switched roles."

There was no anger in the conversation. Quentin and Tallasee never were apart again after that summer. For a while, he spent his weekends in Barrington, driving up on Friday evenings and departing at dawn Monday. Eventually, though, he resigned from the state attorney general's office and opened a practice in a building not far from Tallasee's newly rebuilt studio. They often had lunch together, sometimes in the lunchroom at Corey's department store, and a few times they saw Frances Selkirk there. The first time it happened, Tallasee felt uneasy, but the feeling had not lasted. Frances had waved a cheery hello, and later, when she stopped by their table to fill them in on Charley's progress at college, she had been perfectly friendly, although in a remote and noncommittal way. In fact, Tallasee saw that the passing of time somehow had made Frances seem younger and lighter, as if an ailment of her own had been cured that night when both Tallasee and Lucas showed up at her house.

Tallasee never told Quentin what had happened there. She suspected that he sensed it, and knew not to press for details. Charley also never brought it up. He'd come to understand that their moment together was exactly what she had predicted it would become: a great, nurturing secret, the memory of which could be invoked with only a smile or a look between them. Quentin never intruded on that, and, in fact, became a great friend to Charley. Even before the business with Lucas and Johnny, Tallasee had begun to suspect Charley was in that same deep hole where she'd been. Afterward, she felt guilty for having contributed to it. She had treated him badly all summer, making sure that he understood she thought the search for Pearlie Bullock's phantom grandson was a silly and pointless crusade. Then, when she felt that she was about to fall so far into the hole that she'd never emerge, Tallasee had literally grabbed him to save herself. He was a young man trying to grapple with his own set of problems—and doing it with more grace than most people muster—yet she believed she'd only contributed to his weight.

Her penance was to share Quentin with him. Charley and Quentin found something to do together each weekend, usually involving the death of innocent fish. In addition, shortly after Johnny's death, Quentin had called the administrators of Barrington High School and, after making clear that any clever lawyer would have a field day with their notions of due process, arranged for Charley to take a series of final exams, which he passed because he was smart and because Quentin called him every night to make sure he'd studied. Then, when Charley had his diploma, Quentin nagged him until he applied for admission to the university, and he nagged Tallasee until she agreed to pay for tuition and books during Charley's first year.

"Consider it a penalty for your use of unpaid labor this summer," he said.

"I did pay him," Tallasee protested. It was true: she'd eventually written Charley a check for every hour he'd worked.

"It wasn't enough," Quentin said.

"You don't even know how much it was," she protested. "Besides, what are you contributing to his welfare?"

"I'm his spiritual adviser," he replied loftily. "I'm going to teach him how to meet women."

Tallasee lifted her eyes toward heaven. "Oh, great. The no-money-for-lunch trick gets passed to a new generation."

●

Actually, Charley didn't need Quentin's advice.

A couple of weeks after the fire, Charley came home one afternoon to find Dorothy sitting on his front step, the car she'd gotten as a graduation gift parked at the curb. Unbeknownst to Charley, a bag on the backseat contained a pair of toothbrushes, a change of clothes she'd appropriated from Charley's dresser with Frances's connivance, and a few things for herself. A box and cooler in the trunk held enough food for a few simple meals.

"I've got something I want to show you," Dorothy greeted him.

"Is this your car?" Charley asked, assuming the vehicle was what she had to show. "It's nice."

"Yeah, Daddy got it for me. He says I'll need it at school."

The things Quentin would do for Charley were still ahead of him, so the reminder that other people had happy futures awaiting them made him glum. "I suppose you will," Charley said vaguely.

"We'd better go," Dorothy said.

"Go where?" Charley asked.

She grinned, enjoying his confusion. "I said I had something to show you. C'mon, we'd better get going."

They drove for a long time, into another part of the mountains away from the commune and Pearlie Bullock's home. At a place where several mailboxes hugged the side of the highway, Dorothy turned on to a dirt road that followed a stream spilling down from a nearby ridge. They passed several cabins, then slowed to a crawl as she eased the car over a low spot in the road where a trickle of water found its way to the larger branch. A half mile beyond, the road ended at another cabin, a comfortably rustic place perched over the stream. Dorothy parked by the door and they got out.

"It's my uncle's place," she said. "He lets me use it once in a while."

"Is this what you wanted to show me?" Charley said.

Her talk with Tallasee had made Dorothy bold. "No, not exactly," she said, then took Charley's hand and led him inside. It was hours before they unloaded the car. They stayed for two days, not seeing another soul the whole time, and when they left Charley was confident that no man would ever have the chance to ask what fool had let this treasure slip away.

Years later, in the week following their graduation from the university, Dorothy and Charley were married. Tallasee's present to them was to photograph their wedding.

Her mother was happy to see that Tallasee had finally become a real photographer.

●

One spring morning nearly a year after the fire, Tallasee found a package awaiting her when she arrived at her studio. It was a basket, propped against the front door and carrying no note. She picked it up and took it inside.

It had been crudely woven from twigs, which had not been peeled when they were green and now left flakes of bark in her hand. But someone had invested much care in its creation. It was not utilitarian, having too coarse a weave to be useful, and not particularly ornamental. Yet it clearly had been made specially to accommodate the items it carried. Each of them was nestled in an indentation painstakingly formed to hold it, and all of them sat atop a small cloth spread in the middle of the basket and carefully pressed into the indentations. Tallasee could see that at several critical points, thread had been looped through the twigs to keep the cloth in place.

The items looked like treasures from a boy's secret cigar-box collection: a pocketknife, a pair of baseball cards, a foreign coin Tallasee didn't recognize, a pair of marbles, and a blue robin's egg that somehow had been preserved. She idly picked up the baseball cards and discovered a folded scrap of newspaper between them. Opening it, she saw a photo of a happy man dressed in the clothes of a leprechaun, standing in a stadium full of people. The caption beneath the photo, which had apparently been separated from an accompanying article, only said, "NOTRE DAME MASCOT PLEASED WITH PLAY OVER NAVY."

Tallasee realized that this was someone's memorial to the boy.

Wondering how recently the basket had been placed at her door, she returned to the sidewalk in front of the studio to look up and down the street. She saw no one or nothing out of the ordinary. She went back inside, placed the basket on a table, and sat and stared at it for a long time.

The boy had been a vaporous presence to many people, all of whom had imprinted their own needs or perceptions upon him. To Pearlie Bullock, he'd been an obliging and faithful visitor, a role long since abandoned by her own son. To Johnny Carver, he'd been a slow-witted annoyance, whose passing was of no more consequence than that of an animal that darts from the brush into the road in front of your car. To Lucas, he'd been a second chance, an innocent soul who, unlike Shorty, still could be saved from the horrors that otherwise surely awaited him. To Charley, he'd been a mission, the device by which he could bring some order and meaning to a life that seemed to have lost both. And Tallasee understood that to her, the boy had become a reminder of how quickly events can veer away from happiness and turn inexplicably, irretrievably dark.

"That poor child," she said out loud to herself.

Tallasee never learned how the basket came to appear at her door. She stored it on a shelf in the studio, away from curious eyes and careless fingers. She never showed it to Charley, because she realized that it was a memorial to him, too, in an odd way. But she kept the basket for years, sometimes taking it down and reminiscing for a while, turning over events in her mind and remembering the summer when Charley Selkirk became the best friend that a sad girl could hope for.

Chapter Twenty

Quentin knocked on the door, but Frances was opening it even as he did, as if she'd seen him come up the sidewalk and was waiting for him. For a moment, neither of them said anything, only looked at one another across the threshold. Quentin, as he gazed into her face, could see that she'd given Charley her eyes and nose.

He spoke first. "Mrs. Selkirk, my name is Quentin Mackie and—"

Frances interrupted him. "I know who you are. Please come in."

She had a manner about her that Quentin later would describe to Tallasee as "abruptly congenial," a combination of good manners and the unwillingness to invoke them insincerely. Frances left him just inside the front door as she tended to something in the kitchen, then returned. "What can I help you with?" she asked.

"I wondered if we could talk for a few minutes," Quentin said.

She nodded and led him back to the front porch. Two rocking chairs and a small table, all carrying the shine of newness, sat to one side of the door. "I realized recently I've spent entirely too much time sitting in my kitchen," Frances said as she gestured Quentin into one of the chairs. "I like it better out here. Somehow, wasting time doesn't seem like such a sin if you're doing it where the whole world can watch."

Quentin grinned. "Mrs. Selkirk—"

She interrupted him again. "My name is Frances. If you call me that again, I'll think you're here on official business." She gave him a long, steady look, then said, "Are you?"

"No, ma'am, it's not business." Indeed, Quentin carried no brief-case and had left his suit coat thrown over the seat in his car. It was a Friday afternoon, and he had left his Atlanta office early to drive to Barrington for what had become his regular weekend with Tallasee.

Two months had passed since Johnny Carver's death, and, in that time, the event officially had become a closed file. Its one lingering mystery had been written off as a minor dead end, not enough to warrant keeping open an investigation that otherwise was concluded. Quentin's appearance at her front door was the result of impulse and nonofficial curiosity.

"Then what can I help you with?" Frances repeated.

She seemed to Quentin like someone who appreciated a straightforward approach. "Did you know Lucas was here that night?" he asked.

Again, she held his eyes, only staring at him as several long moments passed. Quentin realized she had an uncommon gravity, the ability to tolerate silences in conversations as she mulled things. Like her face, it was something else that she'd passed to Charley.

"I thought you said this wasn't official," she finally said.

"It's not."

"Then why do you ask?"

"It's my curse to want to understand things," he answered. "The State of Georgia has no further interest in this matter, but I do. There's one thing Charley has told me that I'm not sure I believe. So I thought I'd ask you." He hesitated. "I like Charley. I think he's a fine young man. But this question has become like a stone in my shoe. I just want to know the answer so it'll go away."

"What use will you make of the answer?" Frances asked.

Quentin already had thought about this, already had settled the matter in his mind. His answer was immediate and sincere. "None. This is for my ears only."

Frances nodded, accepting that. "Well, of course I knew he was here. I saw him when he came to the door. But I suspect you actually want to know whether I knew he stayed here for two nights, right?"

"That's right," Quentin said, a little embarrassed by his sloppy question but thankful that it hadn't been asked in front of a judge and jury.

"Yes, I knew," she said.

"Do you know who gave him the gun?"

She was unflinching and direct. "Yes, I do."

Quentin paused for a moment, but Frances's candor made him decide that he could ask the question now. "Was it Charley?"

"No, it wasn't."

As soon as she said it, it hit him. "Did *you* give him the gun?" he asked, knowing what the answer would be.

Her response was no less prompt than the others had been. "Yes, I did," she said.

Quentin didn't speak. He had expected to have to work harder for this, had assumed she would release her secrets reluctantly and only after much prodding. And this wasn't even the secret that he had expected. He had not believed Charley's claim to not know how Lucas came to have the gun, had not been able to shake the belief that it was the one aspect of this whole matter that Charley had lied about. Quentin was accustomed to lies, thanks to a few years in a justice system that formalized and sanctioned the evasion of truth, and while unpersuaded by Charley's lie, neither was he bothered by it. If Charley had been dishonest, it was for a good reason, and all Quentin wanted was to understand that reason. But the fact of the matter was that Quentin until that moment believed Charley—driven by an impulse known but to him—had given Lucas the gun.

Frances, seeing Quentin's confusion, took pity on him. "You'd like for me to explain this, wouldn't you?"

Quentin intuitively knew that there would be no need for him to pry the tale out of her. He simply nodded.

"Yeah, I gave that man Lucas the rifle. Yes, indeed I did. I'd overheard Charley talking to him the night he came to the door. I realized then Johnny had killed that boy. Just hearing Charley tell what little he knew about it made it clear for me, because I knew what Johnny was like. Then the next night, when Charley came home late and told me how you all had captured Johnny and how he'd confessed, I went to see Lucas. I knew he was still there in the shed.

"I asked him if he'd heard about the sheriff. He didn't speak. Just looked at me. Then I said, You knew that boy he killed, didn't you? He still didn't speak, but he nodded.

"It just sort of erupted out of me. I hadn't planned it, but the idea must have been buried deep in my mind. I guess I had been thinking about it without knowing I was thinking about it. Because it's not something a person plans. At least, it's not something I would have planned. But my heart became very dark at that moment. I hated

Johnny as purely as you can hate someone, and it must have been infectious, because that man Lucas's eyes just glittered as I spoke.

"I told him there was a gun in the shed. It was a rifle that belonged
to my husband, wrapped in a blanket, sitting crossways on some of the
overhead beams. There was a box of bullets wrapped up in there with
it. I had wanted that gun out of the house, so I'd put it up there years
ago. I pointed to it and told him anybody could just break in here and
steal it, and I'd probably never even know it was missing.

"He understood exactly what I meant. It's his eyes that I remember
best. It was dark in there, with just a little light coming from the house.
But I could see his eyes, could see there was a lot going on behind
them. I have to tell you, it scared me.

"So he says, 'Yes, ma'am.' He was real polite, but that only made
him sound more ominous. Then he said, 'I believe that's exactly what
happened. That gun was stolen from you.'

"I left and never saw him again. That man was troubled and I feel
bad about him dying. I guess it's something I'll have to account for
someday. Among other things."

Frances sounded regretful, but not in the way of someone who
wished that none of it had happened. Instead, Quentin heard in her the
somber tone of a woman who regrets only that a necessary bit of dirty
business had required her involvement.

Something she'd said early in the tale came back to him. "What did
you mean when you said you knew what Johnny was like?"

It was one question too many. Frances shook her head. "That's
something I'm obligated to explain to Charley," she said. "But only to
Charley."

●

He realized that things were changing when Frances began waiting for
him on the front porch. Whereas Charley always previously had found
her in the kitchen, coffee before her and cigarette in hand, he now
found Frances awaiting him at the end of the day in one of the rockers.
And whereas she once had been a silent and unapproachable presence, lost in her forest of longing and guilt, she now made it a point to

pass time with Charley every afternoon, sitting on the porch with him and savoring the late afternoons of a fading summer. And finally, whereas Frances once had been remote and distant to her neighbors, she now waved as they passed in their cars. In fact, waving had become Frances's gleeful obsession. She had done it the first day she'd sat on the porch as a self-mocking gesture to the townspeople who had grown accustomed to hardly seeing her. But she'd enjoyed herself so much that day that she continued, and after a while Charley had begun waving, too. Sometimes, when Dorothy was with him and sat with one hip perched on the porch railing, all three of them waved.

When they weren't waving, Frances and Charley talked. She asked him countless questions about his job, his college plans, his relationship with Dorothy, and his thoughts on any number of current events. There was a flavor of interrogation at first, until Charley came to see that no answer brought reproval or rebuke. She seemed to be making up for lost years, and only wanted to know things and know him. So he answered, and in doing so discovered that he enjoyed her company.

Two subjects, however, were never broached: Johnny Carver and Shay. But both eventually came up, and on the same afternoon.

Frances wasn't on the porch as usual that day when Charley arrived. He found her upstairs, dressed in old clothes and with her hair tied up. She was tugging at the mattress from Shay's bed, trying to pull it into the hall. Beyond her, he could see that the walls had been stripped of Shay's drawings and that his bug collection was gone.

"Please help me with this," Frances said, clearly talking about more than the mattress.

Together they hauled it to the yard, then followed it with Shay's bedframe and dresser. Finally, they took several large boxes which had been taped shut, but that Charley somehow knew carried a little boy's clothes and toys.

"A man is coming for all this later on," Frances said. She seemed to be near tears, but there had been no hesitancy as she worked. "If you want, we can bring your stuff down, too. I'm going to paint in there, and I'd like to get new furniture anyway." She smiled wanly. "I mean, I know you're going away to school soon, but I'd like you to have a nice bedroom to come back to."

"Why are you doing this?" Charley asked.

"Because it's time. I should have done it long ago." Frances stood for a moment, staring at Shay's things stacked by the curb, then turned to Charley. "Let's sit down, honey. There's something I want to tell you."

They settled into the rockers on the porch. "You're just going to have to let me talk for a while," Frances began. "There are a lot of things knotted together here. I have much to feel guilty about, and I know I'll be called to account for it all eventually. Some things I can explain, some things can't be explained, and some things already have been set right. So if there's a God, we'll have an interesting conversation. It's not as if he doesn't have a thing or two to explain himself.

"Honey, you weren't to blame for what happened to Shay. My God, you were a nine-year-old child who should never have been left to care for a little boy. But I could never make myself say that. I never told you it wasn't your fault, because there was only one other person whose fault it could be. And that's me. It was a terrible thing for a mother to do to her child and I'm sorry for it. I hope you'll forgive me someday."

Charley started to respond, but Frances wouldn't let him. "You don't have to say anything now, honey. Besides, I've still got a few years to try to undo things." She grinned unexpectedly. "In fact, I took care of one of them yesterday. I visited the draft board during one of their meetings. I think I created a bit of a scene. I told them there was no way I would let them take my son. As it turned out, they wouldn't have taken you anyway, because you're the only child of a widowed mother. It seems they give you an exemption for that." She paused. "I surely gave them something to remember, though."

Charley thought of the other person who'd been concerned about his draft status. "Lucas would have been glad to hear that."

Frances shifted uncomfortably in her seat. "Actually, that brings me to the other thing I have to tell you. But let me ask you something first. Do you feel bad about what happened to Johnny Carver?"

"Considering what we know about him now, I'd be surprised if anybody much feels bad about it," Charley answered.

"You don't know the half of it," Frances said. "I'm happy he's dead. If anything, it was a shame that man Lucas was such a good shot. They said Johnny was dead before he fell, which is all the proof you need that justice isn't a very precise instrument. He should have suffered.

"Charley, I'm going to tell you something no mother should ever have to tell her son." Charley saw that a deep blush had consumed her face. "It's a peculiar thing about people that they don't want to even think about their momma or daddy having a sex life. It's one of those things you just don't dwell on. So forgive me for putting you through this, but it has to be said. I was carrying on with Johnny Carver when you were a little boy.

"You could say we were having an affair. But that would make it seem like there was some love involved. Or at least affection. There wasn't. I was just mad at your father because he'd turned into a drinker. We didn't have much money, he was missing work, and it felt like he'd abandoned me. So I guess it was my way of getting back at him. Johnny brought him home one night. He'd found your daddy pig-drunk out on the highway somewhere, and brought him home in his patrol car. I'm pretty sure Johnny saw the disgust and anger on my face. He waited until I'd put your father to bed, then he drove me back out to where our car had been left on the side of the road. I thought it was a nice thing to do, because we would have needed the car the next morning. Johnny seemed to be friendly, and I was . . . well, I guess I was unhappy and lonely and needy, all jumbled up together. That was the first time.

"It happened only twice more after that. The last time, we went to a cabin he'd borrowed or had access to or something. Maybe he'd just broken into it, knowing its owners weren't around. I'd begun to realize by that point Johnny was capable of things like that. Once you got past that happy, friendly exterior, there was something dead inside. And he showed it to me that last time.

"We were still undressing when the phone rang. Johnny must have given the number to his dispatcher, in case an emergency came up, because he answered it right away. Whoever it was, they did most of the talking, because the only things Johnny asked were short questions, like 'When?' and 'Are you sure?' Whatever it was, it didn't seem to bother him much. He hung up after a minute or two and we got into bed. I'm sorry you have to hear this kind of detail, honey, but you need to know.

"When we were finished—and it never took very long—I must have closed my eyes, which caused Johnny to nudge me. 'C'mon, get up,' he said. 'We've got to go.'

"I asked him what the rush was about. He said, 'There's a problem at your house.' He was real matter-of-fact about it.

"He knew about Shay. That was the day it happened. That's what the phone call had been about. He'd been told my child had drowned, and his only response was to finish what we'd gone there to do. He could have taken me home immediately after hanging up, but he didn't. He let me climb into that bed knowing I would eventually learn what had happened. It didn't matter to him. When that call came, he knew it was going to be the last time I would be with him, and he didn't want to miss it.

"So that's what I've had to live with for the rest of my life. That image of me with him is like a snapshot in my mind that can't be erased."

Frances leaned forward in her chair, toward Charley. Her vehemence was almost a physical force. "I hated him for what he did to me. And I've hated myself for what I did to you in return."

Charley didn't want to cry, but felt it coming anyway. "Hush. Don't talk like that," he said.

They were standing by then and hugging, with Frances snuffling into Charley's neck. At that moment a car passed, and the instinct seized them both: they waved.